DRY
HARD

D1125568

ALSO BY NICK SPALDING

NICK SPALDING

DRY HARD

LAKE UNION
PUBLISHING

Text copyright © 2019 by Nick Spalding
All rights reserved.

Published by Lake Union Publishing, Seattle

www.apub.com

Amazon, the Amazon logo, and Lake Union Publishing are trademarks of Amazon.com, Inc., or its affiliates.

ISBN-13: 9781542041652
ISBN-10: 1542041651

Cover design by Ghost Design

Printed in the United States of America

This book is dedicated to anyone who's ever given something up with no problems whatsoever. The other seven billion of us are extremely jealous.

CONTENTS

PART ONE
DRUNK

CHAPTER ONE

KATE VS PROSECCO

As the best man picks up his wine glass and proposes a toast to the happy couple, I am instantly transported back two decades to my own wedding reception.

That's one of the best things about being drunk.

It can bring memories back to the surface that you haven't had in *years*.

And now, as this wedding's guests stand and raise their glasses, I can see all *my* family and friends doing the same thing in my hazy mind's eye.

Beside me is sat the most handsome man I have ever met.

The thick shock of black hair I love to run my hands through.

The kind, clear hazel eyes that always look at me with nothing but love.

In twenty years, that hair will be thinning, and the eyes will need glasses to read, but right now, Scott Temple is *perfect* – and now that I am Mrs Temple, I'm feeling pretty damn perfect too.

I sit next to my new husband as the entire hall stands – and as they raise their glasses to toast our happy union, he leans over and plants the softest and most lovely kiss on my lips. The ghost of that kiss will stay on my lips for a few minutes, and in my memory for two decades.

We then both lift our own glasses to one another, looking into each other's eyes as we do so. I take a sip of champagne, and a warm glow fills me from head to toe.

As Scott rests a hand over mine, I feel the most secure I have ever felt in my life. From this moment on, we will be together, and nothing in this world will be able to tear us apart. He will always be by my side. We will live together, love together, go on wild and crazy adventures together . . . and be *better* together than we ever were apart.

That's what the warmth of his hand tells me as it closes gently over mine, enveloping my new wedding ring.

Then Scott starts to shake my hand for some reason.

He shakes it harder.

And harder.

Why is he shaking my hand like this?

Why is he—

'Kate! Kate! For God's sake wake up!'

My eyes snap open blearily, and I focus on my friend Nadia as she shakes my hand to bring me back to the present.

'What the hell are you doing?' Nadia hisses at me in a rather embarrassed voice. I see her eyes whip round to the other six people sat at our table, a deeply apologetic look on her face.

I let out a low drunken grunt as I remember where I actually am. Not at my wedding, but at the wedding of someone I'm supposed to be making a good impression on. The wedding of a *very important* client of the PR firm I work at.

The shock of this realisation makes my elbow jerk reflexively off the edge of the table.

Sadly, my head has been leaning against my palm, so the instant my arm drops, so does my head, and I soundly headbutt the table and the edge of my dinner plate, sending the remains of my toffee roulade flying into my hair.

'Jesus Christ!' I wail, sitting back in my chair. I now look like I have the worst case of frontal dandruff in history, thanks to the roulade. Marry this with my smeared make-up, bleary eyes and slack expression, and I look a right picture.

The picture, if hung in an art gallery, would come with the title 'Inebriated forty-something in sunken repose' and wouldn't fetch much at auction – other than derisory laughter.

This is no fit state for a woman to be in at five o'clock in the afternoon.

Not in the slightest.

And how did I come to be half-asleep, covered in roulade and reliving memories of a pleasant past?

Well, it goes something like this . . .

***

It's six hours earlier. And I am, for the moment, entirely sober.

I'm stood alone outside a small church in the village of Ropley Heavertide – which is somewhere very expensive in the Cotswolds – waiting for somebody I actually know to turn up. My husband, Scott, was meant to be with me today, but that damned boss of his has made him work at the weekend *yet again*. This has been such a regular occurrence in recent months that I can't remember the last time we spent some quality time together.

Not that today is going to be abundantly full of what you'd call 'quality time' anyway, given whose wedding this is. Poor Scott might be knee-deep in Camberwell Distillery's latest product crisis, but at least he doesn't have to spend his Saturday watching the awfulness that is Annabelle Mastriano getting hitched.

The money Ms Mastriano pays the company to provide her with just the right kind of PR would probably feed a small African village for a year. Mind you, if Annabelle Mastriano did something nice like that, we'd probably have a far easier time creating a positive image for her.

It's quite hard to make somebody look good when they've built a career on buying property out from under people's noses, before renting it back to them at exorbitant prices.

Annabelle Mastriano is the kind of class-A, gold-plated cowbag that makes the rest of my gender look bad. Everyone at my PR firm is so sick of her that if it wasn't for all that lovely money, we would have told her to gazump off a long time ago.

This attitude towards Ms Mastriano (soon to be Mrs Simon Hoffington-Pierce) is the reason I have been sent along to this shindig to make a good impression. I am but a lowly cog in the machine of Stratagem PR, and am entirely expendable if Annabelle fancies a small snack before saying her vows. If she fancies a second snack, she can always take a bite out of my fellow lowly Stratagem cog, Nadia, who – thank God – I can now see walking towards me with a harassed look on her face.

'Morning, Kate,' she says as she reaches me, having successfully negotiated her way around the assembled throng of well-heeled wedding guests.

'Morning, Nads. You look lovely.'

Nadia gives me a withering look. 'I'm wearing a purple dress that's two sizes too big for me, Kate. I look like a half-deflated balloon.' She pulls at a large loose swathe of material around her midriff by way of demonstration.

I give her a smile. 'You could have bought a new one, you know.'

She rolls her eyes. 'For Little Miss Stick Up Her Arse? Not a bloody chance. I can't help it if I've lost two stone since the last time I slung this thing on.' She looks me up and down. 'You *genuinely* look good, though, sweetheart. The flowers suit you.'

I look down at the flowery green-and-white dress I picked up on eBay last week for £15. It's too snug around my backside, but it does a good job of making my boobs look firm. A woman of my age will usually pay a great deal more than fifteen quid to find anything in this universe that makes her boobs look firm, so I'm more than happy with my purchase.

Additionally, the cream clutch bag my mum bought me a couple of years back goes well with the dress too, so I look quite co-ordinated for once.

'Thanks, Nads. It'll do.'

Nadia gives me a look of mock derision. 'Ha! *It'll do*, she says. You look fantastic. I wish I had your hips.'

'No you don't, love. I've developed a strange click in the left one that'll probably mean a trip to the doctor's at some stage in the near future.'

'I'd take a clicky hip over my chubby thighs any time, Kate,' Nadia replies. Then her brow creases. 'Where's Scott? I thought you were bringing him along?'

I heave a sigh. 'He couldn't come. He's had to go into work again.'

Nadia reaches out and places a conciliatory hand on my arm. 'Oh sweetheart. It's getting a bit ridiculous now, isn't it?'

'Yes, it is. For both of us, to be honest. It's a lovely warm Saturday afternoon, and we should be doing something nice with one another – and yet we're a hundred miles apart and both bloody working.'

She squeezes my arm. 'Well, hopefully things will quiet down soon.'

I respond with a smile, but have to confess I don't share her optimism in the *slightest*. I doubt Scott will get much time off in the near future, and while I don't expect to have to attend that many more weddings for Stratagem PR, I still have a fifty-hour-a-week workload to contend with, which I don't see coming down any time soon.

'Maybe,' I eventually reply. I can feel tears start to sting my eyes, and have to blink a couple of times. 'I miss him, Nads,' I finish, in a rather lame little voice.

Nadia looks at me sympathetically. 'I know. It'll get better though.' She pauses thoughtfully for a moment. 'Have to say, hun, I moan about being single a lot of the time, but it does have its advantages.' She offers me a wry grin. 'I don't have anyone to miss.'

I chuckle ruefully, giving myself something of a mental shake as I do. This sad train of thought is not going to help this day go any better, so I'd better snap myself out of it. 'At least you're here, Nads,' I tell my colleague brightly. 'We can get through this nasty thing together.'

'Indeed we can.' Her eyes narrow. 'Not sober though. Definitely *not* sober.'

I link my arm in hers and start to walk towards the entrance to the church. 'That, Nadia, goes without saying, as far as I'm concerned.'

As we walk into the church and take a pew near the back, my train of thought moves away from the pain of missing my husband and on to fantasising about a cool, tasty glass of something fresh and alcoholic. This is a much more pleasant train for my mind to take a journey on. It comes with a well-stocked drinks carriage, for starters.

I have zero intention of getting drunk at this wedding, for obvious reasons, but one or two colourful cocktails are definitely on the cards to help me make it through to the end.

About five minutes after Nadia and I have sat down, the groom arrives with his retinue. Simon Hoffington-Pierce has no chin, the kind of ginger hair they write songs about, and a permanent expression of upper-class befuddlement that speaks of a lifetime spent in the back of a Range Rover, next to the hounds. Simon is also worth approximately eleventy squillion pounds, which may hint at why Annabelle Mastriano has picked him out as her first husband.

Speaking of whom, another *thirty-five* minutes go by before her raven-haired ladyship swans into the church to the tune of the wedding march, played on the harp by a woman who evidently doesn't want to be here, but is being paid more than she's seen in the past six months, so is willing to put up with it.

The church is stifling hot on this late August day, and I can feel the material of my eBay dress starting to bond with the skin on my back. The pew we're sitting on is about as comfortable as watching an adult movie with your grandparents, and the man sat next to me is exhibiting an aroma I can only describe as 'meaty'.

In my head, I have now moved on from images of colourful cocktails to one of a bucket filled with cheap white wine. The more agitated and frustrated I get, the baser my instincts become. If this wedding doesn't begin soon, I'm going to start having fantasies of swigging pure ethanol from a welly boot.

The bride eventually reaches the altar, where a saintly vicar awaits to join her in (un)holy union with her victim.

I have to confess I space out completely during the actual ceremony, which drags on for a further fifty minutes, thanks to a parade of well-meaning religious readings from people who probably haven't seen the inside of a church for decades.

Throughout all this, Annabelle looks decidedly put out, no doubt because she wants to be the centre of everyone's praise and attention 100 per cent of the time, and is rather irritated that our Lord and Saviour is trying to muscle in on the act.

By the time Simon Hoffington-Pierce gets around to giving Annabelle a kiss on the lips that resembles a baby woodpecker tackling its first tree, I have descended into a soup of boredom and irritability that only a welly boot of pure ethanol will bring me out of.

'Are you okay, Kate?' Nadia asks me in a stage whisper.

'Yes. Why?'

'You've scrunched up the order of service into a tight little ball and you're making strange high-pitched noises at the back of your throat.'

I look at her, look down at the crumpled ball of paper and will myself to relax a bit.

I need to be somewhere cool and calm as swiftly as possible, preferably with a drink in my hand. If there are some hors d'oeuvres in that place as well, that'd also be fantastic, as I'm famished.

The vicar pronounces Annabelle and Simon first husband and wife, before taking them off to sign the register. I wouldn't be surprised if there's a document there also making her the executor of his will.

Sweet, sweet relief from this baking church comes ten minutes after this as the happy couple leave via the main doors, allowing the rest of us to scuttle from a side door, out into the cool of the shady graveyard.

Nadia and I position ourselves under, and slightly behind, a large tree as the photographs are taken. We are completely surplus to requirements at this wedding, and only here as lip service to one of our most lucrative clients, so neither of us feels bad about keeping an extremely low profile.

Nadia then comes up with a very welcome suggestion. 'Here, Kate . . . the barn where the reception is being held is only a ten-minute walk down the road. Shall we bugger off there now?'

A beatific smile crosses my lips. 'That is a wonderful suggestion, Nads. Quite, quite wonderful.'

Even more wonderful is the fact that there is a small gate leading out of the graveyard behind us, meaning we don't have to walk past everyone to get out of here.

I breathe an audible sigh of relief as I close the gate behind me with a satisfying click, and start to trot down the cobbled street in the direction of Ropley Heavertide's converted fourteenth-century barn. There are drinks and canapés in my very near future.

There is also a disaster involving a large red tractor in my future, unfortunately, but I am unaware of this fact at the moment, and therefore have a genuine smile on my face for the first time today.

The walk through the village is pleasant, as there are virtually no people about. The peace and quiet is worth every penny of the millions it probably takes to purchase a property here.

By the time we reach the barn at the outskirts, my feet hurt, but at least the eBay dress has finally parted company with my back, thanks to the pleasant summer breeze, and I am feeling relatively comfortable again.

Comfort turns to sheer delight when we enter the enormous barn to find that there is a temporary bar set up at one end. We receive some odd looks from the wedding and catering staff as we walk towards it. They're probably not expecting guests for at least an hour yet, and are still putting the finishing touches to the thirty or so round tables around the barn's interior.

Both sides of the barn are open to let the summer breeze roll through. Beyond the large open doors on the other side, I can see a wide patio with freestanding heaters and lights dotted around it. Beyond the patio there is a gently rising field of closely cropped grass, with a tractor sat at the top end, next to a ramshackle shed.

'Don't mind us!' I say to a particularly disconcerted-looking gentleman arranging an exquisite table centrepiece of lilies and frangipani. 'We are completely unimportant!'

Amazingly, this seems to satisfy him.

Nadia and I get to the temporary bar, which consists of a line of sturdy oak tables, a mobile optics unit and several kegs of beer hooked up to pumps secured to the tables by complicated-looking metal bolts and braces. Easily the most marvellous thing about this set-up, however, is the sign on an ornate silver stand at the end of one of the tables which reads: 'Simon & Annabelle would love you to enjoy this free bar on their wedding day.'

Free bar.

. . . and the angels did sing in their heavens.

Sadly, there is currently no sign of a barman to serve any of this booze.

'Um . . , hello?' Nadia calls, somewhat furtively.

Stuff furtive. I've just had to sit through the most interminable wedding ceremony in history, and still have to get through the reception.

'Hello! Shop!' I bellow, dropping my clutch bag on the temporary bar.

In response to this, a head pops up from behind the stack of beer kegs. The head belongs to a twelve-year-old with sandy hair and a worried expression. I assume I've got the lad's age wrong, given the fact he's here to serve alcohol, but if he's actually a day over nineteen I'd be amazed.

He walks towards us, glancing at his watch.

'Can I help you?' he says – the most redundant question ever asked. Can he not see how parched and discombobulated I am?

'Yes, you can,' I tell him with some enthusiasm. 'You can make this day go from a three to at least a seven in virtually no time at all.'

'Pardon?'

Nadia rolls her eyes at me. 'What my friend here is trying to say is that we'd like a couple of drinks, if that's okay.' Her eyes narrow. 'Small ones though . . . We haven't had any lunch yet.'

'Yes. A small glass of Prosecco for me, please,' I tell him, in a slightly frustrated voice. I'm pushing aside dreams of colourful cocktails here, and heeding Nadia's wise words. Personally, I could go for a very *large* drink right about now, but Nadia's caution is well warranted. We're here to make a good impression, after all.

'I'll have a Pimm's and lemonade,' Nadia adds.

'You'll have to give me a few minutes,' the barman replies. 'I haven't got all the glasses out yet, and the Pimm's hasn't got any fruit in it.'

Nadia waves a hand. 'Don't worry about the fruit, it just tends to get in the way.'

'Take your time,' I say. The poor lad has had two fairly cranky women sprung on him long before he was expecting such a thing to happen, so it's more than fair to give him a bit of time to get himself together.

A mere five minutes after busying himself with our request, Mr Sandy Hair produces our drinks with a small smile. Nadia says thank you. I'd love to do the same, but I'm already drinking. My brain has decided to take matters into its own hands, and has circumvented social niceties in favour of immediate lubrication.

When I've taken a large sip, and felt the Prosecco slip down my throat, I do thank the barman for his efforts, knowing full well that I'd better keep him onside, as he's going to be my best friend this afternoon.

With a relieved sigh, I relax against the bar a little.

There's a joyful feeling of *unwinding* that always accompanies that first beautiful sip.

I might just be able to get through this reception with my soul intact now.

Ten minutes later I've already managed to finish off my Prosecco, while Nads still has a good half of her Pimm's left.

Now, here we come to the central and most obvious problem with alcohol. The problem that leads every single one of us astray – some more than others.

I know I should only have the one drink right now, as I still haven't had anything to eat yet. The smells of cooking coming from somewhere unidentifiable, being borne through the open barn on the light summer breeze, tell me that food is in my near future. This appeals greatly to my stomach, but not so much to my brain, which has now had its first hit of alcohol and wants more.

The sensible, sober part of my brain wants to listen to my stomach and switch to softies until I've crammed a load of food in my mouth. After all, *we're here to make a good impression*, aren't we?

And before drinking that lovely glass of Prosecco, I would have listened to that part of my brain without hesitation.

But – I have now consumed the Prosecco, so *another* part of my brain has come to life, insisting on doing things a little *differently*. The bubbly liquid has gone straight to my head without passing Go, and is already working its magic on me. For that magic to continue, though, more alcohol must be forthcoming as soon as possible.

The world would be a safer, calmer, happier place if alcohol didn't do this.

I turn back to my sandy-haired barman friend. 'Can I have another, please?' I ask him.

'Another one?' Nadia says, concern etched on her face.

I wave a hand. 'Yeah. It's fine. I'll stop after this. Two should get me through the next few hours okay.'

In my defence, when I say this, I absolutely mean it *100 per cent*.

By the time the wedding guests eventually make their way to the barn to join my drinking companion and me, the second Prosecco is history, and I'm starting to get a little buzz on. I've *definitely* entered a far happier state of being.

'What's your name?' I ask the barman as he busies himself checking the beer pumps.

'I'm sorry?' he responds.

'I said . . . what's your name? I can't keep callin' you Mr Sandy Hair all afternoon, can I?'

'Mr What?'

I wave a hand. 'Never mind. What's your name, my bartendery friend?'

'Zane.'

'Zane?'

'Yeah, Zane.'

'That's a very nice name. Very modern. Very . . . zany.' This makes me chuckle to myself. It does not make Zane chuckle. Few things are likely to come out of my mouth that will make poor Zane chuckle today. I point a finger at him. 'You'd like my daughter. Her name is Holly.' I attempt not to leer at him. 'She'd like you too.'

Great. Now I'm pimping out my only child to a complete stranger.

Damn you, Prosecco on an empty stomach. Damn you and all you stand for.

'Oh crap. Here they come!' Nadia says, stiffening beside me.

I look round to see that a long line of people is now descending on the barn.

'Oh bollocks. There goes my good mood,' I grunt.

'I guess we'd better go and sit down,' she replies. 'I think we're at that table right there.' She points to one of the round dinner tables covered in a whole plethora of wedding-day detritus, like disposable cameras, small bags of unpleasant sweets and those irritating little foil bells. Quite why people feel the need to scatter these things everywhere at weddings is beyond me. I've always thought they were secretly invented by vacuum cleaner companies.

It's apparent from the cheapness of these wedding favours that our hosts may be super-rich, but they're also pretty damn super-stingy when it comes to entertaining their guests.

All that mess, along with the crockery and glassware, is arranged around a large table centrepiece consisting of an entire garden. It's bloody enormous. There's every chance if I went searching in there I'd find a garden gnome and a pond.

The table Nadia and I have been placed at is agreeably close to Zane's bar though. This puts a smile on my face.

'Come on, let's go take our seats, before we get noticed,' Nadia suggests.

'Agreed. If anyone looks like they're coming over to speak to us, we can hide in the pond,' I reply, giggling at the mental image this conjures up.

'What?'

'Never mind.'

I give Zane a cheeky grin, before walking over to the table and plonking myself down behind the centrepiece, so that my view of the top table is completely and deliberately obscured.

With a deep breath, and an even deeper sigh, I pick up one of the small foil bells in my hand and start to fiddle with it, wishing I'd ordered a third drink.

The wedding feast and speeches go on for the next *four hours*.

When they bring around the roast duck and vegetables, I hoover it up like my life depends on it, which in a roundabout way, of course, it kind of does. A good half of the toffee roulade barely touches the sides either, before I am feeling comprehensively full to bursting.

You know what also barely touches the sides?

Six more glasses of Prosecco.

Yes, *six*.

It's not deliberate. I don't set out to drink that much. It just *happens*.

Prosecco is an extremely easy drink to knock back, once you're into your stride. It's so damned *innocuous* – sitting there all bubbly and pretty. Nothing that frothy can be all that bad for you, can it? But it is, of course. Especially when your glass is constantly being refilled by the highly attentive waiters buzzing around the barn like black-and-white bees.

So, accidentally, not at all deliberately, and without malice aforethought, after four hours of steady but mindless drinking to fill the time, I find myself completely trashed, and totally unable to *make a good impression* any more.

Then Simon Hoffington-Pierce's best man, Tarquin, stands and asks everyone to raise their glasses to the happy couple for a final toast . . . and I go off into a pleasant daydream of my own wedding twenty years previously.

This brings us bang up to date . . . and covered in half-eaten roulade.

As I sit slumped in my chair with a dazed expression on my face, Annabelle's fat and tanned father, Dimitri, then informs everyone that the speeches are now over, and that the guests should retire to the patio outside to meet and greet the happy couple while the staff clear the dinner tables.

'Here, Nads,' I say to my companion as I rise unsteadily to my feet. 'Do you think they'd let me take the centrepiece home? Our garden is a right shithole, and this would tart it up good and proper!'

Unfortunately, I'm one of those people who gets very *common* when they get drunk. I may live in a relatively middle-class area these days, but I'm a council-estate girl by birth, and boy does that show when I've had a few.

Nadia attempts to lead me away from the object of my potential larceny. 'No, Kate. I doubt they would.'

I contrive to look devastated. 'What, not even the gernomey?'

'The what?'

'The *gernomey*, Nads.' I wave both hands in front of my eyes. 'The little-wittle gernomey that lives inside the table garden.'

'I literally have no idea what you're on about.'

Hand-wave. ''S fine. I don't either, to be honest with you. Shall we go outside and await the comin' of the evil one?'

In my mind I make a small and subtle gesture in the direction of the bride. In reality, I point a wobbly finger towards where she's standing at the back of the barn with a massive arm sweep that makes me look like an air traffic controller with motor function issues.

'Oh God!' Nadia cries in humiliation as the eyes of many wedding guests fix upon us.

I put a finger to my lips. 'Shhhhh, Nads! The evil one will hear you!'

I'm pretty sure the evil one could hear me in the next county, but I'm far too pissed by now to give a toss.

Nadia grabs my arm. 'Let's go outside!' she snaps, and leads me away from the bemused guests.

'Ahhh . . . that's nice, isn't it, Naddy?' I say as we walk out into the late-afternoon sun.

'What is?'

I effect an exasperated expression. 'The sun, Naddsy-waddsy! The fucking sun!' I point at it with the same wobbly fingered gesture I used to pick out the evil one. 'It's *warm*, Nads! I like being warm!'

We've now reached that stage of inebriation where we have become the world's most annoying arsehole.

I do feel sorry for poor Nadia. I will be making this up to her in the office for the next six months at least. She probably won't have to make her own coffee ever again.

'Let's go and stand over there,' Nadia tells me, indicating a patio heater off to the far left. It's miles away from anyone else.

Earlier in the day, I would have happily embraced this suggestion, wanting to stay as inconspicuous as possible.

Inconspicuousness is not something drunk Kate enjoys in the *slightest*, however. Drunk Kate enjoys the attention of all present – which means she has a lot more in common with Annabelle Hoffington-Pierce née Mastriano than she did while still fully in control of her faculties.

Speaking of whom. 'Oi! Nads! Look! It's bloody Annabelle! She's come outside too!' I say this as if it's a massive surprise, and not something her father told us all was happening a mere five minutes ago.

'Yes, maybe we should stay out of her way.'

Nadia attempts to pull me towards the lonely patio heater twenty feet away. I am having none of it.

'I'm gonna go say hello to her. Doesn't she look fuckin' *beautiful?*'

'Yes, I suppose. But—'

'Come on!' I interrupt. It's now my turn to pull Nadia – right towards Annabelle and her new groom/victim.

As we approach I take on a look of mindless delight.

You know the one. You've all seen it before. The one that looks good from a distance, but up close there's a touch of serial killer about it.

'Annabelle!' I cry with happiness. 'You look absolutely gorgeous!'

I stumble into the bride's comfort zone, completely ignoring the two chinless wonders that her and Hoffy-Piss were having a conversation with.

Annabelle, of course, has absolutely no idea who I am.

'Who are you?' she says in her languid Mediterranean accent. The look on her face is not a welcoming one.

I go wide-eyed. 'Me? You don't know *me*?'

Her eyes narrow. 'No, I don't believe I do.'

I slap myself in the chest twice. 'It's *me*, Annabelle! Kate! Kate Temple!'

Nope, still zero signs of recollection.

I sigh theatrically. 'From the *agency*, Annabelle! I'm from Stratatatatagem PR!'

The light of recognition dawns on her flawless face. 'Ah yes.' She looks down at me. This shouldn't be possible, given that we're roughly the same height, but she does a damn fine job of it anyway. 'I was hoping Pierre and Peter would be here,' she says, not attempting to disguise her disappointment in the slightest that the two owners of the company haven't come along – and have instead sent two minions.

I try to look like I'm sorry about this. It looks more like I've got trapped wind though. 'Yeah. Sozzleberries about that! They're very busy at the moment!' I roar at her.

Sozzleberries was a word we used to use with Holly when she was five. My brain has done me a deep disservice dredging it up now.

Annabelle looks suitably confused.

At this point, Nadia steps in. Up until now she's stood in horrified silence beside me as I've shouted at Annabelle. But now, she's intervening before I say or do anything really stupid.

'It's lovely to be here, Mrs Hoffington-Pierce,' she says, eyes full of unspoken apology. 'It really was a lovely ceremony, and we couldn't be prouder than to be here representing Stratagem on your wedding day.'

Annabelle looks a little happier. Flattery will get you everywhere.

'Yeah!' I interrupt. 'We're really happy to be here!' I lean forward, a confiding look on my face. 'Not like everyone else, Belle. None of them wanted to come 'coz they all think you're a witch – but me and Nads . . . we think you're bloody *great*!'

'I think we should leave her alone now, Kate!' Nadia nearly screams at me, as Annabelle tries to process what I've just said. There can't be many brides in the world that get called a witch on their wedding day – not to their faces anyway.

Before Annabelle can say anything, or I can insult anyone else, Nadia drags me bodily away. She's got a good two stone on me, so it's not a difficult job.

She doesn't stop dragging until we're over by that far patio heater, away from the crowd.

I pull my arm away from her. 'Alright, alright! Calm down, Nads! There's no need to be so violent!'

She puts her head in her hand. 'We're going to get fired. Once this gets back to Pierre and Peter, we're *definitely* getting fired.'

'Oh look! A tractor!'

'What?!'

'A *tractor*, Nads! Shall we go and have a look at it?'

Without waiting for my companion's answer, I take off towards the tractor like a gun dog heading for a recently shot pheasant.

I have now entered the stage of inebriation when everything rolls off my back, and I have the attention span of a stunned gnat. I should be exceptionally worried about what's going to get back to Pierre and Peter – the two heads of Stratagem PR. I have a mortgage to pay, after all.

But the Prosecco is reassuring me that everything is going to be perfectly okay on that front, and that a matter of far more concern right now is how cool that tractor is.

When Scott and I were first married, we used to take ourselves off on a lot of spontaneous trips together. This was back when we were young, rather silly and didn't have quite so many large bills to pay.

On one particularly memorable trip to the West Country – which involved some of the best food, drink and sex I can ever remember having – we stumbled on a lively and friendly country fair. At the fair, there was a tractor that you could ride for just a couple of quid, which Scott and I did . . . four times, as I recall.

There's something ever so gigglesome about puttering along on a barking, farting tractor, waving at random bystanders as you go. The fact that we'd both consumed a lot of home-made ale in the drinks tent prior to this probably had a lot to do with our huge enjoyment of the repeated rides we took that day.

I loved that bloody tractor so much. Possibly because I knew Scott loved it too.

The tractor sat at the end of the field outside the barn is the same shade of red as the one from my memories. In fact, my drink-addled brain is insisting it might even be the *same tractor*. This is impossible, of course, but then nothing seems entirely impossible when you're three sheets to the wind, does it?

Nadia gamely follows me across the field with a dismayed look on her face. 'Kate! For crying out loud, what are you *doing?*'

'It's my tractor, Nads! The one I loved so much!'

This makes no sense to her, given that she isn't privy to the internal stupidity currently going on in my brain.

The field is quite large, but the grass is firm underfoot, so it doesn't take that long for me to reach the tractor, even in my high heels. From here, the hubbub of the wedding party is quiet, and I can't see anyone paying that much attention to what I'm doing. A few curious glances are thrown in my direction, but by now, I've resolutely become 'that person' at the wedding. Everybody else usually does their level best to ignore 'that person' as much as they possibly can. Getting involved with 'that person' is never a good idea.

Now I'm up close to the tractor, I can see that it's actually sat behind a barbed wire fence that runs the length of the back of the field. It's parked side-on, but its front wheels are pointed downhill.

Quite why it is here, in the middle of nowhere, I have no idea. Perhaps the barn owners have paid the tractor's owner to leave it here to add to the rustic charm of the barn's countryside location. It certainly does the job quite nicely. What says rustic charm more than an old red tractor parked next to a dilapidated wooden shed?

I must get a closer look.

Luckily, the barbed wire fence has broken right next to the shed, so I'm able to get through to the other side without any problem.

'Kate! Come back! We're not supposed to be over there!'

'Oh, it's fine!' I tell Nadia, hand-waving her concerns away. 'I'm just going to have a little look.'

The tractor really is just like the one I remember from that fun weekend away in the West Country. Massive rear wheels as high as my shoulders, a big exposed engine sat in the bulbous red bodywork, a comedically large black steering wheel, a metal seat that looks like it could give you piles just by looking at it. It's like someone has rifled through my subconscious and picked this straight out of it. Today is apparently a day for reliving happy memories with a clarity that fair takes your breath away.

I pull out my phone and take a couple of snaps. I really must show it to Scott when I get home.

This thought instantly turns my mood sour.

Scott should be here with me, damn it! Having fun with his wife, and drinking Prosecco right next to her – not stuck in an office being moaned at by his fat, sweaty boss!

I stuff the phone back into my clutch bag as my lips purse. I need to do something to restore my happy mood.

Having a sit on the tractor will do the job! It'll help bring back all those happy memories again – of times when life was simple, carefree . . . and powered by home-made ale.

'Here, Nads! Hold this for me, will you?'

I throw the clutch bag at her as she tentatively waits on the other side of the barbed wire fence. She squawks with surprise as the bag sails towards her, but she does manage to awkwardly catch it. 'What are you doing?' she entreats, as I hoick my dress up over my knees and put one foot on the tractor.

'I'm just having a little sit-down,' I tell her confidentially.

'Oh God!'

Ignoring Nadia's shrill tone – I really will be making her coffee for the next ten years, if I actually keep my job – I lift myself up on to the tractor and plonk myself unceremoniously down on to the seat.

I then spot something which is going to make today extremely memorable for all the wrong reasons. 'Here, Nads! They've left the key in this thing!' This is an old tractor, but obviously not so old that they hadn't invented electronics by the time it was built.

Have you ever seen the blood drain from a person's face in an instant? It's quite disconcerting, even when you're pissed.

The now very small sober part of my brain is screaming at me not to do what I now feel overwhelmingly compelled to do.

Drunk Kate thinks that this key was left in this ignition for a reason. It's *karma*. It's *fate*. It's *meant to be*. I was *supposed* to sit on this tractor, and I am *meant* to start up the engine. It's just as simple as that. The universe requires certain events to take place, and who am I to argue with the outer reaches of infinity?

Drunk Kate can be quite the philosopher, in between the swearwords and pointing.

I turn the key with a look of glee on my face.

Nothing happens.

'Oh, thank God for that,' I hear Nadia exclaim.

'No, no!' I say to her, pointing. 'It's not over yet, Nads. There's a clutch pedal down here. I'm going to stamp on it and see what happens when I turn the key.'

I do so, and turn the key again. This time the tractor splutters into life. It seems that a tractor is not all that different to a car, when you get right down to it.

'Aha!' I roar in triumph.

'Aaaargh!' Nadia wails in dismay.

GRUMBAGRUMBABERGLEGRUMBA, the tractor's engine roars with new-found life.

Now, to be fair to me, at this stage all I want is to sit right here with the tractor's engine running and relive the happy early days of my marriage.

It's not my fault that my treacherous right foot decides to depress the accelerator pedal with no input from me whatsoever.

In another, parallel universe, where today just ends with me vomiting behind a tree and taking four ibuprofen when I get home, the handbrake on the tractor still works properly, and somebody hasn't left the tractor accidentally in first gear.

In this universe, however, it doesn't, and they have.

The tractor, set free from the constraints of inactivity, lurches forward about three feet, rolls right through the tumbledown barbed wire fence and then straightens itself – the front wheels following the gentle camber of the field.

'Eep!' I exclaim from my lofty tractor seat.

'Fuck my life!' Nadia screams, jumping out of the way.

I immediately press the large rusty brake pedal next to the accelerator. It doesn't budge.

Actually, tell a lie, it *does* budge, but not much. I can hear the squeal of brake pads, but the tractor is still rolling forward. The guy who normally drives this thing probably has nice big strong legs with which to operate it properly. I do not, however, therefore the tractor's downwards descent is not arrested in the *slightest*.

Thankfully, the slope on the field is not what you'd call pronounced, so the tractor doesn't pick up much more speed. It simply rolls downhill at just over walking pace. However, there is something dreadfully *inexorable* about its progress that cannot be denied.

'Stop the bloody thing!' Nadia cries as she hurries alongside me, flicking her head round to look at the patio full of wedding guests about sixty yards away.

'I can't!' I shout back over the sound of the spluttering tractor engine. 'The brake doesn't work!'

'Well . . . well, do *something*, Kate! You're going straight towards the wedding!'

'I can fucking see that!' I wail, pointing ahead of me like a mounted general starting a very slow charge from the rear.

I stand on the brake pedal again, as hard as I can. This time there's a little movement and the tractor slows a bit, but I can do this for no more than a second or so before my head starts swimming horribly. As soon as I let up, the tractor picks up speed again.

'Stop it, Kate! Stop it!' Nadia screams.

You know how I said that I was being ignored by the wedding guests for being 'that person'? Well, 'that person' is now trundling towards them on two tonnes of out-of-date tractor, so ignorance is most definitely *not* bliss.

'Oh shitting bastard hellfire,' I mutter in terror under my breath as I watch them start to back away, like extras in a disaster movie right before the tsunami hits. Of course, my eye is automatically drawn to Annabelle, who looks like somebody's just told her Versace is *so* last year . . . while simultaneously inserting a large marrow into somewhere uncomfortable.

'Turn the fucking wheel!' Nadia exclaims, still stumbling alongside me.

I look at her in dumbfounded non-comprehension. My brain appears to have locked itself into a death spiral.

'*Turn* the fucking *wheel*!' she repeats, pointing at it.

I look down at the large black steering wheel, and realisation finally dawns.

I give the thing a yank, and the tractor, now a scant ten yards away from the patio, immediately lurches to the left. Instinctively, I wrench it back again to stop the tractor turning over, and the thing lurches back to the right. Now it looks like I'm actively aiming myself at the wedding guests.

Subconsciously, this may be exactly what I'm doing, of course.

I give the wheel a more gentle tug to the left, and the tractor now starts to steer away from the patio. This is good news.

What *isn't* good news is that the slope of the field here is a little more pronounced, so the damn thing starts to pick up speed.

I scream in terror and stand on the brake pedal with all my might, bracing myself against the steering wheel at the same time.

This superhuman effort arrests the tractor's increased speed quite well.

Sadly, it also puts a tremendous amount of strain on my entire body – causing my head to swim viciously, my leg to start trembling uncontrollably . . . and a great wave of alcoholic bile to rise from my stomach *unstoppably*.

I do not projectile vomit. Such is the strain I'm already exerting on my poor body, I just don't think it has the energy to also propel my Prosecco, roast duck and toffee roulade across the tractor's steering wheel. Instead – and for some reason this is even worse – I vomit in much the same way as a burping newborn. It simply spills out of my gob and covers the front of my eBay dress, to the accompaniment of a noise that resembles that sound ketchup makes when you finally get it free of the bottle, after much assiduous bottom-bashing.

As this happens I roll gently past the patio of wedding guests, who all watch my progress in stony silence, and with an understandably high level of revulsion.

In fact, the tractor is now slowing more and more, thanks to the pressure I'm still applying to the brake pedal, so they are all treated to an extremely detailed look at what's left of Kate Temple – a wide-eyed, wild-haired lunatic, covered in vomit, who is standing rigid and gripping the steering wheel for dear, sweet life. There's also a strained expression on her face that she hasn't experienced since she had chronic constipation after giving birth.

I turn my head slowly to look at them all as I trundle past on my way to a small encounter with the wall of the barn.

What exactly can one say or do at such a time as this?

Saying 'sorry' doesn't really seem to cover it, does it? I could spend the next several months debasing myself at their collective feet and it wouldn't be enough.

If I was sober – and *oh my God* I wish I was sober – I would probably choose to just look away in shame and continue my merry way towards the fourteenth-century brickwork, but I'm still pretty damn drunk, so instead I give them all a big, cheesy smile and a hearty wave. It works for the Queen, so why shouldn't it work for me?

Oh yes . . . the vomit and the out-of-control tractor, that's why.

I continue to wave and smile as the tractor finally slows to a halt, but not before bumping serenely into the barn. Initially, this doesn't appear to do any damage, but this is a fourteenth-century barn we're talking about here. It's more or less held together by history and good intentions.

As I sit back down on the tractor seat, an entire section of the wall about two feet across falls inwards, providing me with a peephole view of poor sandy-haired Zane's amazed expression from where he's standing inside, behind his makeshift bar. In deference to whatever comedy gods may be watching, he is so shocked by my sudden appearance that he drops the glass he's been cleaning, which shatters satisfyingly on the floor.

I continue to look at him for a moment, before once more slowly turning my head towards the wedding guests.

I blink a couple of times, wipe the sick off my chin and give them an apologetic look. 'That's not gone well, has it?' I say to the shocked congregation.

So, not only am I rude and impulsive when I'm drunk, I am also capable of feats of gross understatement that I should probably win some kind of award for.

Nadia is my saviour that day, bless her.

As she pulls me from the tractor seat, she makes a point of telling everyone that I'm having a lot of emotional problems at the moment. This seems to quell the rising tide of anger before it has a chance to get going.

By the time Nadia gets around to hinting at the fact that I've just been prescribed *special pills* to help me with my *issues*, and that's why I was so out of control, anger has largely given way to pity.

This is such a masterpiece of outright bullshit that I'm amazed it came from Nadia's mouth – but then I remember that we work for a PR company, where the art of spouting convincing bullshit is in the job description.

Even Annabelle seems slightly mollified by this explanation for my wildly inappropriate behaviour. I still think she'd like to have chewed my head off, but given that screaming at a mentally ill person is probably not advisable in front of your family and friends, she simply tells Nadia to take me away in a curt voice, and that any damages needing to be paid on the barn will be invoiced to Stratagem PR.

Nadia enlists the help of Zane the barman to clean me up, by getting him to fetch as much kitchen roll as he can get his hands on – while the rest of the barn's staff try to move the tractor away, and patch up the hole I've made. By the time I've been de-vomited to an acceptable level, and Nadia is leading me away, the tractor has been pushed back a few feet, and the hole has been temporarily plugged. The damage could have been a lot worse.

. . . to the barn, that is. *My* reputation is so resolutely damaged I may have to move to a mountain in Tibet just to get away from it.

Nadia escorts me down the street and away from the barn, before calling us a taxi. She doesn't speak to me much as we wait for it to arrive.

I don't speak much either, because I'm starting to mildly sober up, and the true import of what I've done is starting to hit me.

As I replay the events of the last few hours, my mouth gapes open like a particularly stupid goldfish.

'I'm in so much trouble, aren't I?' I say in a small, slurred voice.

Nadia looks at me. Do I need to describe the expression on her face? Probably not, eh?

'I should fucking coco, madam,' she eventually says, as the taxi homes into view.

As I clamber into the cab, the driver looks at Nadia. 'She ain't gonna throw up in here, is she? I'm not taking her anywhere if she's going to throw up.'

The disdain on his face as he looks me up and down makes me feel about two inches tall. I would be indignant about it, but really, who can blame him? I'm a mess.

. . . a mess who will have some fast explaining to do on Monday morning if she wants to keep her bloody job.

***

The only reason I *did* keep my job was that Nadia went to bat for me, big style. Also, I immediately offered to pay for the damage to the barn, and sent Annabelle and her new husband a grovelling apology letter that turned my stomach to write almost as much as turning the tractor steering wheel had.

And all of this because there's a thing called Prosecco in this world.

But I didn't *mean* to get that drunk! I wanted to stay nice and sober to make the legendary good impression, but somehow things just got away from me, and the only impression I ended up making was about two foot square, and cost several thousand pounds to fix.

Sadly, I have to confess that this isn't the first time things have got away from me this way – and I'm not sure it'll be the last either.

It's a horrible thing to admit, but when life gets difficult or trying for me, I tend to jump into a bottle of something nice to make it all better. Which, of course, it does – if only for the briefest of periods, until the hangover kicks in the next morning.

I should probably quit drinking. At least for a while.

Prove I don't need it. Prove I can quite easily get through life without a glass of something fun in my hand.

Easy-peasy.

. . . hang on though. Just because I like a drink, and it sometimes leads me astray, it doesn't mean I've got an actual *problem* with the stuff. I'm not a bloody alcoholic or anything. It's just that when I've had a stressful day, nothing quite takes the edge off like a nice glass of red wine. I don't see anything wrong with that!

What is it they say? Everything in moderation, right?

I don't need to quit. I just need to *moderate* a bit more.

And maybe I'll avoid drinking at social occasions when I'm surrounded by complete strangers – that should help.

I'll just drink around the people I know and trust.

I'll just drink when I'm with Scott – because he's always been there in the past to catch me when I fall, and always stops me doing anything too stupid. We're always fine when we drink together.

But, he wasn't there at Annabelle's wedding, was he? a small voice at the back of my head says. *No. His stupid bloody job kept him away from you, when you could really have done with both his company, and his help. He'd have ridden that tractor with you today . . . and stopped you crashing it.*

Oh Christ.

That really bloody *hurts*.

More than anything else, that's the thing that brings tears to my eyes.

When I think back on the way Scott and I used to be in our early years, I feel so sad that we've lost that sense of *togetherness*. The pleasure of doing fun things as a team, like going off to the West Country on a random holiday, where we rode that silly tractor – and then conceived our gorgeous daughter in the bed and breakfast later that same night.

That feeling of being a team has very slowly ebbed away as the years have gone by, and I don't know how to get it back again.

He should have been with me at that wedding, but instead he only got to hear the story about it, which he laughed at – but I could tell he didn't really understand what I'd been through. I should be *living* my stories with him, not just telling him about them!

There's a distance between Scott and me that's been growing and growing, thanks to our workloads and lack of time together. It's not his fault. It's not mine. But the distance is *definitely* there. And it's just getting *wider*. Every. Single. Day. When we're with one another, things are fine. We love, we laugh, we *live*.

But those times are getting very few and far between, and I feel like I'm losing him – I truly do.

It feels like there's a hole in my life where Scott Temple used to be. A hole I feel every night over the dinner table, when I look at his empty place setting, because he's stuck in the office until late *again*.

And right now, I have no idea when things are going to change. I have no clue when Scott will be around more – to stop me getting on another bloody tractor alone.

This is a horrible thing to realise.

Christ almighty.

I could really do with a drink.

CHAPTER TWO

SCOTT VS GIN

'Good fucking grief, this stuff is disgusting.'

I snatch the shot glass away from Matt's hand as fast as I can, eyes darting around the room to make sure no one has heard what he's just said.

'Watch it, will you!' I exclaim through gritted teeth. 'They've been working on this drink for *months*. If anyone hears one of the company's staff saying that, it could sink us!'

Matt looks around the conference room at the gathered publicans and distributors, and sneers. 'Please. This lot are mostly here for the buffet, and are all probably pissed on the bog-standard stuff already. I could throw up all over my shoes drinking this rancid guff and nobody would bat an eyelid.'

This 'rancid guff' is Camberwell Distillery's latest attempt to bring something new to the gin market. A strange amalgamation of the distillery's gin, orange essence and fiery cinnamon – that somebody with deep-seated psychological problems thought should be called 'Gin Fawkes', and should be launched a whole month before Bonfire Night, at a gala event held in the distillery's conference room.

The drink tastes as bad as the name sounds. It's not too awful when it first enters your mouth, but then you start to feel like someone is squeezing a piece of orange peel soaked in dishwater into it, before the final overwhelming hit of cinnamon does an excellent job of shutting down your taste buds for the foreseeable future.

This latest masterstroke follows the disaster that was 'Spring Into Gin', which was Camberwell's last foray into novelty flavours that died at launch back in March. This one featured – and I kid you not – lemon and mint. It was like drinking mouthwash. One of the cheap varieties you always pass over in favour of Listerine. It did a good job of destroying the bacteria in your mouth, that's for certain. It also did a good job of destroying Harry Turner's job – my fellow marketing officer at the company for six years.

I don't intend to follow in his footsteps in the direction of the dole queue, hence my reaction to Matt exclaiming his distaste in front of this crowd of people I'm hoping to convince that buying a metric shit ton of Gin Fawkes is the best idea they've ever had.

'Please don't throw up on your shoes, Matt.' My eyes narrow. 'In fact, don't drink anything else. I need you out there schmoozing, and that's not really doable if you're drunk.'

Matt flicks off a lazy salute. 'Roger that, captain.' Then an eyebrow raises. 'Though I'm not sure I should be taking advice about not drinking from the man who I watched face plant into the pavement last weekend.'

For a moment my hand unconsciously goes to the bridge of my nose, which is still sporting a fading scab. 'That's different. That was fun. This is work.'

Although, I have to be honest, trying to stem the flow of blood from my nose wasn't *much* fun. Neither was dabbing stinging ointment on the cuts and grazes all the way along my arms and legs. Still, it had been a good night up until then. It always is down The Frog.

But today is about selling booze – not drinking it.

'Just please go and mingle,' I tell Matt. 'Charlton will be over here any minute, and you always manage to rub him up the wrong way for some reason. It's better if you're off trying to convince people to buy this drink.'

Matt's face darkens. 'He's a bully, that's why. I always rub bullies up the wrong way. It's why I have that scar on my arse from the compass Blinky Bill stabbed me with at school.'

'Well, he may be a bully but he's also our boss, so sod off and look busy.'

I shoo Matt away. He gives me a reluctant look, before heading off over to the crowd of people who hold my continued employment in their hands.

For a few moments, I fuss around with the Gin Fawkes display I've erected at the back of the room. It's hard to make nuclear orange gin look that attractive, to be honest. The gaudy label on the bottle doesn't help. Somebody might think it's a good idea to feature a painting of Guy Fawkes holding a glass of gin with a cheesy smile on his face, but I am definitely not that person.

I heave a fluttery sigh as I regard the room of people with a critical eye.

I wish Kate was here.

In the past, she's always been good at calming my nerves at these silly bloody events. She also makes them a lot more fun just by being at my side, and making inappropriate jokes under her breath when no one else is listening.

But she's been working her arse off recently, and just couldn't make it. After what happened to her at that wedding, she's doing everything she can to be employee number one at Stratagem PR, and that means working late on one of the portfolios she's had thrust at her in the past few weeks. I could hardly ask her to take the time off to come here tonight.

If anything, I hope she gets out of work early enough to go home and enjoy a nice bath, and some time to herself while I'm out. I think she's been way too hard on herself about that tractor business, so it'll help her relax, with any luck.

I'd still be a lot calmer if she were here though.

Out of the corner of one eye, I see movement from the main doors. The person who is responsible for the horror of Gin Fawkes – and Spring Into Gin, for that matter – has just walked in through the door.

Charlton Camberwell. A man for whom subtlety and social grace are things that just happen to other, less fortunate people. Charlton Camberwell never had a bad idea he didn't love. As such, Camberwell Distillery is having its worst financial run in a decade. Gin Fawkes is unlikely to change this.

Charlton sees me, and marches over, his pendulous gut leading the way from its constraints within the tweed waistcoat he's wearing. My boss ignores every single person in the room, showing the contempt he has for the very people that keep his company afloat. 'Bastard, money-grubbing wankholes,' he called them this morning in the final planning meeting. It's this charming attitude that has compounded the company's problems.

If Camberwell Distillery survives, it won't be thanks to the man who inherited it when his father, Charles, died three years ago.

'Temple!' he barks at me as he crosses the room. Charlton has never bothered to learn my first name. It's frankly a miracle he doesn't just call me 'minion'.

I affect as convincing a smile as I can muster at 7 p.m. on a cold October evening, after a ten-hour workday. 'Hello, Charlton,' I reply, holding out a hand as he approaches.

He ignores this. He usually does, but I always like to make the effort anyway – just in case.

'Everything going alright then, Temple?' he blusters, giving the display a good, hard look.

'I think so, Charlton, yes.'

'By Christ, that bottle looks *fantastic*, doesn't it?'

'Yes. Yes, it does.'

. . . if you're suffering from advanced mental fatigue, that is.

Charlton looks around at the smartly dressed men and women in the room, most of whom are looking back at him the way piranhas would view a passing shark.

'Have the shits had any yet?' he stage-whispers at me.

'A couple,' I tell him. They just about managed not to retch, I'm happy to say. Old Nigel Winters from Drink Lords Distributors actually seemed to like the stuff, but then I have it on good authority that Nigel is partial to a drink of pure ethanol every now and again, so this orange-and-cinnamon disaster zone would probably taste like nectar to him. Still, that's probably at least one distributor we can foist this liquid stupidity on to anyway.

'Do they like it?' Charlton asks, eyes ablaze.

'Nigel bloody loved it,' I tell him honestly, hoping that'll satisfy him.

Charlton laughs. 'Good old Nigel. Knows a decent drink when he gets his hands on one. What about the rest of them?'

'They . . . liked it too,' I reply, hesitantly. 'Not many have had the chance to taste it yet,' I add, which is a big fat lie, as the assembled distributors have all been here for at least an hour, waiting for Charlton Camberwell to grace them with his bulbous presence.

'Well, we'll get it shoved down their throats before this evening's out, you mark my words.' My overbearing boss then looks past me to the large glass double doors at the back of the conference room that lead out on to the distillery's picturesque country garden. 'And the fireworks? They all set up and ready to go?'

I blink a couple of times. I've had little to do with this part of the evening's festivities. Charlton was the one who hired his nephew to do the firework display. The fact he's now asking *me* if everything's set up is a trifle disconcerting.

'Um . . . I think so, Charlton. I haven't been out there for an hour or so.'

'Ah, it'll all be fine, I'm sure!' he replies dismissively. 'Tobias can be an awful little shit sometimes, but he always comes through with the goods if you poke him hard enough.'

I gulp rather nervously. As far as I'm aware, Tobias has no actual background in organising fireworks displays, so I'm hoping he's had more than a poke from Charlton Camberwell to prepare him properly for it.

'Uggh,' Charlton moans, the guttural sound coming from deep within that pendulous belly. 'I suppose we'd better go and talk to the shits for a while.'

I nod, trying to remain calm – on the outside at least. This job would be far easier if I had a boss who could give a toss about actually selling the product.

'Grab a bottle and some glasses then, Temple,' he orders. 'You've got to show the rest of them just how marvellous this concoction is, so they order a load in for the festivities in a few weeks.'

I give Charlton a wide-eyed look. 'I'm sorry, sir, what did you say? You want *me* to drink the gin?'

He leans forward. 'Well, somebody's got to do it, haven't they? To prove it's just about the best novelty gin they've ever clapped eyes on!'

'But, but . . .'

He picks up a bottle of the foul gin and hands it to me with a glass tumbler. 'But me no buts, Temple. You're my number one man on this. I'm counting on you to wow them all with how much you love our new product!'

'But, but . . .'

'We all know how much you like a drink, my boy. Let's put that to good use this evening, eh?'

What?

'I'm sorry?' I reply. 'You *all know* I like a drink?'

'Yes, of course! You're famous for it! And a jolly good job too. Makes you better at your job, man!' Charlton claps me on the back and laughs.

Oh dear.

That's *not good*.

This man is full of bluff and bravado, but if he says I've got a reputation in the company for being a drinker then I guess I have to take him seriously. Charlton doesn't give two hoots about the livelihood of his staff, and probably couldn't tell you much about any of us beyond what we do for a living. If the idea that I *like a drink* has filtered through into that rock-hard head of his, it must be a widely held opinion.

But I'm not *that* bad, for crying out loud!

Yes, I like to drink when I get the opportunity, because I enjoy it – and it's one of the only things I have time to do these days that I *do* actually enjoy, but that doesn't mean I deserve that kind of reputation.

. . . does it?

'Come on, there's that awful woman from Montague's,' Charlton exclaims, breaking my train of thought, 'and that drip from Hammond's. Let's go and show them what's what!'

And with that, Charlton drags me across the conference room floor, me clutching the bottle of awful gin and a glass, with a horrified expression on my face.

I may *like a drink* but I don't want to drink this swill. It's *disgusting*. And now I have to pretend it's the alcoholic second coming, so these people will be persuaded to buy it – even though they've been kept waiting by the pendulous gut next to me, and know that he can't stand to be in the same room as them.

'Ah! Clarissa! Ian! So pleased you could make it!' Charlton booms. 'You two represent our most important business associates, so it's *wonderful* to have you here tonight.' The condescension drips off every syllable like treacle. 'Have you had a chance to try some of our new product yet? It's absolutely fabulous, isn't it, Temple?'

I look at him blank-faced.

He nudges me in the ribs. 'I said, *isn't it, Temple?*' Charlton's eyes expectantly flip down to the bottle I have in my hands, and he waggles his eyebrows.

Oh God.

'Oh yes!' I say in a strangled voice, and pour myself a small amount. Charlton's expressive eyebrows knit together for a moment as he notes the paucity of volume. I pour a little more in . . . then a little more. His eyebrows only achieve equilibrium when I have nearly filled the glass to the fucking brim.

I then look at Clarissa and Ian. She looks at me with obvious pity – I think we can kiss goodbye to any chance of getting Montague's business. It's quite apparent she's already tried this orange garbage. Ian just looks at me as expectantly as Charlton. He's quite clearly not enjoyed the delights of Gin Fawkes, so I still might be able to get an order if I'm convincing enough.

I take a small sip of the gin.

It's like there's a funeral in my mouth and everyone's invited.

. . . and the funeral is on fire.

. . . including some dog shit in a bag just outside the church door.

For a second, I'm unable to hide the grotesque look of intense displeasure that crosses my face, but I gamely try to wrest my facial muscles into something resembling happiness as the cinnamon-and-orange-flavoured gin makes its way reluctantly down my throat.

'You see! It's just a gorgeous, gorgeous drink!' Charlton booms happily, as I try not to puke all its gorgeousness back up again.

'Good then, is it?' Ian asks. This would rather be like him asking a woman in the midst of labour if she's having a nice time.

'Yes!' I gasp, feeling the insides of my cheeks throbbing. 'It's a really interesting and original flavour.'

In much the same way that drinking vodka-infused horse piss would also be an interesting and original flavour.

'Temple can't get enough of it, can you, Temple? It's getting hard to keep the bottle out of his hand since we dreamed up the mix!' Charlton gives me another expectant look. Obviously, one sip of the orange-and-cinnamon hellfire isn't enough for him. I *have* to drink more.

This time I take a larger gulp, figuring that I'm going to have to empty this tumbler before I'm allowed to leave.

If a sip of Gin Fawkes is enough to make you retch, then an entire gulp makes your kidneys want to scramble up the inside of your oesophagus and make a valiant bid for freedom.

'Jesus Christ!' I spit, as I feel my epiglottis melt. Ian looks at me suspiciously. 'I mean . . . Jesus Christ, that's *good*,' I add enthusiastically. I follow this up with a big toothy grin. There's every chance the gin has now stained my teeth orange and is dissolving the enamel as we speak, which would rather destroy the good impression I'm trying to make.

'Ha! Excellent!' Charlton approves, happy with my little pantomime.

'Can I try some?' Ian asks, proving that all my efforts are going to be for nought once anyone actually tastes this rubbish. But what the hell am I supposed to do? Charlton pays my bloody mortgage.

I slowly go to hand the bottle and glass to Ian, but Charlton is one step ahead of me. 'No, no! That's *your* bottle, Temple! Ian can go get his own!'

'Yes . . . that's right. Get, get your own. This one's mine.' I try to say this like I'm being jovial about it, but I sound about as happy as a soldier who's just found that the only remaining foxhole is already full of corpses.

Ian still manages a little, awkward chuckle. Clarissa has remained silent throughout this exchange, and is staring at me. She's just seen me consume an entire glass of the gin, and is probably waiting for my kidneys to appear in my mouth.

'Right then! More people to speak to this evening, so we'll bid you two adieu for now, and hope that a big, fat order for our cleverly named

"Gin Fawkes" will be coming in soon. We can ship to you within the week!' Charlton tells them both. Unless Montague's or Hammond's are thinking of getting into the drain-cleaning business, an order seems unlikely.

I am then dragged across the conference room towards two more likely looking distributors. As Charlton does this I feel my eyesight temporarily blur. I've only had one drink of this hateful orange crap, but it was a big one, and thanks to having had no dinner in the rush to get this evening set up properly, the effects of all that cinnamon gin are already hitting my brain.

I *can't* get drunk tonight. I just *can't*. I'm never going to sell this drink to people if I'm rat-arsed.

Also, I have to get home later, and the taxi fare from here to the house is *astronomical*.

It's an expense I've had to pay out for quite a lot in the past, to be honest. After all, what better way to prove how tasty your product is than to consume a lot of it yourself in front of the right people, eh?

I might hate Camberwell Gin when it's laced with cinnamon and orange, but when it's on its own, with maybe a nice tonic water?

Different story.

There's nothing quite like the cool, crisp taste of this distillery's finest product, mixed with fresh tonic and poured over two spring water ice cubes.

The combination of sweetness and bitterness as it hits your taste buds? Pure *heaven*.

Given my love for a good gin, it goes without saying that this was my dream job when I got it. A dream that only really turned into a nightmare when Charlton was put in charge. His leadership has led to me drinking a lot more of our product over the past few years than I should – which is probably the cause of that disturbing reputation I've earned. It's also meant I hardly see my wife and daughter, which is something I hate Charlton bloody Camberwell for with a passion that's almost holy. He's robbed me of my life – the fat, obnoxious bastard.

And here he is now, propelling me towards more people that I have to drink this execrable stuff in front of.

'Zachary! Paul! Emilia! So pleased you could make it!' Charlton booms again at another three bored-looking distributors and publicans as we near them. They all try to hide their looks of disappointment that the imbecile has turned his attention towards them.

Charlton then proceeds to deliver the same script he did with Clarissa and Ian, with much the same response. None of these people are idiots, and I very much doubt Charlton's fake platitudes are having much of an effect on them.

My boss once again prompts me to drink some of the awful gin to show them how nice it is. Once again I try to take a small sip, and once again I am then forced to gulp a load down to prove that it's like drinking the nectar of the gods.

What choice do I really have?

If I refuse to drink, then I can pretty much be guaranteed to receive a P45 next week. Charlton sacked one of our van drivers a few weeks ago for accidentally nudging his Jaguar in the car park. Oh, he made up some spurious bullshit about the guy taking long lunch hours on a consistent basis, but we all knew what the real reason was.

I'm sure the rotund maniac won't think twice about throwing me under the bus if I don't play out this pantomime convincingly.

I do what I'm told, and again drain the glass of Gin Fawkes, showing the distributors in front of me how delighted I am about the whole thing.

They again look 1,000 per cent unconvinced, but it seems to be enough for Charlton, so we bid Zachary, Paul and Emilia farewell, and move on to a third group of special guests.

These two are from a company called Super Hooch, an alcohol distributor that prides itself on being young and funky. As such, Cordelia and Justin are exactly what you'd expect. Both in their twenties and annoyingly attractive, he looks like he's just left a Harry Styles gig, and she could be Taylor Swift's body double.

Charlton completely ignores poor old Justin, and spends his entire time dribbling over Cordelia. For a brief moment, I think I'm going to get away without having to drink more Gin Fawkes, but my boss eventually manages to roll his tongue back into his head, and has me down another load. Cordelia and Justin are probably no strangers to experimental alcohol consumption, but even they can't hide their combined looks of distress as the forty-something marketing director in front of them tries to fake enjoyment of his company's latest disastrous product.

By the time we hit the fourth and then *fifth* group of guests, I'm actually starting to warm to the Gin Fawkes – in more ways than one.

It hasn't got any better, of course. It still tastes like something you'd clean your best spoons with, but enough alcohol has entered my bloodstream now for the world to have taken on the rosy glow of happy inebriation.

When I was a student, I distinctly remember being plastered one night, and eating all of a chicken doner I'd dropped on the pavement outside the kebab house.

Drinking this Gin Fawkes idiocy is nothing compared to picking old fag butts and grit out of my favourite midnight snack.

At the time it tasted like the best kebab I'd ever had.

It didn't the next morning.

I'm sure I'll feel the same about Gin Fawkes when it hits my bowels at 7.30 a.m. tomorrow. For now, though, I've had *five* large glasses – which amounts to almost a bottle – and no longer need to fake my enthusiasm for it.

'Temple loves this stuff, don't you, Temple!' Charlton roars, clapping me on the back.

'Tha's right, Charltoton, I love this stuff!' I reply, grinning like the Cheshire Cat's drunk uncle. 'I's like there's a partity in my mouth, and all the peoples are invited!'

I don't think I've ever got this drunk this fast in my life. How much fucking gin did they put in this?

There's certainly a lot of cinnamon in it. My stomach lining feels like it's being basted in chili sauce.

Mmmmmm.

Chili sauce.

I wonder if there's a kebab place open nearby?

'Does anybody fancy a kebab?' I ask the people arranged in front of me. I then gaze blearily at Charlton. 'Do you fancy a kebab, boss?' I nod my head once. 'I fancy a kebab. I really do.' I look at our honoured guests. 'Would you lot like a kebab too?'

Charlton gives me a look. It's a look that suggests he's just beginning to realise what a monster he's unleashed on the world.

'Ah no,' he says. 'No kebab shops around here, Temple!' He puts an arm around my shoulder and laughs, looking at the distributors. They do that thing where they politely join in so as not to seem rude. One of them, a portly chap whose name I think is Alberto, looks like he'd quite like a kebab, actually.

I point at him. 'But Alberto wants a kebab too, Charlton!'

Alberto looks deeply confused. 'My name is Stephen.'

I leer at him. 'But you want a kebab, though, eh, Alberto?' I say, looking down at his gut. 'Yeah . . . I bet you do!'

Stephen/Alberto goes immediately red-faced. As does Charlton.

I can see my boss is about to say or do something that could have lasting consequences for my career in the gin industry, when my bacon is saved by Matt, who comes scurrying over.

'Er, Mr Camberwell?' he says in a timid voice.

'Matt!' I bellow at a volume level usually employed by the overbearing maniac stood next to me. 'How in buggery are you?'

Matt looks at me for a second, briefly dumbstruck by my complete change of demeanour. Then he returns his attention to the man who pays our wages. 'Mr Camberwell, we've got a problem!'

'What's the matter? Er . . . Malcolm, is it?'

I'm not the only one who can't get names right. At least I have the alcohol as a defence.

'It's Matt, Mr Camberwell.'

'Well, come on, out with it, what's your beef?'

Matt looks like he wants to start wringing his hands. 'It's Tobias, Mr Camberwell. He's . . . he's gone.'

Charlton's expression turns thunderous. 'What do you mean, he's *gone*?'

Matt looks understandably terrified. 'I went outside to see how he was getting on. He was on the phone with someone. I heard him say something about Granny Wanker's Ashes? Then he put the phone in his pocket and told me to tell you he had to rush off – and to say sorry.'

Charlton has gone puce.

'Granny Wanker's Ashes?' I repeat, my face lit up with amusement.

Matt nods. 'Yeah. I have no idea what he meant, but—'

'The little *scrotebag*!' Charlton spits, before remembering the company he's in. 'Apologies, my good friends,' he says to our guests with an ingratiating smile, 'but something appears to have come up. Please excuse us.' Without waiting for a response, Charlton bodily drags Matt and me over to one corner.

'Granny Wanker's *Ashes*?' I say again, trying not to giggle.

Charlton grinds his teeth for a moment. 'He means cocaine. The little shit has gone off to score some bloody drugs.'

My eyes go wide. 'And he calls it Granny Wanker's Ashes?'

'Yes.'

For a second my alcohol-fuelled brain can't quite grasp the hilarity of this. But then it does, to its fullest extent. I start to laugh so hard that snot comes out of my nose.

'Granny . . . Granny Wankereses Ashes!' I cry with drunken delight.

Charlton is not finding Granny Wanker's Ashes amusing in the slightest, however. 'Pull yourself together, man!' he orders.

I instantly stop laughing. I may be drunk, but I'm not drunk enough for it to completely override my sense of self-preservation.

'What are we going to do?' Matt asks. 'Who's going to do the fireworks now?'

Charlton's brow knits in a mixture of rage and frustration. 'I don't bloody know! He's the only one who knows how to work the flaming things!'

They both lapse into silence.

'I can do it,' I say in a confident voice.

Both of them look at me.

'What?' Charlton says.

'I can do it. I can do the fireworks, Mr Camberwell. Don't you fret.'

'Can you really?' he responds. 'Do you have any experience?'

'Yes! Yes I do!'

There is some truth to this. Three years ago I held a fireworks party at our house. We invited my parents, Kate's mother and sister and some friends around, and had a lovely time, as I recall. I handled the fireworks display. This consisted of a small box of the things bought from Asda, and a row of three empty wine bottles dug into the mud at the back of the garden. I managed to set off the entire box without a hitch. Everyone complimented me on how safely I managed the whole affair.

This can't be that different, *surely*?

Charlton's eyes narrow. 'Are you in a fit state to do it?'

I draw myself up to my full height. 'Of course I am, Mr Camberwell. You can rely on me!'

The reaction from both men is completely different. Charlton instantly looks pleased. In his world, if someone says they can handle something so he doesn't have to worry about it, he's a happy man. It doesn't matter if that person looks entirely unsuitable for the role, and could very well make a complete pig's ear of it. Charlton just doesn't have enough imagination to think about the consequences.

Matt does though.

'Er . . . I'm not sure that's such a good idea!' he says, unconsciously blocking my path to the door.

'Yeah it is!' I confidently argue, clapping him on the shoulder. 'It'll allllll be fine, Matthew.'

This causes Charlton to then clap *me* on the back in exactly the same manner. We now look like we're a terrible three-man boy band from the 1980s, about to break into the chorus. 'Ha! Well done, Temple! I'm sure I can rely on you to get this done!'

'Of course, sir! No problem, sir!' I crow, absolutely convinced that I can handle this with alacrity, grace and decisive positivity.

That's too much alcohol for you. It makes you think you're far more capable than you really are . . . *and* expands your vocabulary exponentially.

'I'm really not sure—' Matt tries to say again, but I cut him off with an upraised hand.

'You stay with Mr Camberwell, Matt. There are a few honoured guests left to schmooze, and you should help him with that while I attend to the fireworks display.'

Ha. That'll teach him to have no confidence in my sterling capabilities.

His face clouds, as I knew it would. The sun has, however, come back out on Charlton's – which is the main thing.

He looks at his watch. 'We'll give you fifteen minutes, Temple. Will that give you enough time to familiarise yourself with the system Tobias has used?'

System? *System?* Why do fireworks need a bloody *system*? You just need a lighter and an empty bottle, don't you?

Anything with a system sounds quite complicated, and certainly not something I can get to grips with in a quarter of an hour.

'Yes! That's more than enough time!' I tell my boss. 'You two go enjoy yourselves while I sort it all out.' I turn to leave, then look back at them. 'And if anyone knows where the nearest kebab van is, be sure to let me know.'

And with that, I'm beetling away towards the glass double doors, safe in the knowledge that I have got this shit *handled*, and handled *well*.

Outside, I march over to the rear of the large garden that the distillery has stood in for the last two hundred years. I'm on the lookout for a row of neatly set-up empty wine bottles, and a box of matches. With any luck Tobias will have nailed a couple of Catherine wheels to the back wall, because they always go down well.

When I arrive at the back of the garden, though, I am met with something that looks decidedly more sci-fi than the picture I had in my head.

There are three rows of fireworks, about six feet away from the back wall of the garden and its small but attractive wooden trellis. All the fireworks are inserted into lengths of plastic drainpipe, affixed in long wooden frames that have been securely driven into the soft earth with big metal spikes.

My drink-addled brain tries to ignore the fact that this kind of security measure can only mean that there's quite a lot of potential explosive energy contained in those drainpipes. Quite clearly a few empty wine bottles could not handle it.

All the fireworks are connected by a spiderweb of thin cord that eventually tangles together and leads to a large black industrial-looking suitcase, parked a good twenty feet away. I wander over to it and open it up. Inside is a very complicated-looking control panel, replete with knobs, buttons and switches that I would not have a hope of understanding if I was stone-cold sober and had a fortnight.

Instead, I'm pissed as a fart on awful gin and have ten minutes.

This should go well.

I do recognise an on/off switch – largely because it has 'ON' and 'OFF' written on it in large, friendly letters.

The rest I haven't a clue about.

Now if I wasn't drunk, at this point I would be taking a sensible decision and reporting to a disappointed Charlton Camberwell that I cannot run the fireworks display as it's too complicated. He'd no doubt be a little mad at me, but better that than try to bodge my way through a process that involves explosives.

But come on . . . I mean . . . look at it! It *can't* be that complicated, can it? I mean, all you're doing is flicking a few switches that'll set a few fireworky-works off. It's not bloody rocket science, is it? It'll all be absolulelely *fine*.

Besides, no one will be close to it, so if anything goes wrong, no one will be in any danger whatsoever.

What-so-ever.

I plonk myself on the ground next to the suitcase trigger and rub a hand over my face.

I then spend the next ten minutes in a daze, fantasising over what I'd put in my kebab.

When I see Charlton throw open the fire exit doors to allow our treasured, honoured and highly valued guests out on the lawn, I have decided that I'm going to have a lamb doner with extra chili peppers and barbecue sauce.

I really should have spent those ten minutes at least *attempting* to understand the complicated control box, but I tend to think with my stomach when I'm hammered.

I stand up, realising that my arse is now soaking wet from the condensation on the grass. Given that it's the end of October, I should also be freezing cold, but the cinnamon inside me is causing some kind of nuclear reaction in my gut, and I'm actually sweating like a pig. Boy, is Kate going to love me when I get home tonight.

'Everything set, Temple?' Charlton calls across to me. 'I've promised these fine people a display that'll send them home happy!'

I throw Charlton the largest thumbs up possible and lean awkwardly over the fireworks control box, hands clasped on wobbly knees. Then, for a few moments, I nibble on a finger as I try to decide what the hell I should actually do here.

First things first. Let's turn the damn thing on, shall we?

A mile or so away, the crew of the local fire station are just settling in to a nice evening of ping-pong and Pot Noodles. It's not Bonfire Night for another month, so they're taking advantage of this relative quiet before the storm . . .

I flick the on/off switch. A green zero appears on the display next to it.

So far so good.

Now what?

Do I press a few of the long line of red switches below it? Or do I opt for the long line of green switches above it?

There's a particularly tempting large black knob to the left of it, and an equally interesting small white knob to the right.

Let's start with one of the knobs, shall we?

The white one turns easily, but appears to do nothing. The black one turns with slightly more difficulty, but now the zero has disappeared from the display, and it now reads minus 14.

Is minus 14 a good thing or a bad thing at this juncture?

Who knows?

Perhaps the long line of red switches might offer some clarity. I flick the first one – and nothing happens. I flick the second with the same result. The third yields a dramatically similar outcome, and the fourth doesn't do anything to further the plot of this story either.

'What's the hold-up, Temple?!' I hear Charlton call out.

I stand and turn to face him. 'Apologies! Having a few te'nical issues with this funny box thing. Should have things underway soon though!' I punctuate my stunning positivity with a gigantic double thumbs up, and return to my musings.

You can only imagine what the collected distributors and publicans are thinking, having heard the man who's supposed to be running the fireworks display refer to the control system as 'this funny box thing'.

So, now there is only the row of green switches to try out.

I flick the first one, and it decides to provide me with much the same response as its red cousins. I flick the second, and the family continues to speak with one voice. I flick the third one, and—

Two small rockets on the end of the first row of fireworks burst into life. Well, I say burst – *sputter* would be a more accurate description.

I wave my arms around excitedly, however. At least something is happening.

'Wahaay!' I shout with enthusiasm borne of terrible gin. 'Here we go!'

Charlton looks delighted.

Everybody else who isn't drunk, or maintaining a tenuous grip on reality, steps back.

They needn't have worried. The two fireworks continue to sputter for a few moments, before one makes a dispirited effort to climb skywards, but only reaches about ten feet before going out with a small flash of light. The other just sits in the plastic drainpipe, farting its way towards oblivion with a slight jiggle and a high-pitched whining noise, before it too ends its short and disappointing life with the kind of burst of light and noise you'd normally associate with pulling a plug out of a wall in a badly wired house.

Oh dear.

This is not going well.

I look over at my boss, whose facial weather forecast has returned to decidedly thunderous.

I crouch and peer down at the control box again, wondering what the hell to do. I have flicked the switches. I have twiddled the knobs. What more can a man do at this point?

Something is going wrong, but I have no idea what.

I stand, wobbling slightly, and think about the dilemma set out in front of me.

Then, inspiration hits!

Maybe the box isn't close enough to the fireworks . . .

This makes no sense whatsoever because the box is hardwired to them, but I am considerably drunk, and therefore sense is not my best friend at the moment.

I throw the punters another thumbs up, and then pick up the box, manhandling it closer to the long lines of fireworks. It's bloody heavy, so I'll probably pay for this move with a few trips to the chiropractor, but my immediate concern is for my future as an employee of Camberwell Distillery, not my lower lumbar region.

I dump the box just ten feet away from the fireworks, and flick a few of the red and green switches again. Frustratingly, this yields no positive result.

If I don't come up with a decent plan soon, I'm going to be in real trouble. I turn my attention to the black knob again, thinking about how humiliating it will be to have to go down to the local job centre and—

Kaboom.

No . . . seriously. *Kaboom.*

It's a bloody good job I'm crouched behind the large plastic lid of the open control box, otherwise I'd be spending the rest of my life getting to know my friendly guide dog.

The entire collection of fireworks goes off at once.

Some ignite the way they should, and would no doubt be flying skywards very soon were it not for the fact that most of them simply explode in the drainpipes, thanks to me inadvertently driving about 1,000 per cent more electronic juice at them than they needed.

The back of the Camberwell Distillery garden is engulfed in multicoloured fire. It's like somebody has committed grand-scale arson in a rainbow factory.

Everyone gathered immediately starts to run away, screaming as they go. I see poor old Nigel from Drink Lords go down on the soft grass in the rush to get back inside, away from this maelstrom of fire and sparks.

Suddenly, from the roaring carpet of malfunctioning explosives, a few of the fireworks make a break for freedom. This happens in multiple directions. Although the one direction they mostly seemed aimed at is my drunken face.

'Holy shitballs!' I cry, as one rocket heads towards me at a frightening rate of knots. I manage to twist my head to one side before it hits me, but I still feel the heat from it as it passes way too close to my left ear for comfort.

Ducking as much as possible, I make a drunken, bow-legged run for the safety of the conference room. As I do this I notice that Charlton has now inexplicably jumped on top of Taylor Swift lookalike Cordelia, and is covering her in the manner of a brave soldier protecting a baby from a hand grenade. She is apparently not entirely pleased with this due care and attention, as she's screaming and kicking her legs and arms around like a freshly pinned insect.

My concern for Cordelia's well-being is rather overshadowed by concern for my own as a particularly large rocket flies past me on the right-hand side, ricocheting off the Camberwell Distillery wall before heading skywards. I follow the crowd back through the double doors of the conference room as Matt starts to close them behind us.

'Wha' about Charlton?' I slur as I rush past. We both look outside to see that our boss has now been thrown off by Cordelia, who is scrambling to her feet, her £500, uber-trendy haircut now in disarray.

Matt looks at me for a moment. 'Fuck him!' he cries in a panicked voice, and slams the doors closed as Cordelia stumbles past him.

I'm rendered completely immobile. In my drunken haze, the shock of Matt's hasty decision simply will not compute. He's just locked the man who pays our wages out of the only place that can offer him protection from the rampant, uncontrolled fireworks display going on outside.

Surely this is likely to damage our chances of a Christmas bonus?

Another rocket flies right towards us and ricochets off one of the glass doors. Matt and I flinch and stumble backwards. As we do this, Charlton rises to his feet, turns to look at the maelstrom behind him and starts to lurch towards us.

'Jesus! Get the doors open, Matt!' I wail. 'We have to let him in!'

This time it's Matt's turn to be rendered immobile. The stress and calamity of the situation have obviously robbed him of motor function.

'Oh, for fuckity fuckingham's sake!' I shout in frustration and stagger towards the doors as my boss nears them from the other side, a look of terror on his dewlapped face.

My hands are extraordinarily sweaty, and my co-ordination is shot to pieces, so it takes me a few moments to gain purchase on the round doorknob. Charlton, meanwhile, is screaming at me to get the door open.

It's like something out of a particularly terrible 1980s horror movie – but one with an inexplicably large pyrotechnics budget.

Eventually, I do manage to wrench the door open, and look up at my boss's relieved face.

From behind him, I see a lone firework erupt from the cauldron of fire and start to fly straight towards us. It takes a split second to cross the intervening distance.

Its aim is unnervingly accurate, as if guided by some unseen force that quite clearly intends for me to lose my job this evening.

It's a good thing the firework is only a very small one, as anything larger would have caused serious injury.

As it stands, however, I'm sure even a small firework isn't something Charlton Camberwell particularly wants fired straight into his bottom.

Nevertheless, this is exactly what happens.

His expression instantly changes from one of relief to one of pained disbelief. It only goes downhill from here as the firework gets caught on the fabric of his trousers.

'Oh, good Lord Jesus save me!' Charlton shrieks as the firework kicks out sparks from his arse. He attempts to run away from it, right into the conference room and towards our horrified guests. He now resembles a celestial comet – if said comet was at least five stone over-weight and had chronic male pattern baldness.

Just before he barrels into everyone, the firework ends its short but eventful life with a large *BANG*, which is enough to nearly cause most of the room premature heart attacks. Charlton jumps about three feet off the floor, which is probably the most exercise he's had in thirty years.

A small, dark part of me revels in my boss's discomfort and humili-ation for a moment.

Yeah . . . I hope your arse is red raw, you overbearing, moronic, fat pig. That'll teach you to keep me at work all the hours God sends!

Outside, the fireworks catastrophe is finally coming to a close, though not before it sets fire to the small trellis against the back wall.

At this point, someone – I don't know who in all the confusion – calls the fire service, who are no doubt very grumpy about having to put down their Pot Noodles when the call comes through.

I scurry over to my boss, who is now face down on the carpet, hold-ing his battered arse, and try to think of some words of comfort. Inside, I may be pleased to see him in such a state, but outwardly, I know which side my gin-soaked bread is buttered on.

'Your trousers aren't on fire, sir,' I say. If telling someone that their trousers aren't on fire is the best you can do, you really need to work on your bedside manner.

I bend over and assist him to his feet. Matt comes to help me do this, which is just as well, as Charlton is a heavy bastard.

'Pbbb pb b ppb bbbp pb,' he says as we do this. Small spit bubbles appear at the corners of his mouth.

'Are you . . . are you okay, sir?' I say, in what must be the most idiotic question ever asked.

'Bppp pbb bpb pb pbp bpbp pp,' he replies. I now feel like I'm trying to communicate with a pan of baked beans on the hob.

'Mr Camberwell? How are you, sir?' I continue in a slow, tense voice.

Charlton looks at me, eyes bulging. 'Temple . . . Temple . . . I . . . I . . .'

Oh dear. I think I'm about to get fired in front of a load of strangers.

Matt, bless him, then saves my life by saying the following: 'Scott made a right hash of that, didn't he, sir?'

I give him a look that screams, *You're not helping.*

Matt ignores this and continues to look at our enraged and embarrassed boss. 'He should never have been allowed anywhere near those fireworks!' He stares at me, his head nodding slightly, goading me to agree. I'm not entirely sure what he's up to, but I might as well play along, given that my goose can't get any more cooked at this point.

'Yes. I shoul' never have been . . . have been allowed anywhere near them,' I say hesitantly.

'That's right!' Matt carries on. 'They should have only been handled by somebody with professional experience. I can only imagine what the fire service . . . and *the police* might say if they knew.'

Aha.

Now I get it.

I grip my boss's meaty shoulder, in a manner he himself is so experienced at. 'Oh God, Mr Camberwell! Matt's right! If the authorities discover that I was allowed to do this display – 'specially drunk off my arse, like I am – then the damage it coul' do to the distillery . . . It doesn't . . . doesn' bear thinking about!'

Charlton Camberwell is a loutish, self-centred oaf, but he's nobody's fool. The import of what I'm telling him manages to break through the tidal wave of rage that's about to break all over me. He instantly changes from puce with anger to white with fear.

Something like this could quite easily get the distillery shut down on health and safety grounds – and he'd be the one ultimately responsible for it. He is in charge, after all.

Charlton takes an extremely deep breath.

'I think,' he begins slowly, 'it might be a good idea to send our guests away, and say no more about this evening's events.' He goes bug-eyed again. '*To anyone.*'

Both Matt and I do our best nodding dog impersonations.

'Let us' – a hand slowly goes to his backside and begins to rub it absently – 'let us send them on their way with sample bottles of the gin, and hope they decide to order a batch.'

Nod nod nod.

There's no chance of this happening, of course, but my job rather depends on maintaining the fiction for the time being.

'And let us do it *quickly*,' Charlton says, eyes narrowing, 'before the authorities arrive.'

He mouths the words 'no witnesses' at us both.

Nod nod nod. Nod nod nod.

Matt and I then proceed to rush around the crowd of traumatised guests, hastily thanking them for their time, thrusting bottles of Gin Fawkes in their hands and ushering them out through the distillery as fast as their legs will carry them. While we do this, Charlton stumbles outside to see how bad the trellis fire has become – which, thankfully, isn't too bad at all. It doesn't look like there's any danger of the distillery going up in flames.

Cordelia and Justin are last out of the door. As they go I hear her say something about being crushed by a hippo. I think it's not only my bacon being saved by initiating this hasty exit. Cordelia may well have grounds for a sexual assault charge, so it's probably just as well she's leaving before she can come to that conclusion herself.

The fire service duly arrives about a minute after the last car has left the car park. We tell them the fireworks went off accidentally, without us touching them. Charlton then proceeds to drop the absent Tobias right in the shit, which I would feel bad about, if the little sod hadn't left *us* in the shit in his desire to obtain the Ashes of Granny Wanker.

'I'm never drinkin' again,' I tell Matt as we watch the fire engine leave, after it's doused the distillery garden in enough water to fill an Olympic swimming pool, and Charlton has gone off to the toilet to rub cream over his ample posterior. 'Not Gin Fawkes anyway,' I add.

'*Nobody* is ever drinking Gin Fawkes again, Scott,' he suggests.

I turn to him. 'Thank you, Matt. You really saved my life back there. You're a good . . . good friend.'

He shrugs. 'No worries. You can make it up to me by buying every single round of drinks for the next year.'

'I said I wasn't going to drink again,' I remind him, waggling a finger at him.

He arches one eyebrow, before slowly turning to walk back in through the distillery's main doors.

I have to concede his scepticism is understandable.

The one thing I've learned tonight – apart from the fact I should never be allowed near fireworks *ever again* – is that I have a 'reputation' at the distillery for being something of a drinker. That's why Charlton wanted me to demonstrate how lovely the gin is, and that's why I nearly burned the whole place down.

This feels . . . *uncomfortable.*

To have a reputation for being a drinker at a *distillery* is deeply troubling. Most of the staff here can drink a majority of the population under the table. If they consider *me* to be the biggest fan of alcohol among them, then I may have *a bit of a problem*. I've always thought my obvious love of our traditional product was a bonus in my job – but maybe it's not so good for my continued health and well-being.

It's certainly something I'll have to give more consideration to, once I've sobered up a bit.

For now, though, I'll have to finish helping Matt and Charlton lock up the distillery for the night. I imagine the cleaners will be having collective apoplexy when they come in tomorrow morning.

Then I'll have to order a cab to take me home.

And *then* I'll have to explain to Kate why I am home so late and drunk after an evening at work . . . *again*.

Mind you, do I even want to tell her what happened here tonight?

I know how guilty I felt about not making it to that wedding – and not being with her when that whole tractor business happened. I imagine she might feel the same way about not being here with me tonight. Kate has the power to charm Charlton Camberwell in a way that's almost magical. She would have made sure I didn't get this drunk. If she'd been here, everything would have been alright.

This leads me to a very uncomfortable conclusion.

Both Kate and I have now brought down near calamity on our heads, because we weren't there to support each other, and stop each other's worst excesses.

We always handle things better as a team. We always have.

I certainly can't remember a time when things have gone so horribly wrong when we've been drinking *together*. No. We've always managed to keep each other out of too much mischief on a night out – and have always been there for one another the morning after as well, when the hangovers inevitably kick in.

But how long has it been since we've done that? How long since we were able to support each other as a couple? To get a bit sozzled together, and then spend the next day curled up on the sofa, trying to wish the hangovers away with copious amounts of tea? How long since we last did something like that with one another?

How long has it been since there was a *Team Temple*?

Too long, mate.

Too bloody long.

I shake my head abruptly, trying to chase these thoughts away. I'm far too drunk to think about it at the moment.

But I'll talk to my wife tomorrow, without a doubt – once I'm sober enough to think straight.

We'll sit down. We'll talk. We'll make each other feel better.

. . . and we'll do our best to *fix* things, to get back the closeness we've lost – before any more disasters befall us.

Everything will be alright then.

Definitely.

. . . I just have to get the time off bloody work first.

CHAPTER THREE

HOLLY VS PARENTS

Welcome to the bedroom of your average seventeen-year-old.

Gaze in awe at the mountain of make-up piled on the dresser. Gasp in amazement at the huge pile of clothes that lies just outside the largely empty wardrobe. Look doubtfully at the precarious position the iPad is in, teetering on the edge of the bedside cabinet. Worry somewhat about the safety of the tangle of electrical charger cords erupting from the plug socket to one side of it.

This is not the room of a person at peace with the universe.

Nobody is when they're a teenager. The universe is a strange and complicated place at the best of times, and being in thrall to raging teenage hormones is *never* the best of times. It's a wonder they're not all on anxiety medication by the age of fourteen.

Holly Temple is a particularly anxious and troubled teenage girl right now.

It's her parents, you see. They drive tractors into walls and nearly blow up distilleries.

Here she is now, sitting down in front of the iPhone video camera that's currently capturing the back of her messy bedroom in glorious high definition.

Included in the aforementioned teenage mess is a small silver Christmas tree sat next to the haphazardly placed iPad, which is as near as Holly can be bothered when it comes to decorating her bedroom for the festive season.

Holly isn't feeling festive. Not at all.

The expression on her face is not a happy one. Most seventeen-year-old girls have perfected the art of looking miserable, of course, but Holly Temple actually has good reason.

Her parents are the WORST.

She looks into the camera, pouting heavily.

'My parents are the absolute WORST,' she says morosely. 'No, seriously – the total and complete WORST PARENTS IN HISTORY.' Holly's brow creases in the kind of irrational fury only a teenager can summon. 'Amber might say hers are worse than mine, but all they do is argue about money and stuff. At least they're *sober* most of the time. And they're around for her if she needs them. *They're* not always working all the time. The last time I remember doing anything with Mum and Dad, it was my fifteenth birthday, when we went to Wahaca for burritos.'

Holly picks out a strand of long dark hair and starts to twiddle it.

'It's getting stupid now. I don't think I've seen Mum or Dad in a good mood for months without a fucking—' Holly's eyes go wide as she realises how loudly she just swore. Her head flicks round to her bedroom door for a moment, before she looks back at the camera and swears again at a lower-decibel level. 'Without a fucking drink in their hands.'

Twiddle.

'In fact, the only time I ever see them anywhere near happy these days is when they're bloody *drinking*. They used to go out, enjoy themselves and have a good laugh. They were fun to be around when I was a kid. But those days are long gone now. It's like there's nothing else left in the world for them apart from work and booze. They seem to have forgotten about everything else . . . including *me*, and maybe even worse – *each other*. The only time I see them actually talk these days is when one of them asks if the other one wants a top-up. It's pathetic.'

She shakes her head in a sorrowful way.

'Do you have any idea how embarrassing it is to tell your mates they can't come round, just in case your parents are pissed up?'

Holly slaps her thigh.

'Why can't they just be more fucking *normal*? Why can't they change? Why can't they stop each other?'

She rolls her eyes and looks towards the ceiling.

'I can't put up with it much longer. I've got to do something to show them what a nightmare they are now. If I don't, I'll end up in therapy – like Dolcis Carter did when her dad went to jail for insurance fraud. It's bad enough being accidentally named after a shoe shop from the 90s, but then having your dad tell you he pretended you were dead to clear a gambling debt? It really finished her off.'

Holly's face sets into a determined look.

'There's no way I'm letting that happen to *me*. I'm going to get Mum and Dad to lay off the booze and start behaving better – before I'm on Prozac like poor Dolcis.' The sheer, unbridled horror of this is writ large on Holly's face.

'Over Christmas I'm going to video them every time they get wasted, just so I can show them how bad they are, once they've sobered up again. That should do it!'

After a last frantic twiddle of her hair, Holly sighs heavily, leans forward and shuts the camera off.

And then it's Christmas Day!

A time for everyone to have fun, make merry and enjoy the company of loved ones.

. . . and also shag the Christmas tree, apparently.

Holly records her father's antics on her iPhone with mounting dismay.

'Kate! Kate! Look at this!' Scott Temple giggles with drunken glee as he thrusts his groin into the large Scots pine sat in the corner of the living room. 'Jus' like that dog we saw last week when we went to get the tree, eh?'

'Scott! For crying out loud! My . . . my mother's here!' Kate cries in mock horror from her position on the blue couch, next to her thrusting husband. As she does this, she spills red wine on the arm of the couch.

Sat next to her is Holly's grandmother, Alice, who is still stone-cold sober, and is probably wishing she'd accepted the lift that Scott's parents offered her an hour ago, when they saw which way the alcoholic wind was blowing.

It's only six thirty in the evening, and Holly's parents have already arrived at the stage of gross, embarrassing behaviour, and carefree alcohol spillage.

This is something of a new record for them.

'Dad! Stop it!' Holly exclaims from behind the phone's camera.

'Jus' jus' get this on film, Hols!' Scott replies. 'It's jus' like that dog!'

Kate points a finger at her husband and laughs. 'He does look just like that dog, though, doesn't he? I'm glad we didn't take the tree he was fucking!'

She then falls into a fit of giggles, spilling even more wine in the process.

'Do you want to come and make a cup of tea with me, Nan?' Holly says to Alice, who gives her a grateful nod, before reaching out a hand for Holly to help her up.

Now it's even later that evening.

Alice has been taken home by Kate's sister, Jenny, who had wisely been with her husband's family this year – leaving Holly and her iPhone alone in the house with her two drunken parents. As the evening slips past ten o'clock, the drunken tomfoolery of earlier has unfortunately given way to something of an argument.

From the ajar living room door, Holly chronicles the heated discussion – which is over the lingerie set Scott has purchased his lovely wife for Christmas this year.

'Why woul' you think I'd *want* something like this, Scott?' Kate asks, waving the black Agent Provocateur box at him.

Scott holds his arms out, palms up. 'I though' . . . I though' you'd like it! You said to me las' month that you don' feel sexy any more! That we don't—' Scott throws a glance over to the door. Holly jerks the camera back for a second, but thankfully her father doesn't see her. 'Tha' we don't have *sex* any more.'

Kate looks half bewildered, half furious. 'And you thought this was the way to fix that?!'

'Yes!'

'Oh *God*. We don't have sex any more because we never *see each other* any more, Scott!' Kate shakes the box. 'This stuff won't fix *that*.' She makes a face. 'And it'll make me look like a bloody prostitute.'

'You – you won' look like a prostitute! You'll look wunnerful!'

Kate throws the box down hard on to the coffee table. 'To *you*, you bloody perv!' She picks up her wine glass and takes a healthy swig, before regarding him with a drunken, critical eye. 'I hope that's not all I am to you now, Scott. A walking sex object.'

Scott bends down and retrieves the box. 'No! No! You're no' an object! You're my wife!' He totters a bit on his feet. 'My sexy, sexy wife . . . who I – I love ver' ver' much.'

Kate stares at him, a dispirited look on her face. '*Do* you, Scott?'

He goes bug-eyed. 'Of course!'

Kate takes another swig of wine. 'Then why do I fee' like you *don't*?' She affects a look of utter misery. 'What's happened to us, Scott? Why do I feel like we're bloody *strangers* these days? And why do you think

I'd wanna wear stuff like that?' She stabs a finger at the box. 'I thought you knew me *better*.'

'But – but . . . this is a *lovely* gift!' Scott continues, his face now darkening. 'It cost me a fortune!'

Kate throws her arms up in drunken exasperation. 'Well, maybe *you* should wear it then!'

Scott goes goggle-eyed for a moment. 'Alright! Maybe I *will*!' he replies, pulling the box open.

'Oh God – *no*, Scott!' Kate wails.

'Oh fuck me,' Holly exclaims in whispered horror.

The lacy black lingerie set falls to the floor, and Scott scrabbles around to pick it up. He grabs the bra and stands up straight. 'Look, Kate! This is a *sixty pound* bra! And I'm going to put it on to show you how lovely and fuckin' *classy* it is.'

'Please, Scott, no!' Kate replies. She still sounds angry, but there's amusement in her voice now. Only being this comprehensively drunk can allow these two disparate emotions to exist together at one time.

Scott then proceeds to awkwardly put on the expensive bra over his polo shirt. He just about manages to get both arms through the straps, but has no chance of doing it up, of course.

Kate now starts to laugh out loud at this. 'Oh my God, you look *ridiculous*!' she screams.

Next, Scott hauls the garter belt up to his waist, the suspenders flying around like the legs of an electrocuted spider.

He then gathers up the French knickers and tries to hoist them over his jeans as well. Given how drunk he is, though, his legs don't want to co-operate with this complicated manoeuvre, and he rapidly stumbles forward, spearing Kate in the stomach as he does so.

The Temples' front room now resembles a particularly cheap wrestling match, involving a highly unconvincing crossdresser called Drunken Scottina and his sworn enemy, the Hammered Housewife.

'Aaaargh!' Kate wails as her husband's shoulder comes into contact with her abdomen. The glass of wine she's holding is sent skywards in a glorious arc of deep-red liquid that will require professional steaming to get it out of the carpet.

Both of them fly back into the couch, sending it rocking backwards. This in turn knocks over the Christmas tree, which crashes against the wall, before falling over in a dispirited Yuletide heap.

Kate is now pinned to the couch with her husband on top of her. Scott appears to have been knocked unconscious.

'Oh God! Oh God!' Kate cries, attempting to push the bulk of her husband off, with little success.

It's at this point Holly decides to intervene, before either parent is carted off to A&E, so she comes into the room in a hurry, ending her recording as she does so.

Two a.m.

The house is silent. Everyone should be fast asleep, but poor Holly is wide awake and prowling about. Passing her parents' bedroom on the way down to the kitchen to get some snacks, she decides to record the aftermath of the Temples' Christmas Day hijinks.

Inside the darkened bedroom, only her mother is visible. She's lying on the bed on her stomach, fully clothed. In front of her, at the end of the bed – on the small and terribly out-of-date TV/video combi that stands on a chest of drawers – a video is playing, which illuminates the bedroom in a cold, flickering glow.

Holly zooms in on the TV with her own camera, and is rather dismayed to see that her drunk mother is watching old videos of her wedding day. The footage is grainy and jumps every few seconds or so – testament to the poor quality of 90s video equipment. Currently, Scott's twenty-two-year-old self is toasting his new bride with a glass of champagne. Both have huge smiles on their faces. It's rather a lovely scene, ruined somewhat by sudden lines of static that crawl up the screen, indicating the VHS tape has chewed itself at some point in the past.

'Oh no,' whispers Holly in a sad little voice. 'She's doing it again.'

She moves the camera back to her mother. Kate appears to have fallen fast asleep, her head lolling over the end of the bed.

Holly moves into the room and zooms in on the thin line of drool now coming from her mother's mouth, which extends in one unbroken line all the way to the floor. It glistens ever so slightly in the flickering light of the TV. Kate is snoring loudly, making the drool dance and jiggle.

Holly backs away before she can disturb her mother, and switches off the TV. She pads quietly out of the room and down the stairs to see if she can find her father.

She comes across him still in the living room, still half on the couch, and still unconscious. Scott's knees are on the floor, but the rest of his body is on the wine-soaked blue sofa, with his head stuffed between the two large back cushions so it's barely visible, and his butt stuck up in the air like a presenting cat. He resembles someone who's just been guillotined, very badly.

For a moment, Holly worries that he might actually be dead, but as she draws closer a muffled snore arises from between the cushions, indicating that he lives.

Scott is still half wearing the Agent Provocateur bra and garter, with the knickers tangled around his ankles.

It is a sorry, sorry sight to see.

As Holly starts to back away, having fully captured her father in his drunken repose, he emits a loud and sonorous fart from his elevated rear end that goes on for a good ten seconds.

'Oh, for fucking hell's sake!' Holly exclaims aghast, ceasing her recording as she makes a break for the fresher air of the kitchen.

Now it's Boxing Day morning.

Weak winter sunshine filters in through Holly's bedroom window, bathing her rather drawn face in a light golden hue that does something to lift the miserable look on her face, but not enough to take it away completely.

She looks down the camera lens and shakes her head solemnly.

'Can I divorce my parents?' she says, only half joking. 'Or can I at least move to another country? Australia's a nice place, isn't it? I could live in Summer Bay.'

The fingers of her right hand start to twiddle her hair again.

'Anyway, at least you can see what I'm on about now, can't you? How bad they are? How awful they can be once they've had a few?'

She rolls her eyes and looks away from the phone.

'Oh, who the hell am I talking to? It's not like I'm actually going to show this to anyone other than them.'

Twiddle.

'I'd be *way* too embarrassed to show it to my friends. Especially Amber.'

Twiddle, twiddle.

Holly looks back at the lens, tears of frustration in her eyes. 'Maybe I *should* though. Yeah . . . that'd show them, wouldn't it? Maybe I *should* show it to Amber, and everybody else!' Her fists clench. 'Maybe I should put the video up on YouTube, so everybody can see just how awful you are, Mum and Dad!'

Now Holly crams the strand of hair into her mouth and starts to chew on it for a moment, before spitting it out in disgust.

'Tyler and Carrie put that video of their dad skiing in his boxer shorts on YouTube. They weren't worried about what he'd say! And that's got to be as bad as what I recorded yesterday!'

Holly appears to think about this for a second, her face stricken.

'No . . . it's nowhere near as bad, is it?'

Her shoulders slump. 'No. My parents really are the *worst*. But I'm going to show *them* this video today, for definite. Nine times out of ten they never remember how bad they were by the time they sober up, but I'm going to make sure that doesn't happen this time! Maybe it'll make them see. Maybe it'll make them *stop*. Maybe it'll make them *change*.'

Holly looks away from the camera for a second, staring down at the floor to one side, before slowly looking back.

'Maybe,' she says, one final time, before leaning forward and switching the recording off.

PART TWO
SOBER

CHAPTER FOUR

KATE HAS A HANGOVER

Oh, good God.

. . . actually, scratch that. He can't be good. No benevolent deity would have designed the human body to respond so poorly to excessive amounts of alcohol.

My head throbs like the malfunctioning filament in an electric heater from the 1970s – the kind we all had before somebody invented health and safety. The filament would always start to burn brighter and harder for a few moments, right before it exploded.

That's my head right now. In exploding filament territory.

The large glass of water I've just poured myself from the kitchen tap might help with the burning headache a little, though I'm not sure how my stomach is going to react to it.

Probably not all that favourably.

Still, somebody once told me that the most important thing to avoid a bad hangover is to drink plenty of water. I'd argue that the most important thing to avoid a bad hangover is not to drink too much alcohol in the first place.

I feel dreadful.

Still . . . at least I didn't spend the night inserted into a four hundred quid DFS couch.

I made a rather half-hearted attempt to raise Scott from his slumber, only to be greeted by a long sonorous snore, and an even longer sonorous fart. It'll be a while before he manages to work his way back to consciousness, I'd imagine. When he does, I'm sure he'll be *delighted* by the taste of cheap upholstery in his mouth, and the women's lingerie wrapped around his body.

Last night's argument is possibly the most *ridiculous* one we've ever had. It even tops the time we decided to argue about the new taps in the bathroom, while standing in line for Colossus at Thorpe Park. I distinctly remember my last words on the subject being something along the lines of 'Fine! We'll go with the fucking stainless steel mixer then!' before being plunged into a series of loop the loops that my new haircut never recovered from.

Speaking of loop the loops, I'd better sit down at the table, before my stomach rejects all that cold water I've just dumped into it.

In a short while, once things have settled down a bit, I will make a lovely cup of coffee for both myself and Scott – but for the present minute, I feel it may be better for my sense of well-being to just stare at the fridge door and try not to make any sudden movements.

At least it's nice and quiet in here. That is something I should be grateful for.

As I take a few deep breaths, and contemplate my immediate future, I close my eyes and lower my head. This feels lovely. So lovely that I think I might continue to lower my head a little more, until it eventually reaches the table.

'Morning, Mum.'

I sit bolt upright, spilling some of the water from the glass I still have clutched in my hand.

Holly is standing at the door, a look of weary exasperation on her face.

This expression tells me that she was witness to her parents' drunken antics last night, the poor girl. I'd better do everything I can today to make it up to her.

Affecting the most natural smile I can with a busted heating filament for a brain, I say good morning to Holly, and rise gingerly from the chair.

'Would you like a drink, sweetheart? I was just about to make coffee for your father and me.'

'No thanks,' Holly replies, as she walks across the kitchen and sits herself down at the table. 'I'm fine.'

Oh dear. She sounds *really* unhappy.

Did something happen last night that I can't remember?

I know Scott and I weren't exactly on our best behaviour, but Holly's demeanour rather suggests that something transpired beyond a few drunken antics and a silly argument. I don't remember anything else happening, though, and I'm pretty sure I wasn't drunk enough to be suffering memory loss.

'Are you sure you're okay, sweetheart?' I ask her, sitting back down again. 'I know me and your dad got a bit silly last night—'

'A *bit*?' my daughter replies, incredulously.

I chuckle ruefully. 'Well, it's Christmas, sweetheart, and people do let their hair down at Christmas, so—'

'You have no idea, have you?' Holly replies, cutting me off again. I'm trying to make light of this situation, but my daughter is clearly having none of it.

I rub my pounding forehead. 'I don't know what you mean, Holly.'

She crosses her arms. 'No. You never bloody do.'

Okay, this is getting a bit much. I don't think my hangover can cope with a row with my seventeen-year-old this morning. If nothing else, we're due at my sister's house in a couple of hours, and I'm going to need at least that long to feel human again.

'Alright, young lady, watch your language, please.' I give her a stern look. Well . . . it's stern-*ish*. It's a little hard to look that authoritarian when you're squinting, and as pale as a ghost. 'What's got you in this mood today?' I continue, leaning forward a little.

Holly looks astounded. 'What's got me in this mood?'

'Yes. What is it?'

'It's *you*, Mum! You and Dad! What you were like yesterday! What you're like a lot these days!' Holly shakes her head. 'Nan didn't know where to put herself once you two got going!'

I wave a dismissive hand. 'Mum was fine, Hols. She had a good time.'

'No she *didn't*!' my daughter replies, shaking her head angrily.

I'm about to reply when a zombie appears at the door.

'Uuuuggghhh,' it says, holding one hand to its head. 'My tongue tastes like I've been licking a wet dog.'

'That taste isn't dog, my beloved husband,' I tell him. 'It's the back of our couch.'

Scott thinks for a moment. 'That might actually be worse.'

He shuffles into the kitchen and plonks himself down at the table, so that the Temple family are united as one in their Boxing Day misery.

Thankfully for all concerned, Scott has managed to extricate himself from the Agent Provocateur lingerie. Holly seems to be in a bad enough mood with us today. I doubt her father sporting a lacy bra and knickers over his clothes would have improved matters.

'Your daughter isn't happy with our conduct yesterday,' I point out to Scott as he leans forward to put his head in his hands.

'Why?' comes the muffled reply.

'Because you were both *awful*, that's why!' Holly snaps, sitting back and folding her arms.

'I'm sure it wasn't that bad, Hols,' Scott says.

'Oh Christ! The pair of you are in such fucking denial!'

My eyes blaze. 'Holly Temple! Language!'

'Owww. Please don't shout so loud,' Scott pleads from behind his cupped hands.

'I'll bloody well shout when our only child comes out with language like that!'

Holly points a finger at me. 'You were saying stuff like it last night, Mum!'

I contrive to look shocked. 'I was not! I never use language like that around my mother!'

Holly bangs her fists on the table. 'Oh my God! You really have *no idea!*'

'Please, both of you,' Scott says in a small voice, 'lower the volume level a little.'

Holy gives her father a disgusted look and then fishes in her jeans pocket, pulling out her iPhone so fast that it brings a load of small change with it. She ignores this and starts stabbing angrily at the phone's screen. 'I recorded you both yesterday. I wanted you to see how bad you both are when you're pissed.'

Oh dear.

Oh dear, oh dear.

Nobody ever needs to see stuff like that. Never, *ever.*

I note that Scott's face has gone even greyer, so I know he feels the same way.

'Oh God, Holly, you need to stop with that phone,' I say to my daughter. 'Not every little thing needs to be recorded. The amount of stuff you post on social media is *ridiculous*. It's getting out of hand.'

Holly's eyes narrow. 'Don't deflect, Mum. I want you to watch this.'

I have a horrible feeling that my daughter is becoming unwholesomely perceptive in her old age.

'If we do, can I make a coffee straight afterwards and get some aspirin?' Scott implores, his bloodshot eyes surfacing from behind his shaking fingers.

'Yes,' Holly tells him. 'The video isn't that long.' She gives us both a long, hard look. 'It doesn't need to be.'

She thrusts the iPhone towards us, and pokes the play button.

A few seconds go by while the captured footage spools out.

'Oh . . . oh my,' Scott says. 'I pretended to shag the Christmas tree, didn't I?'

'Yes!' Holly replies, eyes wide.

Seeing oneself on a video is never the most pleasant of experiences, even at the best of times. I have always been supremely awkward in front of the camera – even when I don't know there's one on me, which is quite inexplicable. I think I have a sixth sense that just seems to know I'm being filmed, or having my picture taken – and any grace, poise or élan I may have goes flying out of the window faster than a freed budgie.

And that's when I'm sober.

I'm not sober in this video. You can tell that by the way I'm speaking at several decibels above normal, and sound like I've suffered a minor stroke.

It's cringeworthy. It's embarrassing. It's eye-opening.

And the look on my poor mother's face!

I shrink into myself like a recalcitrant turtle as I hear myself say the F-word in front of my mum. I'd like to say this is the first time I've ever done this, but I know I've been drunk in front of her before, so I can't even claim that as the truth.

'Why am I still shagging the tree?' Scott says incredulously from beside me.

'I don't know, Scott,' I reply. 'I really, really *don't know.*'

We both watch as Holly offers to take her grandmother to the kitchen to make a cup of tea. The look of gratitude on my mother's face is possibly the worst thing I've ever seen.

Mercifully, the video of this debacle ends at this point.

But sadly, that's not the end of it.

'Oh my God,' I say as my hand goes to my mouth.

'Holly!' Scott says, the most animated I've seen him since he came in through the door. 'You shouldn't have seen any of this!'

'No, Dad! I really shouldn't!' she snaps back. 'But it's a little hard to ignore it when your parents are having a drunken row in the living room!'

I look at myself on the video, where I appear to have turned into a witch. My make-up has slid halfway across my face and my hair now resembles a haystack – if said haystack had been attacked by rabid badgers.

A swift and stunningly awful realisation then occurs. I still look like that *right now*.

I thought I'd remembered the argument Scott and I had last night quite well, but seeing it in all its stark and sober reality on this video reminds me just how much being drunk can colour your perception of events.

For starters, I sound a lot more *ranty* than I thought. There's a whine in my voice I really don't like the sound of one little bit.

When the drunken conversation turns to the fact that Scott and I haven't had sex for months, I turn into a giant ball of cringe, and can't bring myself to look at Holly's face.

My heightened level of shame is then joined by an overwhelming wave of sadness that nearly brings tears to my eyes. Perhaps it's the hangover's fault, but hearing myself and my husband argue over the fact that we've lost all physical intimacy in our relationship makes me want to bawl my eyes out.

What the hell has happened to us?

It's almost a relief when Scott starts to put the lingerie on, moving the argument away from such an uncomfortable area.

Scott isn't relieved to see himself behaving in such a manner though.

'Oh good grief. What the hell am I doing?' he says, aghast.

We continue to watch up to the moment when he shoulders me on to the couch, and Holly ends her recording to come to our aid.

I want to close my eyes in shame and not see any more – but apparently my daughter has turned into quite the mini-Spielberg, and has even more footage to show us.

And what *horrible* footage it truly is.

Horrible because it describes a woman not happy with her world in the slightest, but even more horrible because *I don't remember any of it.*

I don't remember going into the bedroom, I don't remember lying on the bed and I certainly don't remember putting that stupid wedding video on.

My face flames. It's not the first time I've watched that video recently, but it's been something I've tried to keep secret from my family. Having it relayed to both of them in glorious 1080p on Holly's phone is soul-destroying.

'Oh, Holly, just turn it off would you, please?' I ask my daughter, the tears brimming in my eyes.

But before she has a chance to reply, I've disappeared from the screen, to be replaced by my husband's rear end.

What a delightful sight he makes, with his bottom thrust into the air and his upper body rammed between the cushions.

The iPhone's microphone picks up the loud and calamitous fart incredibly clearly, and I have to make a real effort not to glance down at Scott's backside to check if there was any kind of follow through. It's happened to him before when he's been plastered, in an incident I can only refer to now as 'the Premier Inn Thing'.

Scott is clearly thinking the same thing, as I see one hand surreptitiously slide down towards the area for a moment, before a look of relief spreads across his face, indicating that the only thing escaping his bottom was gas and air.

I feel like I need gas and air myself, after watching all that.

Holly drops the phone on to the table, sits back and regards us both with a look that is unwholesomely parental in its construction.

'Well?' she intones.

'Well what, sweetheart?' Scott replies.

'Well, what have you got to say for yourselves?'

Both my husband and I are struck dumb. Partly out of shock at the things we've just witnessed, and partly because our seventeen-year-old daughter appears to have transformed into a nineteenth-century boarding school headmaster.

Scott looks at me.

I look at Scott.

We both look down at the table.

A few excruciating moments pass.

Then Scott looks up again.

'It's that wine,' he says in a firm voice. 'I knew we should have stuck with the Merlot, instead of getting that Cabernet Sauvignon.'

I nod my head. 'It was a bit too strong, wasn't it?' My eyes narrow. 'And we probably shouldn't have opened that fourth bottle.'

Now Scott shakes his head. 'No. That's right. That was a bit silly of us, wasn't it?' He looks back at Holly. 'We're sorry, Hols. We promise we won't buy that wine again.'

Holly's jaw drops open for a moment. And then she makes me jump out of my socks by letting out a short, sharp gasp of exasperation.

'Aaaargh! You just don't *get it*, do you?!'

'What do you mean?'

'It's not the *wine*! It doesn't matter what you're drinking! You always end up the same way!'

'Oh, come on, Holly. We're not *that* bad,' Scott replies, a dismissive note to his voice. 'It's *Christmas*, and your mother and I have had a stressful time of it recently, so we just wanted to let our hair down a bit.'

I don't want to.

I really don't want to join in with the justifications, but I just can't stop myself.

'Your dad's right, Holly. We're sorry you had to see us in a state like that, but it's not something we do all the time. We got carried away yesterday. But we promise it won't happen again.'

Scott reaches out a hand and closes it around Holly's trembling fist. 'Honestly, Hols, we *promise* it won't happen again. We just needed to let off some steam! But we've done that now, so—'

'That's not true!' Holly almost screams, and yanks her hand away. 'You *have* been like this before!' She holds up a hand and starts ticking off on her fingers. 'There was that thing with the tractor, and when you nearly burned down the distillery, and that time you stayed over at the Premier Inn – which you've still never explained properly – and that time at Auntie Jenny's, and—'

'Alright, Holly! That's enough!'

A bolt of pain shoots through my head. I instantly regret losing my temper like that – for more than one reason.

Holly looks startled. I never normally raise my voice to her like that, but the litany of past indiscretions was just too much.

'I'm sorry, Hols!' I exclaim, as I clench my eyes shut to try and will away the pain. 'It's just that I think you're going a bit overboard with this whole thing, sweetheart.'

Scott nods. 'That's right. You really don't have to worry about us, Hols. We've had a stressful time recently, and all of this is just our way of getting through that. Everybody is like it at one time or another, aren't they, Kate?'

I also nod . . . very slowly. 'Yes.' I give my daughter a conciliatory look. 'Trust us, sweetheart. Everything is fine. *We* are fine. *You're* fine.'

I sound as convincing as I possibly can, I think, but I can tell from my daughter's face that she's having none of it.

Holly gives us both a frustrated look. There's something else in her eyes though. Something much, much worse.

Pity.

'You think this is *normal?*' she says, waving her phone at us. 'You think there's nothing much *wrong?*' She stands up straight in one swift motion. The sound of the chair scraping back makes me wince. 'You're both . . . you're both . . .' She throws her hands up. 'Aaaargh!'

And with that, Holly turns and storms out of the kitchen in a spectacular teenage strop that they could write songs about.

Scott, still bleary-eyed and grey, watches her go for a second, before leaning back in his chair and letting out an explosive breath. 'Well, that was relatively unpleasant,' he says.

'Don't worry about her,' I reply. 'She'll be fine once she calms down a bit.'

He gives me a look. 'It's not her I'm worried about, to be honest with you.'

'That video, you mean? Come on, Scott. It looks bad, but it isn't like we behave like that all the time.'

He doesn't reply, but gives me another look that suggests he's slightly more self-aware this morning than I am, despite the grey face and the taste of couch in his mouth. He looks away from me and up at the ceiling. 'I need coffee and aspirin,' he eventually says, which is certainly the most sensible thing anyone has said this morning.

'I'll make the coffee, you get the drugs,' I tell him, and rise gingerly to my feet.

While I'm busying myself making the only drink in the universe that helps a hangover, I start to think of how I'm going to speak to my daughter, when I eventually pluck up the strength of character to do so.

I'm going to have to explain a few uncomfortable things to her, about stress, responsibilities, and the pressure that both can put on you. I don't particularly want to burden her with all these adult concerns while she's still growing up, but I think it's probably necessary at this point, so she can understand why her father and I sometimes get a little carried away with the drinking.

That's for later though.

For now, there is only the smell of finely roasted coffee beans, and the soothing effect of over-the-counter medication.

I think I'll spend the next hour or so in delightful contemplation of both with a bit of Sky News in the background, before having a very, very, *very* long shower, prior to getting ready to go round to see my sister.

This all sounds like quite a decent way to spend Boxing Day, as far as I'm concerned. As long as there's no alcohol in sight, I'll be champion.

***

I don't get a chance to speak to Holly for the rest of the day. It's a whirlwind of board games, leftover turkey, cheese boards and James Bond movies. Boxing Day is pretty much the same for most people. A mixture of pleasure at having another day off work, and disgust at having to take part in prescribed Yuletide activities for the second day in a row.

And let's face it, turkey is just a worse version of chicken, if we're being honest about it. Having to cram dry chunks of vaguely odd-tasting chicken down your gullet on one day is bad enough. Having to consume more of the stuff – only cold and twenty-four hours old – the next day as well is surely some kind of corporal punishment.

Between mouthfuls of chicken's less attractive cousin, I study my daughter closely, to see if I can glean any indication of her state of mind. Holly is seventeen, so has the capacity to either completely forget a grievance the next time a pop video that she likes comes on MTV, or hold on to it for the rest of eternity, should she choose to. Getting an idea of her mood across Boxing Day should give me an idea of which one I'm dealing with this time.

Strangely, though, Holly appears to be acting very coyly around me and her father. Almost embarrassed to be in our presence (which I suppose is fair enough), but there's a high degree of *sheepishness* to her behaviour that doesn't really jibe with this morning's conversation at all.

'How are you doing?' I ask her as we stand beside my sister's heavily laden dining room table.

Holly is spooning a load of cranberry sauce on her dry, day-old turkey as I say this, and I see the spoon visibly wobble.

The look she gives me is one of barely concealed terror. What the hell is going on here?

'I'm fine, Mum!' she says. 'No problems at all!' She sounds less convincing than a bad politician.

'Really? Only you've been avoiding your dad and me all day. Is this about this morning's chat?'

'Er . . . maybe. Um . . . I, er, I don't want to talk about it any more. It's, er, it's done now, Mum. I've done it. It's *done*.'

'What's done?' I reply, my suspicion meter now really starting to tick over.

'Oh, nothing!' she says in a hurry. 'Just the conversation! Nothing else!'

And with that, Holly carries her cranberry-slathered turkey back to her chair, and I get no further chance to question her on her strange behaviour.

The rest of Boxing Day passes (as does much gas from the bottoms of the males in the room), and by 7 p.m. I'm feeling like I could sleep for several months. Hangovers are bloody exhausting when you get right down to it.

We get back to the house at seven thirty, and I make a beeline for the bath. This morning's shower woke me up enough to deal with Boxing Day, but now I want a bath, purely for the indulgence of it.

There will be expensive Waitrose ginseng bubble bath involved here, people. You mark my words.

I leave Scott crouched over his laptop in the study – where he's no doubt looking at work emails, despite me telling him not to until tomorrow – and my daughter equally lost in her iPhone, and go to enjoy some quality time on my own. Holly is looking even more nervous and discombobulated than she was earlier, but I just don't have the capacity to glean what afflicts her this evening. It'll have to wait until tomorrow.

As I'm resting my head against the back of the bathtub and feeling the warmth penetrate my aching bones and muscles, I hear my mobile phone text alert from the bedroom. This I ignore, for obvious reasons. I remembered to mute my ringtone, but not my message tone, which was an oversight on my part.

I ignore the second text alert, and the third.

By the time the fourth one comes along, I'm sitting up in the bath and am not feeling relaxed at all any more. Four text alerts in the space of ten minutes is probably not a good thing.

I then hear Scott's phone ring, and put two and two together. Something bad must have happened. Someone is trying to get hold of me and Scott. They failed with me, and have gone to him.

I'd better get out of the bath and find out what the hell is going on. As I do, I hear Scott speaking to someone on the phone. His voice is starting to take on a sharp tone.

Something bad is most definitely afoot.

I wrap the towel around my dripping body and hurry into the bedroom, where I snatch my phone up from the bedside cabinet.

What greets me are *six* missed calls, and four text messages that are as terrifying as they are confusing.

The first is from Lisa, my hairdresser. It reads: 'OMG! Your a star! OMG! How drunk r u???'

This makes no sense. I'm stone-cold sober.

The second is from my sister, Jenny. This one reads: 'Sis. What the hell have you done? It's all over the internet. Max saw it and came running to tell me! Call me!!!!'

Max is Jenny's youngest, and is glued to the internet even more than Holly.

The third text is Lisa again. This time she's really excited about something: 'Fuuuck! This'll be on TV! I never thought I'd know a YouTube celebrity!'

What the hell?

It's the fourth text that really puts the cat among the pigeons. This is from Nadia, and is most definitely the clanging chimes of doom. It reads: 'Kate. You'd better have a chat to Holly, if you haven't already. There's a video up on YouTube that's starting to go viral of you and Scott. It's not good. Call me when you get the chance.'

My heart simultaneously plummets and leaps into my throat as my brain processes this development.

'She's done fucking what??' I hear Scott scream from the study.

From upstairs, I hear the front door slam.

My hand starts to shake, and I drop my phone on the bed, before I leave the bedroom and walk into the study to see Scott standing by the laptop, one hand clasped to the phone held to his ear and the other grabbing at the hair on the side of his head.

'YouTube?? It's on fucking *YouTube*??' Scott squawks with dismay, as he sits himself back down with a thud and starts to frantically push the mouse around the table in quick, jerky movements.

On wobbly legs, I join him and look down at the laptop, just as the YouTube website page loads.

'What's it called, Matt?' Scott asks, before making a face and holding the phone away from his ear for a moment. 'Stop laughing, you arsehole!' he then exclaims into it. 'What's the video called?' He pauses for second, listening. 'What?!' he screams in horror.

'What is it?' I wail. 'What's the bloody video called??'

Scott angrily pulls the laptop closer and starts to type. '*My . . . Parents . . . Are . . . the . . . Worst*,' he parrots as he stabs at the keys.

Oh, for crying out loud.

'Thanks, Matt,' he says into the phone, before cutting his friend off in the midst of another gale of laughter.

'What the hell has she done, Scott?' I ask my husband with understandable distress as the page begins to load.

'Made us a laughing stock, apparently,' he replies.

We both watch as Holly's YouTube channel – entitled *TheTempleGurl* – loads fully on to the screen.

I don't think either of us has ever been that concerned with our seventeen-year-old daughter having her own YouTube channel before. Holly is a sensible girl, and in the past has never put anything up on it that wasn't appropriate. There's nothing on her Facebook, Twitter or Instagram feeds I've ever had an issue with either. I know this because I check all of them at least once a week. You can never be too careful in this day and age. My knowledge of modern technology isn't great, but I've educated myself enough to keep tabs on my only child's exploits, for reasons which should be quite obvious.

TheTempleGurl is largely typical of a video blog for the modern teenager – full of clips of her and her friends singing, dancing, acting like mild fools . . . that kind of thing. All pretty innocent, to be fair.

And none of those previous videos have ever had more than a couple of hundred views, given how uncontroversial they've been.

You can imagine my anxiety then when I see that 'My Parents Are the Worst' has already had twenty-seven and a half thousand views.

Twenty-seven and a half thousand.

'Press play,' I demand of my husband, in a shaky voice.

He does, and we're forced to relive the video Holly showed us over the kitchen table, only this time in a heavily compressed format, and with additional footage of Holly sat in her bedroom, talking straight to the camera.

Her explanatory narrative before and after our drunken exploits only serves to make the whole thing worse. Here we have a clearly distraught teenager introducing the world to her even more clearly alcoholic parents.

I can feel my face going white as we get through all ten minutes of it. By the time we're done, the view count has risen to over twenty-nine thousand.

'How?' Scott cries with panic. 'How have so many people *seen* this?' He looks up at me. 'You told me her videos didn't get watched much!'

'They bloody didn't, Scott! Not until this one!'

'Then why is this one so different??'

'I don't know! It must have gone viral somehow.'

I'm no social media expert, but I'm savvy enough to know how these kinds of things work. If a video is funny enough, clever enough or embarrassing enough, it'll start to get shared over and over again, until it's seen by thousands of people.

I remember laughing at such things as 'Charlie Bit My Finger' and the one with that kid coming out of the dentist. I also seem to remember nearly wetting myself watching a musical one with a baby monkey riding backwards on a pig. I think I was pretty drunk at the time.

And now *I'm* in a video on YouTube that looks to be rapidly going viral itself.

I'm certainly not laughing now.

Scott looks up at me again. 'What . . . what do we do, Kate?'

My eyes narrow. 'We get hold of our daughter and get her to take it down!'

'Where is she?'

'I heard the door slam just a minute ago. She must have gone out when she realised we knew what was going on.'

'I'm going to *kill her*,' Scott says in a flat voice. 'She's grounded for a fucking year!'

'Hold your horses. Let's talk to her first. She might be able to explain what's happened.'

'What's happened?? What's happened is that our daughter has turned us into fucking *laughing stocks*, Kate!' He points at the screen. 'Look at the comments below the video already!'

He begins to read a few off the screen.

'*ROFL! Look at these pricks!*' Scott narrates, his voice high and tremulous. '*OMG . . . wot a pair of drunk twats.*'

'Oh shit,' I say, watching as more and more comments appear on the screen as Scott scrolls down.

'Here, listen to this one,' he says to me in a feverish tone. '*. . . dat girl don't know what her life is. Dem parents be fucking off the chain hilaz.*'

'That literally makes zero sense,' I tell him.

'I know! But it's been upvoted a hundred and fifty times!'

I then spot a comment that makes my skin clammy and my blood boil at the same time. '*I don't know about nothing else,*' I read, '*but I would totally do her mum. She's got nice tots. Total milf.*'

I assume this paragon of social virtue means that I have nice *tits*, but was too caught up in his own masturbatory fantasies to notice his poor spelling.

I instantly feel sick.

Turning away from the laptop, because I simply can't look at it any more, I pick up Scott's phone and call Holly. I get no answer.

I call a second time, with similar results. Scott continues to read out more of the YouTube comments. Barely any of them are grammatically correct, and all of them are tiny pieces of character assassination that continue to make my stomach churn as I listen to the tinny ringing tone go on and on, until Holly's message cuts in.

I guess I can understand why she wouldn't want to talk. This is a truly terrible situation – and one she's directly responsible for. The thing is, though, I *know* my daughter. I know she wouldn't have planned for something like this to happen. She's just not built that way. I can't see her uploading that video hoping it'd be seen by so many people.

I need to get some answers.

I call her phone a third time as Scott continues to experience apoplexy beside me. This time when I get Holly's voicemail, I leave a message. 'Holly . . . Please call us back. I know this is bad, but I don't think it's something you'd do deliberately. Just call, so we can sort through this. *Please.*'

I hang up, and turn my attention back to my husband. 'Try to calm down a bit, Scott. This can be fixed.'

'Can it?! Really?? The damn video's been watched over thirty thousand times now!'

Oh, good grief.

I nearly jump out of my skin when Scott's phone starts to ring in my hand. It's Holly, thank God.

'Hols, where are you?' I say as I answer.

'I'm going to Amber's house,' the reply comes. Holly sounds a little out of breath. She must be hurrying down the road. Her friend Amber only lives a few streets over, but I'm not happy about my only child wandering around in the dark on her own.

'Well, don't, please. Come back here so we can talk about this.'

'I . . . I don't think that's a good idea, Mum. I want to stay away tonight.'

I close my eyes and try to remain calm. I can tell when my daughter has developed a bee in her bonnet, and it sounds like this is a very large and buzzy one. 'Look, sweetheart. You're not in trouble. We just need you to come back and remove the video from YouTube so that—'

'I don't want to.'

'What?'

'I don't want to take the video down. Not now.'

Okay. This is going *very* badly. 'Why not, Holly? Why would you want to do this to us?'

'Because . . . because I love you, and I need you to *change*!'

'And you think causing us all this embarrassment is the way to do that?' I'm trying to keep the anger out of my voice, but I'm not sure I'm all that successful.

'Maybe. I'm sorry, Mum. I never meant for the video to get so popular so fast. I've been watching it all day. It got shared by this massive vlogger, and that's why so many people are watching it. I kept wanting to take it down, but then I keep thinking about the way you and Dad are these days . . . and I think this might be the best thing for you both.'

'Trust me, Holly, it's *not*!'

'I'm sorry, Mum. But I think it might be. And I can't go on with you the way you both are any more.' She pauses to catch her breath. 'I'm going to sleep at Amber's tonight. I'll speak to you in the morning. Please leave me alone until then.' She pauses again. 'I love you, Mum. I really do.' I can hear the tears in her voice.

And with that, Holly ends the call without giving me the chance to respond.

I stand there for a moment trying to process all this.

My daughter is so distraught about our drinking habits that she felt the need to broadcast it across the internet, and doesn't appear to regret the decision, even though it's got way out of hand.

Things may be even worse in the Temple household than I'd feared.

Holly is a *good girl*. There's no way she'd do something like this, unless she felt she had no choice. Could it be that Scott and I have been turning a blind eye to what is obviously a more serious issue than either of us believed?

I want to think that Holly is just overreacting – that she's just being a typical teenager. But my daughter is *not* a typical teenager. She's smart. She's brave. She's wise beyond her years.

Maybe it's time I started listening to her.

'Oh fuck me, *thirty-five thousand* people have seen it now!' Scott wails from beside me. He looks up at me with an expression of combined fury and dismay. 'PinkyPud!' he screeches into my face.

'What?'

'PinkyPud!' he repeats, even louder.

'What the hell are you talking about?'

His face has gone red. 'Pinky – *fucking* – Pud!'

Oh no. I think my husband has suffered some kind of extreme mental breakdown. He's clearly unable to form proper sentences any more, and has resorted to spouting gibberish.

'What's a PinkyPud?' I ask him, looking for signs of foam coming from his mouth.

'The bastard who shared the video! I've found his YouTube account. He's got five million followers, Kate! FIVE MILLION.'

What little strength I have left in my legs fades away, and I have to lean against the desk. How many of those five million followers will see the video of my husband rugby tackling me in a pair of Agent Provocateur knickers? How many will watch me dribble into my eiderdown? How many will have to bear witness to the antics of two people with a real drinking problem before I can convince my stubborn and upset daughter to remove it?

'What are we going to do, Kate?' Scott asks me in a pitiful voice.

'I don't know. I really don't,' I reply in a flat tone.

. . . except I *do* bloody know what I want to do, don't I? I want to go downstairs and crack open that last bottle of red wine we've got in the kitchen cupboard. That's what I want to do more than anything else right now.

'All these people, Kate. All these people *watching* us,' Scott says, sounding quite incredulous. 'Some of the things they're *saying* about us.' He rises from his seat and looks at me mournfully. 'Have we . . . have we got a real problem with booze, do you think?' he asks, as the comments continue to scroll up the screen.

'I don't know,' I tell him.

But deep down, I know that's a lie.

Christ on a bike. We really *do* have a problem here.

All of us.

All three members of the Temple family.

And I have no idea what we're going to do about it . . .

CHAPTER FIVE

SCOTT HAS A PLAN

I have learned a lot about YouTube in the past few days.

For instance, I've learned that there's no real point in taking down an embarrassing video you're in, because the bloody thing will already have been shared and reposted countless times by other people before you do.

Holly came home at 4 p.m. the next day, and by that time 'My Parents Are the Worst' had been viewed *one hundred and eight thousand* times.

One hundred and eight thousand people had watched me fart, with my head stuck in a couch. And by then, the video had proliferated like a virus across more YouTube channels than I could keep track of. Holly did take the video down, but by that time the damage was done.

Another thing I've learned about YouTube is that it's full of people called 'vloggers', who appear to be making a great deal of money by doing very, very little.

A large selection of enthusiastic young people are making a lucrative living sat in front of a camera, talking about the things that they like doing, watching, eating, hearing, wearing or shagging.

I used to do that with my mates in the pub. None of us gave much thought to how we could make money out of it, though, more's the pity.

The vlogger that caused 'My Parents Are the Worst' to go horrifyingly viral is a strange creature called PinkyPud.

PinkyPud is a fresh-faced twenty-something, who seems to have made a bloody fortune making videos of himself doing absolutely nothing constructive. It's quite incredible.

His YouTube channel has hundreds of clips of him playing video games, watching movies, eating pizza, riding a skateboard, eating a pizza while riding a skateboard, eating pizza while riding a skateboard and playing a handheld video game . . . and so on and so forth.

For some reason, five million people think that watching PinkyPud doing these asinine pursuits is worth their valuable time.

I fear that Western civilisation will soon collapse in on itself, and none of us will notice it happening, because we'll all be sitting at home watching somebody else noticing it happening.

Another thing PinkyPud loves to do is share 'hilarious' YouTube clips that he discovers in the many, many idle hours he has free to him – thanks to the fact that so many people like to watch him eating a deep pan pepperoni with extra olives. He uploads a video of himself telling his vast audience all about them, and then prompts them to go check out the clip for themselves.

And guess what? The Pinkster stumbled across the video of Kate and me a mere hour or so after Holly had secretly uploaded it, following her conversation with us on Boxing Day morning. It turns out PinkyPud is friends with the older brother of one of Holly's old school mates, and it's those two degrees of separation that means we're laughing stocks to thousands of strangers, rather than just thirty or forty of Holly's immediate friends.

Thanks to PinkyPud informing his loyal following about the drunken antics of two forty-somethings on Christmas Day, our video started to rack up hits and views like they were going out of fashion.

I initially wanted to ground Holly for the rest of her life, but Kate managed to talk me down, thankfully. She reminded me that Holly isn't the type of girl who'd put us through this level of humiliation willingly. I'm still angry at my daughter that she decided to upload the video at all – even a few people seeing it is a few too many – but I can't be mad at her for what happened subsequently, which was entirely out of her control.

I can be mad at the reaction the video got online though.

Not just from Pinky fucking Pud, but the social media sphere in general. People are quite comprehensively *awful* when they have the anonymity of the internet to hide behind. I feel like my wife and I have had our reputations and characters dragged through several layers of mud over the past week. We've been insulted, laughed at, sexually objectified (in Kate's case anyway), ridiculed, judged and psychologically dissected by a bunch of keyboard jockeys who think they are about 1,000 per cent more witty and clever than they really are.

It's the judgemental attitude of so many that really makes me sick. The number of times I've been called a 'raving alky' or a 'drunk prick' on the internet recently is soul-destroying.

There was one particular comment from someone called Smells Like Teen Danny (no, I don't know why either) that really hit home hard. He went into a lengthy and rather rambling diatribe about how Kate and I reminded him of his own parents, who would routinely bounce Danny off the walls of their Louisiana trailer after they'd spent the night drinking Wild Turkey.

The intimation that we are anything like people who would treat a child that way made my blood boil.

But . . .

I can't deny that reading a lot of those comments – the slightly more sensible ones anyway – has made me start to seriously question my relationship with alcohol. You can only read so many times that people find your behaviour shocking before it starts to sink in that something might be amiss.

I became obsessed with picking out the posts from YouTube subscribers who seem to have a grip on their sanity, and their thoughts about Kate and me do not make for comfortable reading. The general consensus from those who can spell and form proper sentences is that we're not acting like people who have a decent grip on life.

In fact, it appears that as far as the YouTube community is concerned, we're either acting like a pair of teenagers who need to grow the hell up, or a couple of total louts, who most people would cross the street to avoid.

The one thing everyone seems to agree on is that we've both got a drinking problem, and are psychologically scarring our daughter.

Jesus Christ.

'You need to stop looking at those posts, Scott!' Kate snaps at me as I read another one out to her that describes us as 'the Christmas Cretins'.

'I'm not sure I can,' I reply truthfully. 'I think I've become addicted to reading how awful people think I am. I never thought I had a masochistic streak in me before, but apparently I have.'

'Well, I don't have a masochistic streak in *me*, so please stop telling me about them.'

'It makes for some pretty hard reading though.'

'Yes! I know it does. That's why I'd rather you didn't do it any more!'

I shake my head. 'But I don't think we can ignore what they're saying.'

Kate's eyes blaze. 'Yes we bloody well can, Scott! Those idiots don't know us! They don't know who we are!'

'No, I know that. But some of the things they say . . . about how drunk we get. About how we're treating Holly . . .'

Kate rubs her eyes and sighs. 'Yes. I know. I'm not denying that we might have an issue here, but I still don't need a bunch of random whiners on the internet to remind me of it. Please, Scott . . . turn off the bloody computer.'

I do as I'm told, because I know which side of the bread the butter's on. I then rise from the laptop and give Kate a hug. I think we both need one right about now.

'It'll be okay, sweetheart,' I tell her comfortingly.

'Will it?' she replies in a disbelieving tone.

'Yeah. People get bored with these viral videos. The view count is slowing down all the time.'

Kate shakes her head. 'I'm not worried about that, Scott . . . well, not that much anyway. I could do without the embarrassment, but there are *deeper things* wrong here that aren't just going to go away when the next stupid video hits YouTube.'

I nod my head slowly. 'Yeah. I know what you mean. Maybe we need to do something about how much booze we're knocking back. It's not doing us any favours, is it?'

'No.' Kate breaks the embrace and starts to pace up and down the study. 'But when the hell did it become such a problem, Scott? Can you remember? When did our drinking get so bad that it ruins Christmas Day, and causes our daughter to make a video of it public because she's so traumatised?'

'I have no idea,' I tell her. 'I never thought it was really an issue. We like to have a drink, but it never occurred to me it might be such a bad thing. I always thought it was just a way for us to let off some steam. Get rid of stress.'

'So did I.' She gives me a troubled look. 'Somewhere along the way, it's gone from the thing that makes us feel better, to the thing that makes everything *worse*.'

'And we've been making excuses for it ever since,' I reply.

'What do you mean?'

'You know what we said to Holly after we first saw that damn video. We made light of the whole thing. Defended ourselves. Made out it wasn't that bad. We've spent years condoning each other's behaviour, and now it's come back to bite us on the arse.'

I lean against the desk and look up at the ceiling, deep in thought for a few moments. When I look back at Kate, she is staring into space and nibbling on a fingernail. 'What are we going to do?' I ask her.

'I have no idea,' she replies, still staring and nibbling.

A few more moments of uncomfortable silent contemplation go by before I come out with a suggestion that makes my skin crawl, but it's the only real solution I can think of for our predicament.

'We'll have to stop.'

Kate finally breaks out of her contemplation and looks directly into my eyes. 'We will, won't we?'

The cold, hard truth of it is as undeniable as it is distressing.

I don't think either of us realised up until this point just how much we've been relying on alcohol to keep us going.

'I feel sick,' I say to her.

'I feel . . .' Kate pauses and takes a big gulp of air. 'I feel *scared*.'

Fuck me.

I know *exactly* what she means.

Is that how bad it's become? That the prospect of not drinking any more is actually a *scary* thing to contemplate? That we're so . . . so . . .

The word you're looking for is 'addicted', you idiot.

. . . addicted to alcohol that the mere thought of not having it in our lives is enough to send us to the nearest bottle?

Kate walks over to me and gently takes one of my hands. She looks into my eyes, a mixture of sadness, fear and resignation in hers. 'How did we get here, Scott? How did we get to such a scary place?'

I shake my head. 'I don't know, sweetheart.'

'Do you think we'll find our way out of it again?'

I want to tell her yes. I want to tell her that everything will be alright.

But I'd be lying to myself as much as to her.

***

I didn't get much sleep last night.

A great many thoughts roared around my head for far too long, stopping me from drifting off.

Most prevalent among them was the fact that it's New Year's Day in two days . . . the day when people customarily make resolutions to change something about their lifestyle.

The timing could not be worse for this to come around. If my daughter and YouTube haven't made it already plain enough that I should stop drinking, the infinite universe itself has also decided I should give it a go, by bringing all this to a head at this most difficult of times.

Because what kind of arsehole would I be if I didn't at least give quitting the drink a go? I've been given ample evidence that it's doing me no good, and is affecting my only child's mental health, so what possible reason could I – and my wife, for that matter – have for not embarking on a teetotal lifestyle once the clock strikes midnight?

There are *two* reasons, actually.

The first is fear.

The second is stubbornness.

I don't like to be told what to do with my life – outside the confines of my gainful employment anyway.

You're talking to someone who once refused to throw away a carton of eggs that was a month out of date, simply because they were expensive organic ones that I didn't want to waste. Kate repeatedly told me to chuck them out, but I wouldn't have any of it. I also wouldn't have any solid food for the following four days after eating one of them, thanks to the rampant food poisoning it gave me.

Mind you, Kate's not exactly easy-going herself sometimes. She once refused to leave a branch of New Look until the shop girl apologised for calling her a moany bitch under her breath, when Kate took a pair of sandals back because they had frayed straps.

We were in there nearly an *hour* before the shop girl eventually gave her a desultory apology, which was only forced out of her by the manager. I never find clothes shopping with my wife to be the most pleasant of experiences at the best of times. You can imagine how cringeworthy I found that whole experience, as I tried my best to hide behind a row of maternity dresses while my fuming wife stood at the returns counter with her arms folded implacably in front of her.

Neither of us are easy to get moving once we've decided to dig our heels in. It's one of the cornerstones of our relationship – but I'm self-aware enough to know it'll make giving up the drink even harder.

So, we're both terrified *and* extremely reluctant. Two emotional states not commensurate with carrying out a New Year's resolution to stop drinking.

But we've got to do it. We really, really do.

And it's something we have to do *together*, for once. We'll need each other's support, and God knows that's been in short supply in the past few years. We can't just drift apart on this one. It's too damn important.

So how can we make sure we actually get on with it, stick together and don't back out – thanks to a fear of being sober and a natural pig-headedness?

This is the question that stopped me getting to sleep until long after 4 a.m.

The answer hits me about three hours later, when the winter sun wakes me from my restless slumber.

I sit up in bed and gently poke Kate. 'Are you awake, sweetheart?' I ask her, to a muffled response. 'I said, are you awake, Kate?'

She rolls over and looks at me blearily. 'Well, I am now, you idiot. Why have you woken me up? I've slept like crap.'

'Me too. Too much going on in my head.'

Kate sits up as well, rubbing her eyes. 'Yeah. I know what you mean. The past few days have just been running round and round in mine all night.'

'It's because we both know what needs to be done, but neither of us want to do it. Consciously, it's obvious what steps we need to take, but our subconscious minds are railing against it.'

She gives me a perplexed look. 'When did you become an expert on psychoanalysis?'

'About the same time someone called me "the Farting Transvestite" on YouTube.'

'Fair enough. I see your point though.'

'It's New Year's Eve soon, and I think we should both stop drinking.'

Kate squirms a bit before replying. 'Yeah, yeah. You're right. I know you are.' She grabs me by the arm. 'I don't want to though. And I don't know if I *can*.'

'Me neither, but we've got to give it a go.'

She drops her head. 'I just don't know . . .'

I take her hand in mine. 'I think I've thought of a way we can make sure we stick with it. An incentive to keep us both on the wagon.'

'And what's that?'

I then say seven words to my wife that make her respond with this: 'You want to fucking do *what*??!'

I can see this is going to take some explaining . . .

Which is something I need Holly's help with, so a bit later I sit her and Kate down on the wine-stained living room couch, and stand in front of them with my hands clasped together.

Kate is sat with her arms folded and a disgusted look on her face. Holly just looks a little bemused, and not a little tired, given that I've just dragged her out of bed far earlier than she usually gets up. I could have waited until this evening to relay my little plan to her, but I wanted to get it off my chest before both Kate and I have to go into work.

Quite why employers think there's any point making their staff go to work between Christmas and New Year is beyond me. Unless you're in the emergency services, it's an entirely pointless exercise, because no work gets done, and people tend to just shuffle around the office drinking coffee and trying not to think too hard about how much turkey they've consumed recently.

Kate and I are dreading having to pop in to our respective jobs even more than usual this morning, thanks to the fact we've become internet sensations in the past few days.

Which brings me back to the point of this impromptu family meeting.

'Holly, your mother and I have decided that we're going to give up the drink for a while.'

Her face lights up. 'Really?'

'Yes. Your video has shown us that we quite obviously have something of a problem . . . and while we wish we could have realised that in a less chronically embarrassing manner, we can't deny that something has got to change.'

She looks up at me with the same expression she used to use when she was a little girl and wanted a bedtime story. 'So, you're not mad at me any more?'

'Well . . . we're still a *bit* pissed off you thought it'd be a good idea to YouTube a video of us to your friends, but we know you didn't deliberately set out to make us unwilling internet stars. Besides, the whole debacle may have made your mum and me face some . . . *unpleasant home truths.*'

Holly smiles, a little sheepishly. 'So, are you quitting tomorrow then?'

'That's the plan,' Kate says. 'For a . . .' – she goes a little pale-faced – '. . . for a *year*, at least.'

'A *year*?' Holly says with amazement.

'Yes. I'm not sure we can do it for that long either, but your father wants to share a wonderful idea he's had about the whole thing that'll make it easier for us.'

'That's right.' I pause for a second. 'This is going to be hard for us, Hols. Your mum and I are both sensible enough to realise that, and I don't want us to backslide a couple of days into it. But to do that, we need some sort of *incentive*.'

'To stop you falling off the wagon, you mean?' Holly surmises.

'That's right. And we need your help with it.'

'What can I do?'

'Well . . . I think it would be a good idea for you to upload the video to YouTube again.'

'What?!'

Kate throws her hands up. 'You see? It's a bloody *crazy* suggestion!'

'Hang on! Hang on! Let me finish!' I say, as Holly looks at me with disbelief. 'Look, the video has made us see that we have a problem that needs addressing, but if we're not constantly reminded of that problem, we *will* backslide. I just know we will. So, having it up on YouTube, with people able to see it, will remind us of how important it is that we stick to the plan. Also, I think you should do *another* video at the end of the year, to show how we've improved. A sort of before-and-after deal, if you like.'

'To show everyone how you've changed?' Hols suggests.

'That's right! That'll give us a good incentive to stick with it, because we can eventually upload a new video of us looking all sober and healthy. Then people will hopefully see that we're not a couple of drunken losers any more.'

Kate looks at Holly with disgust. 'You see? Absolutely bloody *mental* idea!'

Holly thinks for a moment. 'I'm not so sure, Mum.'

'What?!'

'I actually think Dad might be on to something.'

'You do??'

'Yeah. I mean . . . it would be a good way for the both of you to make sure you stay sober. The video would be a constant reminder.'

'Exactly!' I add. 'Any time we feel like cracking open a bottle, we can just watch it, read the comments and go make a cup of tea instead.'

Kate looks furious. 'But I don't *want* to be on YouTube! I don't *need* to be on YouTube!'

'Nor do I, sweetheart,' I tell her, 'but I also don't want to carry on with my life the way it is. I want to change, and I think this will help me do that.'

'It won't help me!' she fumes.

Holly turns to her. 'I think you should give it a go, Mum. I know it's embarrassing . . . even for me. I'm on the video being all mopey in my bedroom, remember? But I do like Dad's idea of doing another video later on, to show how well you've done not drinking.'

Kate appears to think for a second. We might actually be getting through to her.

'No! I'm not doing it!' she snaps.

Apparently not.

She rises from the couch. 'This situation is bad enough without piling more pressure on. I can go teetotal quite alright on my own, thank you very much. I don't need to be splashed across the internet while I do it.'

I try to conceal my look of grave doubt before Kate catches sight of it, but fail miserably.

'I'm going to work,' she tells us in a cold voice, before storming off out of the living room.

'Well, that went well,' I say as I watch her go.

Holly gets up and gives me a hug. This is something of a rarity these days, so it catches me off guard a bit. 'I think it's a great idea, Dad,' she says. 'Give Mum a little time, she might come around to it.'

'I'm not so sure. Your mother can be a very stubborn woman.'

'Yes. But she's also a *smart* woman. Just see how it goes.'

Smart wife. Smart daughter.

'I hope you're right, Hols. I really do. I want us to quit drinking *properly*. Do it right first time.'

'Me too, Dad,' she replies. 'Me too. I might go and make sure the video is still ready to upload . . . just in case Mum comes around.'

I admire my daughter's optimism, if not her grasp on the realities of the situation. She does know her mother well, but I know her even better.

Luckily for my continued sense of well-being, the only people at the distillery are me, Matt, a couple of cleaners and One-Armed Jeff, our head distiller. The cleaners are busy with their job, and One-Armed Jeff wouldn't know what YouTube was if you held a gun to his head. The only person whose derision I have to put up with all day is Matt's. And boy does he let me have it with both barrels.

'And when you fell over in those panties? Oh my God . . . Oh my Go—'

Matt cannot finish, thanks to a paroxysm of laughter that renders him unable to communicate in any meaningful way.

I sip my coffee and return to looking at the three emails I've had over the Christmas period. I've already read through them six times, but there is quite literally nothing else to do, other than listen to Matt laughing his arse off.

'And the *fart*, Scott! Oh, Jesus Christ, it sounds like you followed through! Did you follow through, Scott? Did you?' he asks me, his face full of glee.

'No, I did not,' I tell him with a scowl.

The scowl manages to send him into another gale of laughter.

'I'm quitting, you know.' The laughter cuts off, and Matt looks at me with utter and total disbelief in his eyes. 'Drinking. I'm going to quit drinking for New Year.' I sound pretty convinced.

Matt is not.

He starts to laugh so hard now that he rocks back on his office chair. It tumbles from under him and he goes sprawling to the floor. Even this doesn't stop his mirth. He's still chuckling as he climbs to his feet. 'You? Quit drinking? No fucking chance!'

'Piss off, Matt.'

Thankfully, he does so at this point – though the sound of his raucous laughter continues to ring in my ears even after he leaves the office.

When the clock strikes four thirty, I've had enough. Of Matt. Of work. Of emails. Of the sound of a vacuum cleaner. But mostly of Matt.

I lock the place up until New Year, and wend my way home with my knuckles gripped so firmly on the steering wheel that they turn white.

When I get through the front door, all I want to do is march straight to the kitchen and pull out one of the six bottles of red wine we have stashed in the cupboard above the microwave. My feet are so familiar with this time-honoured post-work routine that they take me over to that cupboard before I've even had time to consider what I'm doing. It's only as I'm reaching my hand up to open the door that I realise what I'm doing.

I step back.

This takes an awful lot of willpower.

I then make myself a cup of tea.

I'm sipping the tea with something of a grimace on my face when I hear the front door open, and then slam shut heavily.

Oh dear.

I then watch as my wife enters the kitchen . . . and makes a beeline for the same cupboard I've just avoided cracking open.

'Hi, sweetheart,' I say to her as she flings the door open. 'Good day at work?'

'No!' Kate snaps, and yanks out one of the bottles of red. I watch her with consternation as she pulls a glass out of the dishwasher, and pours herself a glass of Merlot.

She then throws back a huge glug of it, and I can see the effect it has on her the second she does it. This stuff is really quite obvious when you find yourself actually looking for it. Her face seems to relax. Not completely. It'd take more than one gulp of wine to do that, but imperceptibly I see her brow start to uncrease, her cheeks fall and her eyes widen.

With the second gulp her shoulders lower, and her whole body language softens.

I'm silent as she walks over to me and sits down at the table.

'Bad day?' I ask.

'Oh yes,' she replies. 'Terrible.'

'Why?'

She rolls her eyes. 'That bloody video. That bloody, fucking, arsing stupid video!'

'Went around the office, did it?'

'Of course it did!' Kate throws back another gulp of wine.

'Embarrassing?'

Her fist clenches around the wine glass. 'So *incredibly embarrassing*.' Her face darkens. 'Pierre called me in to his office to discuss the whole thing. He was trying to be nice about it, but I got the impression he was just trying to make sure I hadn't come in drunk to work. I now appear to have a *reputation*.'

'I know exactly how you feel.' I pause for a moment and lean forward. 'We probably should make sure nothing like that happens again, shouldn't we?'

She looks at me with brow creased. 'Oh, it won't. I'm going to confiscate Holly's phone.'

'That's not quite what I meant.'

Kate takes another large swallow of wine. 'What did you mean then?'

I lean forward and grab the wine glass out of her hand. This spills a little of what's left in the bottom of the glass.

'Hey!' Kate protests. 'Give me that back!'

'No,' I reply curtly, and rise from the table. I take the glass over to the sink and dump the contents in. I then grab the bottle and upend it into the sink as well.

'What the fuck are you doing?!' Kate screams. She rushes over to me and attempts to take the bottle before I can pour all its contents away. 'Stop it! Stop it!'

We wrestle with the bottle for a few moments, before I lose my temper. 'For fuck's sake, Kate, stop it!!' I roar at her. She stumbles back, a look of frustration and rage on her face.

For a second, we lock eyes. Hers are full of anger. Mine are full of shock.

Then, something seems to reassert itself in my wife's mind, and the look of rage disappears, to be replaced by one of horror.

It's quite strange watching someone have an epiphany right in front of you.

'Oh, for the love of God,' she says, before making her way to sit down on the kitchen chair with a thud.

I join her, and take one of her hands.

'It's not Holly's video that's the problem, sweetheart,' I tell her softly. 'It's *us*. *We're* the problem.'

I let this sink in for a moment.

Kate squeezes my hand. 'I know. I know.'

I lean forward and plant a kiss on her hot forehead. 'It's time to make a change.'

She nods slowly, her eyes full of tears. 'But I don't know if I can . . .' she says, trailing off.

'Nor do I,' I confess. 'But we have to try . . . and we have to make sure we have an incentive to keep us going.'

Kate knows exactly what I'm driving at. Her eyes narrow again. 'But it was *awful* today, Scott! They laughed at me.' Her eyes widen and her mouth downturns. 'None of them believed I could stop drinking!'

'And they'll keep laughing,' I tell her, 'and they'll keep not believing, until we prove them *wrong*. Until we show them that we've *changed*. All of them. Not just the people at your work. Not just the people at mine. Not our friends, or family. I mean all one hundred and eight fucking *thousand* of them. Let's show all of them that we can do this.'

The look in Kate's eyes changes slowly from fear and shock to stubborn resolve. It's the same expression I saw in New Look that day. I'm much more pleased to see it now than I was then.

'Holly!' she calls loudly, without taking her eyes off me.

I hear the sound of my daughter thumping down the stairs. She appears at the door. 'Hi, guys! How was work?'

Kate growls. 'Holly. Your video. You still have it, right?' she says, looking directly at me.

'Yeah. I've got it.'

I feel Kate squeeze my hand tightly. 'Put it back up,' she says in a flat voice.

'What?'

'Put the damn thing back up on YouTube.'

CHAPTER SIX

HOLLY HAS A HASHTAG

As New Year's Eve parties go, the one at the Temples' house this year is pretty subdued. Holly records the festivities on her phone, as she usually does with these kinds of events, but to tell the truth, there's not really that much to chronicle.

You see, it's a *sober* New Year's Eve this year. For all three of them.

Holly was invited to a party at her friend Amber's house, and there was a part of her that wanted to go, but while Holly Temple loves a good party as much as the next teenage girl with an iPhone fixation, she loves her parents even more.

Besides, Holly is not a girl who enjoys alcohol herself, you'll be *amazed* to discover. There's something about putting up with two drunk parents for years that really puts you off the stuff. If she had gone to the party it would have been to get selfies, not to get wasted.

But her parents really need her moral support this evening, so she stayed home.

You've never seen a pair of people less happy to be celebrating the turning of the year in your life. Three hundred and sixty-five days ago, they were both trollied by 9 p.m. and having a whale of a time. This year, the clock has struck 11 p.m., and Holly's phone is recording a scene of utter despair.

The Temples are watching *Jools Holland's Hootenanny.*

Nobody in their right mind watches *Jools Holland's Hootenanny.* It's one of the rules of New Year. The BBC broadcasts it – as is their right – and the entire population of Great Britain completely ignores it, as is theirs.

Only those suffering severe infirmity, or suicidal loneliness, have ever actually sat through *Jools Holland's Hootenanny.* To do so under any other circumstances would just be plain *wrong.*

And yet, here we find ourselves . . . on the couch with the Temples, who are sipping tea and watching Jools Holland bounce up and down at a piano, while The Proclaimers belt out their most famous song.

'I'd walk five hundred miles to punch Jools Holland in the tits,' Scott says, taking another dull sip of tea.

'I'd crawl across five hundred miles of broken glass to stop The Proclaimers,' Kate adds, also sipping.

From behind the camera, Holly tries to inject a little levity into the situation. 'It's only an hour until New Year, though, guys! New year, new start!'

Her parents' eyes swivel from watching two middle-aged Scottish men herk and jerk around on stage like their pay cheques depended on it to alight on the camera's lens.

Have you ever seen such derision? Have you ever witnessed such disdain?

'Maybe I should stop recording?' Holly suggests. Both her parents start to nod slowly up and down like ruthless automatons.

Holly does as she's told.

Only for about an hour though.

It's now a few seconds before midnight.

The scene on the television has changed to the BBC's coverage of Big Ben.

As enthusiastic TV presenter Konnie Huq gyrates up and down with excitement, while the last seven seconds of the year dribble out of the metaphorical hourglass, Holly captures her parents sat stock still on the couch. They both look like they're watching a *Saw* movie.

'It's coming, guys!' Holly says, trying to insert a little gusto into the proceedings. 'Nearly here!'

Kate gives her a wan smile, but Scott doesn't respond at all.

Five! Four! Three! Two! One!

Happy New Year!

The crowd along the Thames goes wild. The fireworks start to light up the night sky behind Big Ben in a glorious technicolour display. Konnie Huq starts to vibrate with excitement at such a speed that the molecules of her body begin to phase out of this corporeal dimension.

'I'm going to bed,' Scott says flatly, and rises to his feet.

'I want to eat some cheese,' Kate adds, and also gets up.

Holly's camera watches them both leave the living room in silence, while the rest of the United Kingdom explodes with unfettered joy. Joy which will last for approximately seven or eight hours, before everyone gets up the next morning and realises everything is exactly the fucking same.

'Oh, good grief,' Holly says quietly to herself, before shutting off her recording.

Welcome back to the bedroom of your average seventeen-year-old.

. . . except Holly Temple is anything *but* average – especially when it comes to taking risky decisions about her parents' welfare.

Her actions on YouTube have persuaded her mother and father to give up the drink, which is great. Though they both appear to have become walking bags of misery because of it, which is not.

Something has to be done to pull them out of the malaise they've fallen into in the three days since Kate asked her daughter to re-upload that most embarrassing of videos.

Holly sits herself in front of the camera and starts to twiddle her hair almost immediately.

'So, Mum and Dad have quit the drink. I'm so, so happy about that. The only problem is they've now become almost suicidal. I've never seen them act like this before. It's like something's been . . . *unplugged* inside them. I don't think putting the original video back up has helped. I thought not many people would want to watch it now, but I was wrong about that. The view count is up to over one hundred and fifty thousand.'

Holly looks a little sick.

'My YouTube channel subscriptions have exploded as well. I'm not sure how I feel about that. It's nice to get some attention . . . but maybe this is a little too much.'

Twiddle.

'I almost didn't do *this* video, but I've thought of a way to help Mum and Dad feel a little more encouraged about not drinking any more – and it means making and uploading *more* videos, including this one.'

Holly leans forward.

'I've had a really good idea, but it's something I'm going to need *your* help with.' She points down the camera. 'Yes, *you*. All of you sat watching this on your computers, phones and tablets. You've all seen my parents at their worst, and now I need you to help me get them back to their best.'

Holly leans forward even more and picks up the phone, making the image joggle and wobble around quite drastically for a moment before she holds it out in front of her to show her hastily tidied bedroom. 'Come with me,' she says as she walks out of the room and down the stairs.

She turns the camera back to show her face, in a startling effort of teenage co-ordination that if tried by anyone over the age of twenty-two would result in a broken phone and a trip to the accident and emergency department.

'I'm going to run this idea by them, and then I'm going to upload the video to YouTube. When I have, I want *you lot* to tell me what you think.'

She flips the phone around again as she walks into the kitchen.

There, she comes across two badly functioning robot approximations of her parents shuffling around as they make themselves lunch on the first day of the New Year.

There's an almost visible dark cloud hanging over them, which might explain the gloominess in the kitchen.

'Mum? Dad? I need to talk to you,' she tells them. They look up from buttering bread at the counter, their expressions full of dull resignation.

'I know quitting the drink has already been very difficult for you,' Holly says as the robot Temples continue to stare blankly down the camera lens, 'and that the whole YouTube thing has been horrible.'

'You could say that,' Kate mumbles.

'Right . . . so I think I've thought of a way to get you more support, restore your online reputations and cheer you up a bit.'

Scott Robot actually manages to contrive a look of faint horror, which must be a strain on his circuits. 'We have *online reputations*?' he says. 'It was bad enough having one in the real world, now I have to worry about digital Scott looking stupid too?'

'Yes. You've both become internet stars because of all this,' Holly replies. 'Sorry about that.'

Kate puts down her knife carefully. 'And what are you proposing to do to change that?'

'Well, I thought that it might be a good idea to chronicle your efforts to stop drinking on *TheTempleGurl*, and get all the viewers out there to post their encouraging comments!'

Kate and Scott look flabbergasted. Well, as flabbergasted as two robot facsimiles can look anyway.

'You think people will post *encouraging* things?' Scott says in disbelief.

'Yes!' Holly tells him, the camera bouncing up and down a little with her barely controlled enthusiasm.

'And you want to do a lot more videos?' Kate adds.

'Yes! Like . . . one every couple of weeks or so. Let people see how much *better* your lives are now you've given up drinking!'

Scott swallows and grimaces. 'Hmmmm. *Better*,' he says in a rather bitter tone.

'And this is something you really want to do, is it?' Kate asks her daughter.

'Yeah, Mum! I think it'll really help you!'

Kate stares down the camera lens for a few moments, contemplating this.

Maybe this isn't just about helping her and Scott, she's probably thinking. Maybe Holly needs this just as much as they do. Perhaps more.

Kate eventually shrugs her shoulders. 'Why not,' she says, and picks up her knife again, plunging it into the butter.

Scott looks at her aghast for a moment, before turning his attention back to the lens, a look of resignation now on his face.

He sees how important this is to his daughter just as much as his wife does. 'Alright, Holly, we'll do it. It probably can't make things any worse at this point, can it?'

'No!' Holly says excitedly. 'Brilliant!'

'Will you start with what you're recording right now?' he asks.

'Yeah, that was my plan.'

Scott's eyes narrow and his brow furrows as he points his buttery knife straight at the camera. It's the most animated he's been in days. 'Right, listen up, all of you watching this. My wife and I are going to go along with this hare-brained scheme of our daughter's, because we have nothing to lose. But I don't want to see any more nasty, horrible comments that are just meant to troll us, alright?'

'Well said, Dad!'

'Thanks, Holly. And I have a special message for PinkyPud, if he sees this. You helped turn us into laughing stocks. It'd be nice if you helped us turn that around.' Scott punctuates this with a particularly hard stab of his knife towards the camera, sending a large gob of butter splashing over the lens and completely obscuring the view.

'Dad!' Holly exclaims, as the shot cuts immediately to black.

A short time later, and the iPhone has been cleaned of butter.

It now rests back in the bedroom, with an animated and excited Holly Temple sat in front of it.

'Okay, so . . . so, they've agreed to it, and that's great! I really think it'll help them.' Holly leans forward. 'But that's where you guys come in. I'm going to post this video up on my account, and I need you to leave a comment letting me know you'll be watching as I chronicle their new sober lifestyle. Can you do that for me?'

There's a hint of pleading in Holly's voice that conveys just how important this is to her.

'I really need your help with this, guys. Without you, I don't think they'll stick to the plan. I love them both, but they're really hard to get through to sometimes. It's not something I'm very good at doing on my own.'

Holly looks a little lost for a moment. A sight that is sure to make Scott and Kate feel quite awful when they see this video.

She recovers quickly, though, and the enthusiasm returns.

'So, I'm going to video their progress as much as I can. Probably weekly or every other week. I'll post all the vids right here on YouTube, and I'll stick stuff on social media too.' Holly's eyes light up. 'I'll think up a hashtag for it! Yeah . . . that'd be great!'

The excitement in Holly Temple is quite palpable now. This is a girl who feels like she's made a breakthrough – and when Holly makes a breakthrough, you'd better believe she's going to make the most of it.

'So, that's it for now, guys. Please leave your comments below, and I'll speak to you again soon!'

Holly quickly reaches over and shuts the recording off, no doubt wondering what the end result of this rather crazy experiment will be. Inadvertently allowing thousands of people into your embarrassing private lives once is one thing. Actively inviting them in repeatedly for a period of several months is quite another . . .

A while later, Holly is back.

Now she looks even more excited.

'I've thought of a hashtag!' she exclaims, a huge grin crossing her face. She sits up straight and puts both arms out wide. 'Hashtag DRY HARD!' she crows with delight. 'Every time I post on social media, I'll add #DryHard – so if you see it, make sure you spread the word!'

It's quite unbelievable to see such a change in Holly Temple – no longer the sad and distracted girl from Christmas Day. This project of hers has given her a new lease of life.

If only her parents were as enthusiastic about the plan as she is.

. . . but it might turn out okay.

Perhaps this video diary about trying to stay teetotal *will* help them get through it.

Maybe the viewing audience out there *will* be encouraging, to make up for all those insults and character assassinations they dealt out previously.

Time will tell.

For now, though, there is a plan, an excited teenager, two melancholy adults, an expectant audience and a brand-new hashtag.

From such things great epics are wrought.

. . . or massive and catastrophic disasters, depending on your perspective.

PART THREE
STRESS

CHAPTER SEVEN

KATE GETS THE ELBOW

'How many?!' I cry with unfettered disbelief.

'Half a million,' Holly repeats, a grin splitting her face from ear to ear.

'I think I'm going to throw up,' Scott says in a weak voice, carefully putting his Costa coffee back on the table before he spills it.

I knew I shouldn't have asked Holly to check her YouTube subscriber count this morning. I fucking *knew* it.

I've done my level best to ignore this whole scheme of hers as much as I possibly can over the last few weeks, but my curiosity got the better of me today as I sat sipping my flat white, after a hectic morning's shopping at the tail end of the January sales.

Thus far, my daughter has made three videos of my new sober lifestyle. In none of them have I done anything even *remotely* interesting. We've been on a nice walk in the country. We've done a bit of light baking in the kitchen. We've played on Holly's Nintendo Switch, which we bought her for Christmas. None of these videos have been that fascinating to watch, I assure you.

Okay, Scott did tread in that cowpat . . . and I did bake a flapjack that you could use in the foundations of a large country house . . . and

Scott did die repeatedly over and over when he kept getting stuck in the corner of one room in *Super Mario* . . . but none of this should be required viewing for anybody.

And yet – there's those half a million subscribers. It's quite ironic that I've built a career trying to make other people popular, spending a lot of my company's money in the process, but here I am, a freshly minted YouTube star, and all I've done is overcook some oats.

'How in the name of Christ can half a million people care about what we get up to?' Scott asks, with his head in his hands. 'We're *boring*.'

'People are interested in how you're doing, Dad,' Holly replies. 'Whenever I use the Dry Hard hashtag, I always get a load of responses from people willing you on. And they all like listening to the both of you talking about being off the drink too.'

I suppose that's fair enough.

Holly has developed almost Dimbleby-like levels of interview technique, apparently out of nowhere. Scott and I get bombarded with questions every single time she records us. Scott only trod in that cow-pat because he was thinking long and hard about how much his energy level has changed in the several weeks that have gone by since giving up alcohol.

I have to say that this project has allowed a side of Holly I've never seen before to flourish. That's almost worth the horror of being watched by half a million people, who really should find something better to do with their time.

But while the new world order in the Temple family is making my daughter well and truly come out of her shell, it's not been quite so positive for me or my husband.

In fact, it's been a *nightmare*.

When we're not being recorded for posterity, Scott and I have to get on with our lives, with the knowledge that the main emotional crutch we used to rely on has been pulled away.

I still have to go to work. Being sober twenty-four hours a day hasn't changed that.

And work has gone from bad to worse since the New Year.

We found out two weeks into January that Stratagem PR would be losing Annabelle Mastriano-Hoffington-Pierce as a client.

Thankfully, this had nothing to do with me crashing a tractor into a barn, and everything to do with the fact that Simon Hoffington-Pierce was a lot less rich than he made out. It transpires that he had invested heavily in all the wrong places, and those investments have all crumbled in the past few months, plunging him and his new wife into the deep waters of potential bankruptcy.

And while there's some delightful *schadenfreude* to be had from the situation, it's also *a very bad thing indeed* for me financially, because it mounts pressure on everyone at the agency to retain new clients to make up for the shortfall.

And all this right around the time I stupidly agree to stop drinking.

I am, in a word, stressed.

Really, really fucking *stressed*.

I feel like a string on an overwound guitar. Like a cat with a firework up its arse. Like a pot of boiling water about to overflow.

I'm so stressed I can't stop thinking up appalling similes for how stressed I am.

Usually this would all be resolved (temporarily anyway) by the consumption of much fine Italian wine. This, however, is an avenue no longer open to me, and I have as yet not found anything to replace it.

Coffee certainly isn't the answer. If anything, it sends my stress levels even *higher* – but I needed *something* to drink after wandering around in a morass of overburdened shoppers for the past three hours.

'How many more people do you think are going to subscribe?' Scott asks Holly, returning me to the present.

She shrugs. 'Who knows? It shows no signs of stopping at the moment.'

'Oh, good grief,' her father responds, shrinking in on himself a little.

Funnily enough, I'm not feeling quite the same level of dismay as my husband.

I think – and I'll whisper this so only you can hear it – I think *I might quite like the attention.*

While I was mortified that the first video went as viral as it did, I can't say I'm having the same reaction to what's happening now. Okay, the shock of being told half a million people are watching your exploits was a little hard to take, but I have to confess that I feel a small thrill at the idea that Kate Temple is doing something that so many people are interested in.

I keep these thoughts to myself, of course. Scott clearly doesn't feel the same way as me, by the looks of his ashen expression. I have to conceal a small grin of excitement as I sip on my flat white again.

There are no grins to be had of any kind two days later, though, when I walk into a maelstrom of pain and suffering at work. An email has gone around from our flamboyant bosses, Pierre and Peter, which features the dreaded word 'redundancies' in the title.

This causes my constant baseline stress to skyrocket. I doubt I'm the golden girl in the office at the moment, thanks to Tractor-Gate and Holly's video, so I could well be one of the ones up for the chop.

By 6 p.m. that evening I am a jittery mess, and have taken to chewing my index finger until it looks like minced beef.

'Are you okay, Kate?' asks Ester the receptionist, as we both wait for the lift. Ester is a quiet, small mouse of a girl in large spectacles. The kind of person it's easy to forget about unless they're standing right in front of you.

'Been better, Ester,' I reply, resisting the temptation to nibble my finger even more. For some reason I decide that Ester may find this offensive. She might take my rodent-like nibbling as a slight against her mousey demeanour.

'The email?'

'Yeah. The *email*.'

'It was a stupid thing to do. They should have been more tactful about it, the fools,' Ester says with uncharacteristic bluntness, her slightly exotic accent heightened by this display of displeasure. I blink a couple of times in surprise. To hear this come out of Ester's mouth is a complete surprise. She's usually so calm and timid.

. . . hang on. Is she though? I don't actually know that much about her at all. I know she's from another country, and looks like she's timid and placid, but I have no idea what type of person she actually is. I feel instantly awful for judging her, and start to subconsciously nibble my finger again as we step into the lift.

'They could have done it better, yes,' I eventually reply. 'It's caused everyone a great deal of unnecessary stress.'

'Agreed. Luckily, I'm going to my class tomorrow night, which will help me relieve some of that stress, I think.'

A stress-relieving class? Sounds like something I could do with . . .

'What is it you do?' I ask her.

She gives me a shy smile. 'It is called Krav Maga. It's Israeli. I learned it at home, and am delighted to find they do classes here now. It's very good for relieving anxiety and tension!'

'Oh . . . gosh, that does sound good.'

Ester's smile broadens. 'Perhaps you'd like to come with me?' she asks. 'They are always keen to have new people along.'

Okay, that's unexpected. I barely know this tiny little woman, and yet she's kind enough to ask me along to this Krav Maga thing. I feel quite touched. In fact, I can feel tears welling up in my eyes, which is pathetic. The stress, lack of sleep – and most importantly, lack of *alcohol* – in my life have evidently made me somewhat emotionally unbalanced.

'Um, I'd love to,' I tell her with genuine pleasure. I need something to help me with all this stress and tension. Maybe Krav Maga can do that.

You'll notice here that I'm not asking Ester to give me more details about what Krav Maga actually is. She's told me it's a stress-relieving activity that originates in the exotic climes of Israel – and I have made some fairly unsubstantiated assumptions based on this scant information. I am assuming that Krav Maga is probably a lot like yoga – all stretches and becoming one with your inner self. After all, Ester is a small and mousey-looking little woman. I can't imagine that her hobby would be anything *too* strenuous, right?

'Great!' Ester exclaims with delight. 'The class starts at 6.30 p.m., so I'll be going straight from work tomorrow. If you'd like to come, just bring some gym clothes with you. It's only a couple of miles away at Fitness4All – the gym next to the multi-storey car park.'

'Okay, that's fantastic, Ester! I'll definitely be there. It sounds like just the kind of thing I need.'

'That's lovely to hear.' Ester pauses and gives me another shy look. 'I have been watching your videos on YouTube, Kate. I think what you are doing is fantastic.'

'Do you?' I say, face flaming red.

'Oh yes. It's very strong of you to stop drinking and let people see your progress. I think it's quite inspirational.'

'Really?'

'Absolutely!'

Well, I'll be damned.

'Thanks, Ester . . . that means . . . that means a lot.'

The door to the lift pings open at the car park before I have a chance to respond further. Ester wishes me a good evening, and walks off towards her car.

As I climb into mine and begin to make my way home, I feel a small sense of happiness that I've bonded with a new person today. Ester has never really been on my radar as friend material, so I'm pleased we might have a new pursuit to do together.

I don't think my small happiness is just about that though. I also think that for the first time since quitting the booze several weeks ago, I may have found something that I can at least try to replace it with. Something that will do me some physical and mental good, rather than damage.

'Hi, Holly,' I greet my daughter as I walk into the house and see her climbing the stairs.

'Hi, Mum!' Holly replies, turning to face me. As she does, a sudden and wild idea occurs.

'I'm doing something tomorrow night that might make a good video for *TheTempleGurl* and Dry Hard.'

'Really?'

'Yep. Some kind of yoga class. A friend from work is taking me.'

Holly's eyes widen. 'You . . . doing *yoga*?'

I put my hands on my hips. 'Yes, young lady. I thought it might help take the edge off being so bloody sober all the time. I figured you could come along and watch with your camera. Your dad can bring you along, and he can watch it as well. You never know. It might inspire him to join in.'

'Okay, Mum,' Holly says, obviously surprised at this turn of events. I don't think she was expecting me to be as proactive about finding things for her to record, but right now I am full of both excitement about a potential new hobby and the desire to show all those bastards on the internet that I am doing something constructive with my new sober lifestyle.

They are going to watch me do Israeli yoga instead of drinking red wine, and they are going to bloody well *like it*.

So am I, I fervently hope. This could be the first proper step I take in dealing with my increasing stress levels, and to dispel the aching need I constantly have for a large and soothing glass of something alcoholic.

The next day, I make sure to chat to Ester at lunchtime, just to check she's still okay with me coming along, and also that she doesn't mind me bringing my family with me.

She doesn't mind at all. In fact, the idea that her Krav Maga class might feature in one of Holly's YouTube videos makes her almost as excited as I am.

At no time at all do I think to ask her more about what Krav Maga is.

That evening, Ester and I meet Holly and Scott in the car park of Fitness4All, and after introductions are made, we make our way to the large hall at the rear of the building where the class is being held.

Scott and Holly go and sit on the raised seating near the back, while Ester and I go to get changed into our gym gear. When we emerge from the changing room, I can't quite help but notice just how toned and strong Ester looks. Her arms and legs are lithe and limber, with lines of rope-like muscle. I start to feel quite inadequate. My muscles are less like rope and more like strained spaghetti.

Still . . . I'm sure if I get into this Israeli yoga thing, I can start to look as toned as her, eventually.

As we walk into the gym hall I see that we are joined by ten other people. All of them are men, which is surprising. I always thought this kind of thing was for women. More fool me for being so old-fashioned and out of date.

Ester greets a few of them, and introduces me. They all look like quite nice people, which is good, as I may be seeing a lot of them in the future, if I get into this. They all seem to show Ester a great deal of respect, which is good to see in this day and age.

One particularly large gentleman, who introduces himself as Tomas, almost seems a little scared of my new friend. Maybe he harbours some kind of romantic affection towards her and doesn't know how to express it. I'm trying to picture this man-mountain in an embrace with all five foot three of Ester Hirsch, and have to supress a smile.

'Evening, everyone,' I hear a voice say from behind me. I turn to see a one-eyed pirate coming towards me. At least, that's what this gentleman looks like. He's about fifty, deeply suntanned and equally wrinkled, is wearing a dark-blue bandanna, and his left eye has a patch over it.

'Who's this?' I ask Ester.

'It's Dabney.'

'Dabney?'

'Yes. Dabney. He's our Krav Maga instructor. He was in the special forces for twenty-five years. Really knows his stuff.'

'Ahh . . . that's interesting. Wouldn't have expected somebody like him to be teaching a class like this.'

Ester gives me a confused look. 'Why ever not?'

Before I can answer, the pirate Dabney barks at us all to stand in a line. The men and Ester do this almost instantly. I stand immobile for a second, staring dumbly at the bandanna-wearing instructor.

He then gives me a thin smile. 'Ah. You are Kate, yes?'

'Yep. That's me!' I say, trying to sound natural.

'Welcome, Kate. Please stand next to Ester. She'll partner with you this evening and help you through everything.'

I nod, and walk to stand next to my new friend. As I do, I see some of the men in the row give me mixed looks of pity and fear.

Somewhere far back in the vaults of my subconscious, something stirs.

A thought. An idea. A realisation. I turn to Ester. 'Er . . . what exactly is Krav Ma—'

'Right!' Dabney roars at us. 'Pair off for a basic drill! We're going to concentrate on elbow strikes, throat punches and eye gouges for the first part of tonight's session!'

What?

. . . *what??*

Elbow strikes? Throat punches? *Eye gouges?*

Where's the downward-facing dog?

Where's the extended child's pose?

Where on earth is the soothing mantra?

Ester said this was a great way to relieve stress. How does performing an eye gouge lead to stress relief??

I don't have time to voice any of these concerns, as Ester has bodily swivelled me around to face her. The usually calm and collected expression she wears has been replaced by one of knotted fury.

I don't want knotted fury in my life. I don't want anything knotted in my life.

Knotted things are stressful.

'Ester, I'm not sure what's going on here,' I tell her.

The knotted fury uncoils slightly for a moment. 'Don't worry, I'll take you through it. Hold your hands up like this.' Ester raises her arms, and her hands instantly harden into fists. I try to duplicate this, but my fists don't so much harden as solidify slightly into a jelly-like substance. 'Now brace your legs like this,' Ester instructs, bending her knees and spreading her legs so she looks like a prize fighter. Again, I try to emulate this, fearing that I look less like a boxer and more like someone in dire need of the toilet.

I look over at Holly and Scott for a moment. Scott is wide-eyed with what I'm sure is a mixture of confusion and some amusement (damn him). Holly's face is obscured by her bloody phone, which is recording everything.

'Basic elbow strikes to the temple. Get into position!' the pirate Dabney orders.

Hang on. *I'm* the Temple here. It says so on my wedding certificate.

I don't want basic elbow strikes anywhere in my vicinity!

Ester reaches forward and grabs me by the shoulder. I blink a couple of times in rapid succession.

'On the count, ladies and gentlemen!' Dabney screams. 'Begin with . . . ONE!'

Ester's right elbow comes whistling towards my left temple at a speed Usain Bolt would be jealous of.

'Aaaargh!' I screech, fearing an oncoming severe brain injury.

Thankfully, Ester's elbow stops a scant few millimetres from my head.

'And TWO!' Dabney barks. I watch as Ester's elbow flies back, and straight at my head again. The look of aggression on her face is *terrifying*.

'And THREE!' Dabney screams again. This time I actually feel a light gust of wind against my head as Ester barely avoids knocking me into the middle of next week.

This isn't stress-relieving in the *slightest*.

I can hardly think of anything *less* stress-relieving, in fact.

Maybe if somebody intravenously fed espresso into my bloodstream, while a small Israeli woman mimicked bashing my head in with her elbow, it could be worse, but not by much.

No wonder the men in the class are all so respectful towards Ester. She's quite clearly a martial arts expert, given how accurate each one of her simulated blows is.

Oh, blimey. Is that what we're doing here? Martial bloody arts?

I wanted to learn how to embrace my inner goddess, not smack her in the face.

Dabney gets to ten, and yells 'SWAP!' at us.

Now Ester stands back a little and beckons me on.

'I'm sorry, what do I do now?' I ask her, blinking like a deer in the headlights.

'Grab my shoulder with your left hand, and simulate elbow strikes to my temple,' she hisses back, as if either of these is the most natural thing in the world.

'Really? That's what you want me to do?'

'Yes!'

'Can't I just sing you a nice mantra?'

'No, Kate!'

'ONE!' Dabney screams.

Ester reaches out and grabs my hand, wrenching it forward to place it on her shoulder. 'Now, Kate! Elbow strike! Do it!'

'I can't!' I wail.

'Yes, you can!' Ester yells. 'That's why you're here!'

'No, it's not!'

'TWO!' Dabney screeches.

'Oh God! Oh God!' I simper pathetically.

'Do it, Kate!' Ester demands. 'Do it!'

'THREE!'

Oh fuck me!

'FOUR!'

'Kate!! Kate!! Elbow strike me!!'

'FIVE!'

With a high-pitched keening noise I hold up my right arm and attempt to copy what Ester was doing. Sadly, I have no idea what *I'm* doing, so instead of administering a swift and deadly simulated elbow strike, I flap my right elbow out at a sharp angle, mimicking a distressed chicken with a broken wing.

As this occurs, I lose all control over my hand, which flails around in the air for a second, before I manage to poke Ester in the eye with my pinky.

'Aaaaaarrggh!' she wails in pain, one hand flying to her eyeball.

'Hey!' Dabney shouts. 'We haven't moved on to eye gouges yet, new girl!'

'Oh God! I'm sorry, Ester!' I cry.

'Bloody hell, Kate!' she replies, her palm massaging the eye socket.

'I'm sorry! I'm sorry! I don't know what I'm doing! I tried to do the elbow strike thingy, but I don't know how to do things with my elbows. I've never needed to do anything with my elbows before. They're just elbows!'

Dabney walks over, gives me a disparaging look and turns to Ester. 'Let's have a look,' he says, and pulls Ester's hand away roughly. This is not a man with a natural bedside manner. Ester's eye looks red and watery, but otherwise undamaged, thankfully. 'You're fine, Ester. Just blink it out, and we'll move on.'

Move on?

He wants to *move on*?

I've just nearly blinded someone, and am obviously not cut out for this Krav Maga business in the slightest, but he wants to move on and *do more*?

'Um. I don't think I can do this,' I point out.

Dabney's disparaging look deepens. 'Of course you can. Besides, Ester needs a partner.'

I look back at Ester's watery eye. 'Okay, but maybe she'd prefer someone else?'

'No, it's fine. You're a beginner,' Ester says. 'No real harm done. We should keep going.'

'Oh . . . okay.'

I do not want to *keep going*. Nothing would give me greater pleasure than to not *keep going*. But I also don't want to just run off in shame and humiliation. It's my own stupid fault for not realising what Krav Maga actually is, and I owe Ester.

Damn me and my sense of fair play.

Also, I have a daughter recording all this. I don't want the last thing people see on YouTube to be me running off in defeat. I have started to repair my reputation with the viewing internet audience, and I don't intend to damage that repair job by chickening out of this ridiculous class.

I take a deep breath and clench my fists a few times in rapid succession. 'Right, let's carry on then.'

Ester nods at me in approval, as Dabney returns to the front of the group.

The next quarter of an hour is quite exquisitely painful.

For Ester.

While she pulls every single one of her blows without so much as putting a scratch on me, it appears that my complete lack of co-ordination during the elbow strikes is a recurring theme. My throat punches are largely feeble affairs that result in Ester receiving a sharp blow to the chin on no less than three occasions. My eye gouges (deliberate ones this time) are just as unfocussed and shabby. I don't poke Ester in the eye again, but I do inexplicably manage to pick her nose for her.

Twice.

Dabney then moves us on to leg sweeps, during which I whack Ester on the shin and tread on her big toe.

We then move on to shin drags and foot stamps, where I manage to accidentally perform a leg sweep, proving that I can't take instructions for love nor money.

Then it's time for some knee strikes to the groin, in which I get up close and personal with poor Ester's left breast when I completely lose my footing on the mat and reach out for the nearest available handhold.

By the time Dabney calls a halt to proceedings, Ester is black and blue, and all my muscles are aching like a rotten tooth.

'I just . . . I just can't apologise enough for this,' I say to Ester as we both gulp down water.

'It's okay,' she says sullenly, clearly indicating that it's not.

Dabney gets us back on the mat after a ten-minute break and announces that for the second part of the session we're going to be doing a little light freestyle work with one another.

I don't know who receives this news with less enthusiasm – me or Ester.

'Right, we'll take this *really* easy,' Ester tells me, as we square up to each other again. 'Just . . . try to remember what we've been doing, and use a few moves on me. We'll do it slowly.' She swallows hard. '*Very* slowly.'

I nod silently, brow knotted in concentration. I don't find having my own brow knotted any less stressful than seeing Ester's in that state.

I didn't want to be knotted tonight. I wanted to be *unravelled*.

Still, if I can just get through this, I might be able to go home for a long soak in the bath, and a nice glass of wi—

Oh *fuck it*.

Dabney starts to count rhythmically to us. Ester comes in close to my body, and starts to simulate strikes against me again. This gets no less disconcerting, to be honest with you. She's very good at not actually hitting me, but I can't stop flinching anyway. You would too, given how fast and powerful each one of those strikes and punches looks.

Flinching repeatedly is incredibly tiring, so by the time Ester tells me it's my turn to do a little freestyle on her, my whole body is a mass of tense, shaking muscle.

This evening has become a fried slice of hell.

But, I must try to at least end it well. I must try to leave here with a little dignity, having shown Ester that I am not completely useless, and that I have learned something tonight.

I then proceed to spend the next five minutes accidentally beating her up in slow motion.

I manage to just about remember all the violent manoeuvres Dabney has taught us this evening – hypothetically speaking, at least. I know what an elbow strike is now, it's just that I have a hard time relaying that knowledge into useful physical practice.

'Ow!' Ester bellows as I jam my elbow into her shoulder.

'Aaaargh!' she exclaims as I inadvertently insert my thumb into her ear.

'For fuck's sake!' she wails as I poke my big toe up her arse crack.

Steam is erupting from Ester's ears as we enter the final stage of our freestyle practice. She's angry with me – and who can blame her?

No one can be this bad at simple martial arts, surely?

Anyone who can manage to commit such acts of apparently accidental violence on another person must be *actually quite good* at martial arts, otherwise they wouldn't be able to look so *bad* at it. Kind of like the way Les Dawson had to play the piano extremely well to do that funny routine of his.

This is probably what Ester is thinking.

I know the truth though.

I am a klutz of the highest order – but one stubborn enough not to admit she's crap at something, and therefore willing to make just enough effort to cause poor Ester a great amount of pain.

Her anger has been building all evening, and I'm afraid to say the dam breaks when I commit my final atrocity upon her person.

She lunges forward with her fists raised. It's at this point I am supposed to push her back by planting a firm hand on her chest. Sadly, my eyes are half closed in fear as she comes at me, and my hand does not come into contact with Ester's chest. Instead it hits her square in the forehead. Given that her forehead is extremely sweaty, my hand flies upwards and over her head, causing me to lose my balance, fall forward and plant my equally sweaty armpit in her face.

This is the final straw for Ester. She can take being smacked around a bit, but having her nose smooshed into the armpit of a woman who probably should have shaved at least two days ago is more than she can tolerate. It probably doesn't help that I had a curry the night before.

'You fucking idiot!' she screeches, as she backs away in disgust.

'I'm so sorry!' I repeat for the umpteenth time.

Ester looks at me with unholy rage. Israelis are usually extremely friendly people, so unholy rage should come with some difficulty. Not for Ester tonight though. She's experienced more than any woman – Israeli or otherwise – should have to. I fear her sanity may have broken.

'You're a fucking *idiot*!' Ester tells me in no uncertain terms.

'I didn't mean to!' I try to explain.

'Yeah? Well, I didn't mean to do this!' she cries.

'Do what?'

. . . I had to ask, didn't I?

Ester kicks me on the shin. It's not a Krav Maga move, thankfully, otherwise I'd be in A&E with a compound fracture. It's more like something a six-year-old would do to an annoying playground companion.

It bloody hurts though.

'Ow! Bloody Nora! Why did you do that?'

'Ladies! Ladies!' Dabney exclaims. 'Calm yourselves!'

This falls on deaf ears. Ester kicks me on the other shin.

'Ha! There!' she crows. 'See how you like it!'

I'm now hopping around on one leg and then the other, trying to grasp my two painful extremities at once. I rather resemble a Morris Dancer who's just been poked with a cattle prod. 'Stop it!' I cry in pain and anger. I didn't mean to hurt Ester, but now she's doing it deliberately to me, and that's just *not fair*.

She moves forward again, to no doubt give me another childish kick, but I'm feeling a burning sense of injustice racing through my veins now, and do not intend to let her get in another blow. Just as she sets herself to deliver the kick, I flail out a hand, which connects with her face.

This successfully enables me to pick her nose for a third and final time.

'Fucking hell!' Ester screams.

'Jesus Christ!' I bark, as I bring my snot-covered hand away.

'Ladies! Ladies!' Dabney shouts, trying to bring back some order.

'Why you little—' Ester snarls, in a passable impression of Homer Simpson, before lunging at me again.

At this point, I decide it's best for me to start running like blazes. With a squawk of terror, I'm off – pelting across the gym floor like a thing possessed.

Behind me *is* a thing possessed.

Where once there was a small, happy Israeli lady with a friendly demeanour, there now exists a ravening monster from beyond the limits of hell. A monster of my own creation.

I'm like an accidental Victor Frankenstein, with stubbly armpits.

I run straight towards my husband and daughter, both of whom have stunned expressions on their faces. Holly is still recording all this on her phone, more's the pity. My antics here tonight are likely to get an awful lot of hits, but they're hardly going to show the viewing public that I'm getting my life back on track.

I pass the members of my immediate family as I start to run in a circle around the edge of the gym floor, all the while pursued by the Ester Monster.

'Help!' I scream at Scott.

'How?!' he shouts back, giving Ester a fearful look as she closes the gap a bit.

Before I have a chance to throw a few choice epithets at him for his lack of assistance, I am forced to accelerate, given that Ester is gaining on me.

I catch sight of Dabney, who is trying to pick his jaw up off the floor. 'Stop her! Please!' I entreat as I sprint towards him and the other equally dumbfounded Krav Maga participants.

Ester points a finger at him. 'Don't you DARE!' she commands, spittle flying from her lips.

For a moment it looks like Dabney is going to leave me to my fate, but then he steps forward with his arms outstretched as I hurtle past him. A moment later I hear Ester bellow in absolute fury as her path is blocked by Dabney. From the corner of my eye, I see several of the others move in to help him stop my pursuer.

As I run straight at the exit, I begin to hear the screams of men echoing around the hall.

Oh, the horror.

I can only imagine how many testicles are currently being sacrificed so that I may escape.

Without looking back at the nightmare unfolding behind me, I clatter out of the hall and into the changing room.

I can still hear the cries of terror and pain as I grab my street clothes and my handbag, and rush headlong towards the changing room doors, and the freedom of the gym's foyer.

The final terrible thing I hear as I fly out through the door is poor Dabney's voice, raised in the kind of pain and suffering which no mortal man should ever bear witness to.

'Oh God, my fucking plums!' he screams.

If I had plums myself right now, they'd be shrinking down to nothing.

In the car park, I have time to see my husband and daughter scuttle towards me as I start the car. They both keep throwing looks over their shoulders, as if awaiting the arrival of the terrible creature chasing them across the concrete.

'What the hell is wrong with her??' Scott yells as he approaches my wound-down window.

'No time! Talk later!' I scream back at him. 'She's coming! They won't be able to stop her!'

Sure enough, as soon as I've finished speaking, Ester appears, covered head to toe in the blood of her victims.

'Oh, my fucking Christ!' I wail, and floor the accelerator.

I speed past Ester, whose fists clench in impotent fury as she watches her quarry escape her.

She'll just have to satisfy her bloodlust over the corpses of my husband and child.

They've both had a good innings, to be honest with you.

I'm sure they'd be happy to lay down their lives for me, so that I may live to fight another day.

Yes.

It's what they would both want. I'm sure of it.

***

Somehow, Scott and Holly arrive home a scant ten or so minutes after me – proving that I may have exaggerated the threat from Ester *just a tiny bit*.

'I thought she was going to beat me up for a moment,' Scott tells me, as I sit quivering on the couch, 'but Hols threatened to call the police if she didn't back off. That made her see some sense.' He then gives me pitying look. 'I'd steer clear of her at work tomorrow though.'

My eyes widen in terror at the thought of this.

They stay wide with terror all through that evening, until I fall into a fitful sleep at about 3 a.m.

I'm so bug-eyed with terror as I sidle up to reception the next morning that I'm half afraid my eyes are going to fall out and roll across the carpet.

The reception counter is gratifyingly Ester-free as I hurry past it.

But just as I grab the handle to the door that leads into the Stratagem PR offices, little maniacal Ester pops up from behind the counter like a malevolent jack-in-the-box.

'Good morning, Kate,' she mutters darkly, freezing me to the spot.

'Eeeep.'

'How are you this morning?'

'Eeeeeep.'

Ester pauses, looking at me the way a spider sizes up a particularly juicy fly. 'I do hope you have a *good day*,' she finally says, weighting the final two words with portentous dread.

'You . . . you too, Ester,' I manage to squeak, before hurrying through the door without a backwards glance.

So that all went *exquisitely* well, didn't it?

I set out to do something to relieve my work-based tension, but all I actually managed to do was add to it by creating a mortal enemy for myself.

Not only do I have to worry about client deadlines, I now also have to constantly keep one eye open for the company's receptionist, who might be about to drop-kick me into oblivion at any given moment.

Holly tells me that her hastily edited video of last night's cavalcade of idiocy and casual violence is already racking up the views on YouTube. There was part of me that didn't want her to upload it, obviously, but there was another part that felt comprehensively guilty about the damage I did to both Ester's body and mind, and figured the light humiliation was probably a decent amount of penance.

There's a silver lining to all this, in the respect that I now need to stay alert twenty-four hours a day, just in case Ester is lying in wait for me somewhere – so the chances of me backsliding and having a drink are now zero.

The lesson I've learned here is that the next time someone invites me along to something I have no previous knowledge about, I will make sure to do my research properly.

I've already got one mortal enemy; I don't need another one by mistaking a sword-fighting class for an evening of light knitting.

CHAPTER EIGHT

Scott Gets a Good Sucking

Do you have any idea what it feels like to be teetotal when you work for a gin distillery?

No. Of course you don't.

You are no doubt a perfectly *sensible* human being, with a decent grip on life. Someone who has managed to carve out an existence that more or less makes sense – most of the time anyway.

You are not the type of person who would, let's say, get a job at McDonald's when you're allergic to beef. Or sign yourself up for five years at sea with the navy when you get seasick in a child's paddling pool.

You wouldn't be stupid enough to be a pilot when you have a fear of flying . . . and you certainly wouldn't be idiotic enough to quit drinking when you work for a company that sells nothing but alcohol.

Trying to explain to Charlton Camberwell that his marketing director has gone teetotal was like pulling teeth . . . while a hippo savaged my leg.

'Quit drinking?!' he roared with disbelief, his slug-like eyebrows knitting in Charltonesque fury. 'What the bloody blue blazes are you blithering on about, Temple?!'

'My wife and I, sir. We've stopped drinking. After that video came out on YouTube, we thought it might be best.'

Charlton's eyes knitted even further. 'What the bloody hell's a "YouTube"?'

It took me a good half an hour to explain the situation properly to the point where Charlton stalked away in a massive huff. I'm sure he'd probably like to sack me (when doesn't he?), but he also knows the legalities enough to realise that I could sue his big fat arse should he try to.

The rest of my work colleagues took the news with a mixture of confusion, disbelief and not a small element of betrayal. When you work your socks off five days a week for a gin company, it doesn't sit particularly well when one of the higher-ups turns around and says he doesn't want anything to do with it any more.

Matt, of course, just laughed at me. Over and over again.

He has about as much faith that I can hold out as an atheist does in Jesus appearing in their bath.

I'm pleased to say the vast throng of YouTube viewers on Holly's channel has been more supportive of my efforts. Okay, we still get a lot of people who want to talk about Kate's breasts, or criticise me for my dress sense – but, by and large, we've gained ourselves quite the supportive following in the past several weeks, as we attempt to keep up this sobriety thing against all the odds.

Kate's taken to the whole Dry Hard thing like a duck to water – at least in comparison with me anyway. It's the PR professional in her, I think. She knows the value of a good promotional campaign as much as the next person, and what is Dry Hard now but one big promotion for our new healthier lifestyle? I think Kate finally has a client she likes dealing with. Herself.

I can't say I am as enthused as my wife though. The whole silly thing was my idea, but it's definitely me who struggles more with the attention than Kate or Holly. It's all so bloody *stressful*. Trying to live an ordinary life while thousands of people watch your every move is enough to make anyone's blood pressure skyrocket.

In fact, if it weren't for the supportive feedback from the community that's sprung up on *The TempleGurl*, I'd be seriously questioning my continued involvement.

When you've had a day dealing with Charlton Camberwell and his lunacy, it's nice to come home and read a few of the more positive YouTube comments that accompany Holly's videos. Reading that Claire in Daventry thinks you're a superstar for staying sober for three months really does help you to grind your teeth a bit less at night.

It's no substitute for a large gin and tonic, but it'll do at a pinch.

It's not just your regular, run-of-the-mill YouTuber that appears to have taken an interest in our ongoing sobriety either. No, it seems like we've caught the attention of the professional vloggers out there in the vast sea of video content that is YouTube.

There's PinkyPud, of course, who's responsible for making us go viral in the first place. He's continued to comment on, and link to, Holly's uploaded clips as the weeks have gone by. He nearly choked on his pizza with laughter watching Kate's attempts at Krav Maga. Without his input, I doubt we'd be getting anywhere near the amount of hits that we are.

We also wouldn't have come to the attention of a lot of his contemporaries.

Like BucketFace.

Yes . . . *BucketFace.*

BucketFace appears to be a young man of indeterminate age, who sits in his bedroom with a large black bucket over his head, reviewing all the best YouTube clips of the week. He also reviews movies, video games and TV shows. All done behind the bucket – on to which he has painted a rather childish smiley face with Tippex, so you know what to look at.

This person has a quarter of a million subscribers. So, you know, everything is fine with Western society, and we have no problems *whatsoever*.

BucketFace very much enjoyed watching me spear myself into the sofa. Repeatedly. In slow motion. For some inexplicable reason he even added the *Superman* theme over it, which made it all so much *worse*.

And then there's Zooby.

Zooby is a young black woman who sports multicoloured dreadlocks and the kind of radiating youthful energy that you could probably plug into the national grid and run a decent-sized detached house off.

She's earned herself over a million YouTube subscribers, thanks to her ongoing health and lifestyle channel. *Lovin' Life with Zooby* is a brightly coloured hellscape of youthful enthusiasm, pop music, occasional guest stars and dubious health tips – all presented by Zooby, who bounces around like someone has genetically spliced her with a ping-pong ball.

Zooby knows how to wear Lycra, of that there is no doubt. She also knows how to think up a shedload of new and interesting ways to get healthy. The irony here, of course, being that her viewing audience is predominantly comprised of healthy young people, who have absolutely no need of her tips and tricks. The people that could actually do with her help are us fat, unhealthy, old bastards – but none of us would ever tune in to a YouTube channel run by somebody called 'Zooby', and therefore the entire thing is rendered pointless.

Or, at least, you'd think it would be – but she has those million or so subscribers to her name, so I'm obviously way off the mark, and have no idea what I'm talking about.

You may be wondering at this point how Zooby and the Temples have crossed paths. What do two middle-aged fools who have quit drinking have to do with a YouTube health channel run by a woman in her early twenties, who has never known the pain of a four-hour

Sunday hangover, and wouldn't have a clue what a colonoscopy was if you bashed her over the head with the camera?

Well, cast your peepers back a few sentences, study the words 'occasional guest stars' good and hard . . . and please do start to form your own conclusions.

'You want to do *what*?' I ask my wife in horror.

'I want to go on *Lovin' Life with Zooby*.'

'What the hell is a Zooby?'

'Not a what, a who. Here . . . look.'

Kate hands her iPad over to me. For the next five minutes I watch Zooby and her special guest of the week – PinkyPud. In this edition of the show, Zooby's decided to try to make some healthy snacks to accompany her fitness tips, and the Pudster is along for the ride. I scowl enormously as I watch them make some kind of edible ball-shaped object out of quinoa, lentils and falafel. These fartballs look about as appealing as licking an actual ball of farts, but both of them seem delighted to be cooking them.

I hand the iPad back when the video has finished and provide my wife with the stare of a thousand yards. 'You have got to be kidding me.'

'Nope.'

'But *why*?' I implore. 'Why on earth would you want to subject us to such a waking nightmare?'

'Because it'll be an excellent way to promote Holly's channel. We should leverage opportunities like this as much as we can. It'll increase our exposure and open up potential revenue channels.'

I give her a withering look. 'You're not at bloody work, you know.'

The look she returns withers my withering look so fast it gives me a momentary headache. 'I know that, Scott. But if we're doing this bloody thing, then I want to do it *right*. I want us to look like we're engaging positively with the process, and going on Zooby's show is a good way of doing that.' She rolls her eyes. 'God knows I could do with something that makes me look good, after that disaster with the Krav Maga.'

'And you think making fartballs with this Lycra-clad maniac is the way to do that, do you?'

The look I get this time has gone way past withering and has entered into the uncomfortable realm of full-blown scorn. 'Zooby seems like a lovely girl, Scott. The email I got from her was very sympathetic to our cause. She says she can help us cope with the stress of being teetotal with some lifestyle tips, and I'm willing to give it a try – especially if it'll help Holly gain more subscribers as well.'

'But—'

'But me no buts, mister. This is worth doing, and I need your support.' She gives me a rather arch look. 'After all, staying on YouTube was your idea in the first place. Don't blame me if I want to make the best of it.'

'I hardly see how becoming involved with Zooby and her fartballs is making the best of it.'

'Scott!'

'Alright! Alright! I'll go along with it! Stop looking at me like that!' I fold my arms in disgust. 'I'm not wearing any Lycra though. I draw the line there.'

Kate smiles. 'That's fine, dear. I don't think YouTube needs to see you in Lycra any time in the near future. It has enough problems coping with things like BucketFace. You squeezed into a Lycra body stocking like an overstuffed sausage would probably send them all over the edge.'

About a week later, I'm stood under a large gazebo in Zooby's back garden, dressed – I'm delighted to say – in regulation blue jeans and black T-shirt.

. . . I say it's Zooby's back garden, but it's actually her *parents'* back garden.

They seem like a very nice couple. Both of them have the vaguely stunned look of people who have no idea what their daughter is up to, but are willing to let her get on with it as she's already managed to pay the mortgage off.

I have to admit, I'd very much like to be in their situation . . . and maybe one day I will be. I have my own very talented and entrepreneurial daughter, after all.

Being on Zooby's silly show might be comprehensively awful in every measure for me, but Kate does have a point – it might bring even more subscribers to Holly's YouTube channel, and that can only be a good thing for our girl . . . and one day hopefully for my mortgage payments.

Holly and Zooby have become instant best friends, as you might imagine. Holly has come along today to film our exploits for #DryHard, and has already thoroughly bonded with the tall, energetic girl.

Zooby has asked us on the show to talk about our struggles with sobriety, and to offer us some helpful lifestyle tips. There has been no mention of making fartballs, so far. A million people seem to think she knows what she's talking about, so I should probably put my distaste to one side as much as I can, and give the girl a chance. Who knows? Maybe she does have some advice that'll make the long, alcohol-free days pass a little easier.

I could certainly do with something to help with my general stress and anxiety levels. Most days I tend to feel like the proverbial cat on a hot tin roof – especially when I'm at work, and Charlton is within shouting distance. I never really appreciated just how important drinking was to keeping my stress under control, but now it's gone from my life, I see it very clearly. If Zooby has a way to replace it – and bring my general sense of well-being up a few notches – I'd be willing to eat an entire plate of fartballs, with a side order of peechips.

There are two massage tables arranged in front of us on the well-manicured lawn, giving some hint of what Zooby has planned for us. And I'm not averse to having a nice massage, it has to be said. If a little back rubbing can alleviate my pent-up levels of tension, then I'm all for it.

'So, once I start the camera rolling, I'll leave it going until we're done,' Zooby tells us as she unrolls some towels on the massage tables. 'I'll edit it later, so don't worry if you stumble over your words, or things go wrong.'

'You do that all yourself?' I ask her, in wonder. You'd have thought there would be someone else helping her with her videos.

She smiles at me, with a rather confused look in her eye. 'Of course. Why would I need anyone else's help?'

I go a little wide-eyed. These kids know so much about all this modern technology that they can produce broadcast-quality footage without anyone else's help, which then goes out to millions of eager viewers. It's both terrifying . . . and rather incredible, when you get right down to it.

'So, we're getting massages then?' Kate asks Zooby, as Holly walks around us all, filming everything on her phone.

'Not quite,' Zooby replies with a broad smile. 'I'll fill you both in on what's happening once we get the camera rolling. I like to keep things spontaneous.'

Hmmm.

I'm not sure spontaneity is exactly what I'm after here. Spontaneity is never something that lowers my stress levels. I like things laid out for me in advance, preferably in writing.

'Okay,' Kate says, sounding a little unsure. She obviously feels the same way I do.

'Great!' Zooby says, flashing that million-dollar smile again. 'I'm all ready to go now, so if you both stand just behind the two tables, we'll get started.'

I blink a couple of times. We've only been here for about five minutes. I was expecting some kind of rehearsal, or at least a summary of what we're going to be doing. But that's not the way the YouTube vloggers of the world work, apparently. It's all a lot more seat of the pants in the twenty-first century.

God help us all.

Zooby picks up a small remote and points it at the tiny camera sat on a tripod on the other side of the two massage tables. She presses a button and the camera whirs into life.

'Hey hey hey!' Zooby screeches at the top of her voice. 'And welcome to another bangin' episode of *Lovin' Life with Zooby*!' The girl throws her arms into the air and starts to jog on the spot – for some unexplained reason.

A magical transformation has happened to our host. At the press of a button, she has gone from a relatively calm and stable young woman into a wailing, flailing maniac.

'Today's show is going to be off the chain, guys!' Zooby assures her million subscribers. 'Totally off the hook!'

I fear Zooby may be hyping this up a little too much. I have never done anything in my life that has been *off the chain* – unless you count the time when I was thirteen and fell off my bike outside Bejam, while I was on the way to return some rented videos.

'I got some special guests for you today!' Zooby continues, enthusiasm unbridled. 'They're two great people, who have decided to quit drinking before it kills them!'

Er . . . I'm not actually sure it was going to kill m—

'And they're here on our show today to see if there's anything we can do to turn back the clock a little, and undo some of the horrible damage that years of drinking have done to them!'

Here, steady on, love. That's a bit—

'You'll know them from their mega-viral hashtag Dry Hard. Please welcome Kate and Scott!' Zooby turns to look at us both, clapping her hands as she does so.

'Er . . . hello?' I venture, trying to keep at arm's length from Zooby's flapping hands as best as I can.

'It's lovely to be here!' Kate tells Zooby, trying her hardest to match the girl's boundless energy . . . and failing miserably, because she's in her forties, and is constitutionally incapable of doing so.

'Great!' Zooby cries happily. 'And we've all seen you guys struggle badly with coming off the booze, haven't we?'

'Um. I suppose so,' I say, a little offended. I thought we'd been doing quite well, to be honest.

'And we've all seen just how hard it's been for you to function as normal human beings, without having alcohol to fall back on, to make your lives better, haven't we?'

'Well . . . er . . . I . . .' Kate says, not sure how to react to that. Zooby's tone of voice is now full of pity for us.

'It's okay, guys!' she assures us, placing a comforting hand on each of our shoulders and looking back at the camera once more. 'We're here to help you get back on track, and to show you that there is life after alcohol . . . even for people at your advanced age.'

Now, wait just a fucking min—

'Yay!' Zooby screeches, and pumps both fists above her head wildly. 'And how are we going to do that, guys?' she asks of her unseen audience. 'Well, we're going to explore some really great ancient relaxation techniques, which will hopefully help Kate and Scott reduce their stress levels, leach out the toxins from their bodies, and help them back on the path to being happy, healthy . . . and almost *young* again!'

For the love of fuck.

'Now, Kate. I'd like to try some hot-stone therapy with you today,' Zooby explains to my wife. 'All you have to do is lie face down on your massage table, and I'll apply a few hot stones to your lower back. These stones will release tension, improve blood flow and help reduce toxin levels!'

'Er . . . okay,' Kate replies. 'I won't have to take anything off, will I?'

'No! Just lie down on your chest, facing the camera for me! I'll take care of the rest!'

Zooby points at the massage table and Kate does as she's told. She looks a little reluctant about it, but this whole thing was her idea, so she's going along with it . . . for now anyway.

'What about me, Zooby?' I ask her.

'Oh, Scott! I've got something really great in store for you!'

'And what's that?'

'Cupping, Scott! We're going to do some cupping on you!'

'Cupping?' I reply with confusion.

As far as I'm aware, there's only one part of the human body where you can achieve 'cupping' . . . and I have no desire to rest my testicles in the hands of a girl who's young enough to be my daughter, on YouTube. That's how you get yourself on to a register.

'Yeah! Cupping! It's an ancient art, where cups are placed on to your body with suction! They'll help to leach out all the toxins in there thanks to your decades of alcohol abuse!'

'I wouldn't quite call it alcohol abu—'

'Lie down for me, Scott! And we'll get started!' Zooby demands. She does it in such a commanding tone that I'm halfway to being sprawled out on the massage table before I know what's happening.

I throw a glance over at my apprehensive wife. She attempts to provide me with a comforting smile. I'm having none of it.

I look back to see Zooby's mother and father approaching us. She is carrying a large metal pan of water, which is evidently quite hot, as she's wearing oven gloves. He is carrying a small wooden box. I can't see the contents of the small box. This worries me greatly.

Zooby thanks her parents, and then starts to talk at length about the details of both relaxation techniques to her hoard of followers. She talks about toxins a great deal while doing this.

I've never really thought much about toxins – but my God, Zooby certainly has. To listen to her, you'd think the human body was awash with so many foul and pestilent toxins that it's a wonder we don't all dissolve into unpleasant puddles of filthy goo.

And apparently, these toxins must be driven from our bodies, like a priest exorcising a particularly stroppy bunch of demons.

And Zooby intends to do this to Kate and me today, by popping a load of hot bits of rock on to my wife's back, and sticking a load of glass cups on to mine. Quite why this will have the desired effect of toxin drainage is beyond me. It all sounds so bloody random. Zooby could have told us that she'd be driving the toxins from our alcohol-soaked flesh by covering Kate in gravel and sticking a load of rusty old spoons to my back and it wouldn't sound any less or more convincing. I do hope Kate isn't falling for any of this claptrap.

'First, let's get some of these lovely rocks on you, Kate,' Zooby tells my wife, who looks mildly terrified.

She continues to look terrified as Zooby pushes her shirt up to expose her lower back, and then lifts a small flat black rock out of the metal pan of hot water.

Terror turns to instant pleasure, however, as the rock is placed on the small of her back.

'Nice?' I ask warily.

'Oh yes,' she tells me. 'It's not too hot at all. Very pleasant, in fact.'

'Oh. Okay,' I respond, somewhat surprised, but also quite pleased that Kate is enjoying it.

She appears to enjoy it even more as Zooby applies several more rocks. 'How's that, Kate?'

'Mmmm. It's very nice, thanks.'

'Great! The warmth of the rocks will help to melt away tension. Those toxins will be coming out of your pores in no time!'

'I'm sure they will,' Kate replies with a contented smile. She does indeed appear to have fallen for this claptrap.

'I'll leave you for a few minutes then, as we turn our attention to Scott!'

Zooby turns to me, and unceremoniously pulls my T-shirt up to around my neck. She is surprisingly strong for such a thin girl. 'Okay,

Scott. I'm going to start applying the cups to your back now. We start by filling the cup with a little alcohol . . .' Zooby pauses and waggles her eyebrows at me. 'Not the type you can drink, though, you silly man!'

Oh, bloody hell.

'And then we set alight to the alcohol to draw the air out of the cup, and apply it to Scott's back.'

I hear a lighter being lit, a small *floomp* noise as the alcohol in the cup is lit, and then feel Zooby stick the cup on to my lower back. The cup feels warm, but not entirely uncomfortable. I start to relax a bit, thinking that this may not be so bad after all.

Then Zooby applies another cup . . . then another . . . and then another. Within the space of a couple of minutes, I have a good dozen of the things all over my back. I can feel a weird pulling sensation from my skin under each cup, but otherwise things are still more or less okay.

'And now we leave the cups on for several minutes, to allow the sucking motion to pull the toxins from Scott's skin. This will leave him refreshed, happy and looking a little less haggard.'

Good fucking grief, I can't believe—

. . . oh. Hang on a moment . . .

Something *unpleasant* is happening. The soft sucking sensation has suddenly developed into a prickly stinging feeling that I'm not at all happy with. It feels like the level of suction has ramped up under each cup.

'Er . . . I'm not sure this is so great, you know,' I say, pushing myself up on my elbows.

'It's fine, Scott!' Zooby reassures me. 'This is how the cups work! Just let yourself go with it!'

'But they're starting to feel quite painful, and I—'

'Scott!' Kate hisses. 'For the love of God, just do as Zooby says. We're on camera, *remember?*'

I look up at Zooby's tiny digital camera, and then over at where my daughter is also filming from the sidelines.

Just look at that expression of happiness on her face, would you? How could I ruin things for her? I'm not going to get my mortgage paid off if I wimp out now, am I?

I grit my teeth and lie back down, trying to ignore the increasingly sharp pain coming from each and every one of the dozen points across my back where the sucking cups have been placed.

This feels like I'm being hugged by a squid.

Probably a giant one.

Like the kraken from *Clash of the Titans*. That was one of the videos I was returning that day I fell off my bike outside Bejam.

. . . was the kraken actually a squid though?

I really can't remember.

It had big long tentacly arm things, didn't it?

There were probably suckers on it somewhere . . .

Now the pain is starting to get *proper nasty*. Instead of several small points of great discomfort, I now have one large one that extends across my entire back.

The hug from the kraken has now turned into something a lot worse. We've moved on from a vaguely unpleasant embrace into something that's bordering on squid-based molestation. In my mind's eye, I can see the kraken tighten its grip as it goes in for a big wet kiss . . .

Oh God, I have to get these things off my back!

'Can I please get them off?' I plaintively cry to Zooby.

'Scott!' Kate barks, her eyes flying open.

'No, Kate! This is getting *really* painful now!'

'It can't be that bad!'

'No, no! It really is! I feel like I'm being touched up by a horny squid!'

This is the single dumbest sentence that anyone will ever hear uttered on YouTube . . . and it has a lot of competition, let me assure you of that.

'The process isn't complete yet, Scott!' Zooby cries, trying to push me back down on to the massage table.

'I don't care if it's not complete! I don't want to be hugged by the kraken any more!'

Zooby's brow creases in confusion. 'The what?'

'The kraken! You know . . . from *Clash of the Titans*!'

'Clash of the who?' Zooby continues to look thoroughly confused.

'Titans! It's the giant squid monster from that film!'

'The kraken isn't a squid, Dad,' Holly helpfully points out.

'Isn't it?'

'Nope. I did a bit on Greek mythology at school.'

'Then what is it?' My rising levels of pain from the cups have momentarily been superseded by my rather baffling and intense need to identify the species of animal that the kraken belongs to.

Holly shrugs. 'No idea. It's just a sea monster thing. Zeus used it to kill people who defied him, as I recall.'

I look at Kate. 'Do you know what the kraken is?' I ask her.

'Nobody cares what the bloody *kraken* is, Scott!' she replies with barely concealed fury. 'You're ruining this!'

'No, I'm not!'

'Yes, you are! Nobody on YouTube gives a shit about stuff from a bad fantasy movie!'

I could have assured her at this point that at least 65 per cent of YouTube cares about nothing *but* stuff from bad fantasy movies, but the pain from the cups has ratcheted up a level, robbing me of my train of thought.

I look at Zooby again, and this time it's with an expression devoid of embarrassment or indecision. 'Get these bloody things off me please, Zooby!'

I jump up from the massage table and turn my back towards her.

'I'm not supposed to do it like this! It might hurt a bit . . .'

'I don't care! I want the sucky cups off me before the kraken gets too fruity!'

. . . that's the second dumbest sentence anyone will ever hear on YouTube, in case you were wondering.

Because I sound half hysterical and half enraged . . . and because she is just a young girl with a YouTube channel, after all, Zooby panics, and starts to yank the cups off me like her life depended on it.

Sccchlllllluuurrrpppp – pok!

'Ow! Oh, fucking hell! Ow!' I cry, as the first cup comes free.

Sccchlllllluuurrrpppp – pok!

'Jesus fuck!'

Sccchlllllluuurrrpppp – pok!'

'Ah! Ah! It hurts!'

Sccchlllluuuurrrrppppppppp – pok!

'Oh God! Make it stop!'

But Zooby has another eight cups to go, of course, so it doesn't stop.

Not for another hideous *minute*, during which all thought is blasted from my head . . . other than the vision of Laurence Olivier dressed as the mighty god Zeus, commanding that somebody release the kraken to bring fear and pain to the people of Greece.

I could have told him that all the seventy-foot-high sea monsters in the world are no substitute for a skinny girl with neon dreadlocks and a very dubious form of massage therapy. He could have just thrown Zooby and her cups at the Greeks, and those bastards would have stepped into line without hesitation as soon as they saw her coming at them with her lighter.

'Are they all off?' I cry in exhausted agony.

'Yes! They're all off!' Zooby tells me, backing away towards where her parents are standing. The poor girl is probably regretting ever starting her own YouTube channel. I'm sure if she'd known it would eventually result in her yanking glass cups off the back of a sweaty, screaming alcoholic in his mid-forties, she might have taken up knitting instead.

Kate, her expression filled with consternation at her husband's antics, sits up as well. Not only have I suffered the torment of the sucky cups, it appears I must also now deal with the wrath of my unhappy spouse.

'For God's sake, Scott! Why couldn't you just have gone through with this, like I asked you to? It really couldn't have been all that bad, you know!'

'It was! Look at my back!'

'Oh, stop being such a – *bloody hellfire! What the hell has happened to you??*'

'Dad! Your back!' Holly cries.

'What? What?' I shout, craning my head to see what has caused my precious loved ones to recoil from me with horror. I can't see what the problem is, though, given that it's impossible to look at your own back unless there's a mirror handy.

. . . or a video camera.

'Holly! Give me your phone!' I order my daughter.

'Why?' she replies, her eyes still full of fear, and with a queasy expression on her face.

'Because I want to look at what those cups have done to me!'

She shakes her head. 'You really don't!'

'Yes I do!'

I grab the phone, stop the recording and bring up the footage she's just captured.

As I freeze-frame on a shot of my poor back, the blood drains from my face.

Standing out on the pale white flesh are a dozen large, angry and extremely painful-looking red welts.

It's like the kraken has administered a series of gigantic love bites to my person, before plunging back into the icy depths to eat a few Greek virgins for dinner.

I look over at Zooby . . . the architect of all this misery. 'What have you done to me?' I ask her, in dumbfounded disbelief.

Zooby – who up until now has been a bubbly, happy, energetic girl with a bright life ahead of her – bursts into tears and buries her head in her mother's shoulder.

I have this day robbed her of her innocence about the world. Before I came along, she was 'Lovin' Life'. She was making people happy and healthy, secure in the knowledge that her efforts were all for the betterment of her fellow human beings.

But now, she sees what she has truly wrought upon the world. She sees how much pain and suffering she can inflict. My hideous red welts are testament to her downfall. Zooby has this day *released the kraken*, and now things will never, ever be the same again.

'It was a squid in *Pirates of the Caribbean*,' Zooby's father says, a thoughtful look on his face.

'What was?' I reply, looking at him with flummoxed wonder.

'The kraken. It was a squid in *Pirates of the Caribbean*, I think. It's been a while since I saw it, but I'm pretty sure I'm right.'

'Oh yeah,' Holly adds. 'It was in the second one, wasn't it?'

'Yes. That's right,' Zooby's father agrees. 'Definitely a squid in that.'

I hold out a hand. 'Thank you! I knew I was right!' I look at Kate, who has now got to her feet. 'You see, Kate? The kraken *is* a squid.'

She looks at me wide-eyed for a second. 'I don't care what the fucking *kraken* is, Scott!' she screams, and immediately stalks off, passing the wailing Zooby and her parents without a glance.

The rest of us stand silent for a moment, stunned by my wife's outburst.

'Well,' I eventually say to no one in particular. 'I guess that concludes this episode of *Lovin' Life with Zooby*.'

Holly takes her phone back from me, and throws a look over at where the young vlogger is still wailing into her mother's shoulder. 'Yeah. I think maybe we should go.'

I nod my head. 'Agreed.' I turn to Zooby's parents. 'Well . . . thank you for your hospitality Mr and Mrs . . . er . . . Zooby.'

'It's Eldridge,' Zooby's mother says as she pats her distraught daughter on the back.

I lean forward. 'Is it? Well then, thank you Mr and Mrs Eldridge then.' I look at Zooby. 'And no hard feelings, Zooby. I'm sure the mess you've made of my back will improve in no time.'

Yes, it's a little cruel to put it that way, but the girl did pretty much describe me as being old and haggard before the cups came out, so I'm not going to feel too bad about it.

Zooby ignores me and continues to cry.

'Holly? It's time to leave,' I tell my daughter as I move towards the house in pursuit of my irate other half.

'I've got it on DVD, if you want to borrow it,' Mr Eldridge says.

'Excuse me?'

'*Pirates of the Caribbean.* The one with the squid.'

'Ah . . . no, thank you,' I reply, before hurrying away as fast as my legs will carry me.

The last thing I want to look at is a giant bloody squid. Today has already been hard enough on my sanity, and if I have to sit through a film that reminds me of my brief experience with the joys of *cupping*, then I really will be kraken up.

***

You'll be amazed to know that Zooby did not put our episode of *Lovin' Life* up on YouTube. In fact, it was a good two weeks before she returned at all. When she did, she seemed quite subdued . . . and had developed a slight twitch in her left eye.

Holly *did* upload the footage she had caught with her camera, using the Dry Hard hashtag.

BucketFace absolutely *loved it.*

So did everybody else.

Even Kate managed to see the funny side, after her towering rage had subsided. After all, the video led to a massive uptick in our subscriber count, so the guest appearance achieved exactly what she wanted it to . . . in a roundabout kind of way.

I have had to endure endless tweets and Facebook posts featuring a large variety of giant squid, of course. This was rather inevitable. My social media feeds have been about 90 per cent kraken for the past few weeks, but I'm willing to put up with this, as the red welts have almost faded and I've suffered no ill effects from my cupping experience.

. . . other than becoming allergic to calamari, for some reason.

Sadly, the trip to Zooby's world did nothing to alleviate my ongoing struggles with sobriety. I'm still stressed and anxious pretty much every day, and still gamely searching for some kind of solution. It's quite clear that I'm not going to find one on YouTube though.

Having said that, BucketFace always seems quite happy with the world. Maybe if I pop the orange bucket I have in the garage on my head, it might improve my sense of well-being no end. I wouldn't be able to see Charlton Camberwell any more – and that could only be a good thing, surely?

When I mention this to Kate, she looks at me like I've gone mad.

This is entirely understandable.

What on earth am I thinking?

. . . the bucket in the garage is way too small for my head. I'd need to go and buy a new one from B&Q.

CHAPTER NINE

HOLLY GETS AN ADMIRER

There's never been a teenager quite as excited as this one.

Not since the last iPhone came out anyway.

'Oh my God! Oh my God!' Holly cries enthusiastically into the camera that's been chronicling her parents' struggle with sobriety for the past five months, which has thus far included aggressive nose picking and imaginary squid assault.

'PinkyPud has emailed me!' Holly exclaims, wide-eyed with exhilaration. '*PinkyPud!*'

She says this name with the kind of reverence only a tech-savvy teenager could have for a skinny twenty-year-old with a very popular YouTube channel. Where once the youngsters of this country deified pop stars, they now worship people with green screens, HD webcams and rather silly nicknames.

'I can't believe it!' Holly says, as if the Pope had dropped her a text. 'He's invited me – and Mum and Dad – along to Control, Alt, Del-Eat! That's the restaurant he owns in the city!' Holly is pulsating with excitement over this prospect. 'He said in his email that – oh, hang on . . .' She picks up her iPad from the bed and looks at the screen. 'He says . . . *I'd love to invite you and your parents to meet me and have a free meal!*

I've really enjoyed following your vlogs, and love the Dry Hard hashtag . . .'
Holly looks back at the camera, still goggle-eyed. 'Can you believe it?
He's following me on Instagram and Twitter! He's even asked me to be
his friend on Facebook! Seriously . . . can you believe it?!'

It's no wonder Holly has been contacted by such an august member
of the online community. PinkyPud has been doing pretty well in the past
few months out of his association with #DryHard. A rising tide floats all
ships . . . and a virally popular hashtag makes for more website clicks.

PinkyPud is someone who understands this (underneath the oh-so-
cool exterior of 'PinkyPud' lies a shrewd young man called Jasper Peabody,
who knows the power of both a strong image and a large public following).

He sees the angles here better than Holly does. Where there's popularity, there's money to be earned. Jasper has made a career of aligning
himself with what's hip and happening online, and what's been going
on with the Temple family is no exception.

And it's probably no coincidence that he's got in touch not that
long after Kate and Scott were guests on Zooby's YouTube channel. The
idea of a rival vlogger muscling in on what he probably thinks of as his
territory probably didn't go down well at all.

Holly's exuberance about PinkyPud's interest is entirely understandable.

At seventeen, you tend to take things at face value, and as far as
Hols is concerned, she's just been acknowledged by one of the coolest
people in her world. Nothing else matters.

'I've got to tell Mum and Dad!' she tells the same viewing audience
that PinkyPud is no doubt planning to exploit as much as he can in the
very near future. 'I hope to God they want to go!'

Holly's enthusiasm for this new scheme may be understandable, but
whether her parents will feel the same way is *highly* debatable.

Downstairs and a little while later, Kate and Scott look decidedly unsure
about the whole thing.

Not entirely unwilling to go along with the plan, but not entirely happy about it either.

'And PinkyPud says he wants me to record it all for my YouTube channel!' Holly explains to her parents from behind the camera, her excitement unfettered. 'And he's going to post it to his channel as well! All of his five million subscribers will be able to see it! *My* video, guys! *My* video! He even said he's going to *pay* me!'

'That's . . . er, lovely, Hols,' Kate replies from her customary place on the (still slightly wine-stained) couch.

'And he also said he'd help me monetise my channel better, so we can start making some proper cash from this whole thing!' Holly continues.

'Really?' Scott pipes up, sitting bolt upright. 'We can actually start to make money from this?'

'Oh yeah, Dad! With PinkyPud's help! He makes loads with ad revenue and merchandise. He might be able to do the same for us.'

This is a far more interesting notion.

Good old PinkyPud has amassed himself quite the fortune from his YouTube exploits. If he can help the Temples amass their own through advertising and monetisation, then this dinner invite is not something the Temple Twosome can really turn down, is it?

Besides, Holly's excitement at the prospect of her video being on PinkyPud's channel is palpable.

This could mean the start of something big in her future. She's a bright, smart and dedicated kid, who just needs a push in the right direction. Maybe that push will come from this PinkyPud person . . .

All this is somehow conveyed in a single look that passes between Scott and Kate as they contemplate their daughter's latest piece of news.

Eventually, it's down to her mother to give Holly the reply she's looking for.

'Okay, Hols. We'll go along and meet PinkyPud.' Kate sighs. 'We could do with a nice meal out anyway.'

'Woo hoo!' Holly cries.

'Just don't stick that damn camera in my face too much while I'm eating,' Scott tells her. 'The world doesn't need to see me chewing on a chicken leg.'

'No worries, Dad!'

Holly then plonks her iPhone on the coffee table and goes around to give her parents a hug. The camera catches this – including the slightly uncertain looks on the faces of both elder Temples as Holly grasps them tightly in her arms.

And so, to a dinner date at Control, Alt, Del-Eat.

Opened about a year ago with the help of his father, Gerrard, this *achingly* trendy two-floored bistro has become a nice little side earner for our new benefactor, PinkyPud. Jasper Peabody fancies himself as a member of the restaurant elite, and is willing to use some of his online fortune to facilitate this.

Here, you can masticate on a variety of foods you wouldn't find in any other high street restaurant. Fancy a fried tarantula? Control, Alt, Del-Eat is the place for you. Want a crocodile burger? Then step right on in. Have an overwhelming desire to drink a cocktail that inexplicably marks *bacon* as one of its main ingredients? Then pull up a stool, the waitress will be with you shortly.

The décor matches the alternative cuisine on offer. You've never seen so much reclaimed driftwood in your life. And are the tables all made from recycled aluminium cans? Of course they are!

Don't dwell too much on what some of the optics behind the bar are made of, because a lot of those glass bottles and valves have a decidedly *medical* look about them. It really doesn't bear thinking about what they might have contained before they became receptacles for flavoured vodka and botanic gin.

All this strangeness is captured by Holly's phone as the Temple Twosome descend on Control, Alt, Del-Eat for their free meal.

They've both dressed up for the occasion, that's for certain.

After all, the opportunities for a posh night out in recent months have been few and far between, thanks to their heavy workloads – and the desire to avoid social situations where alcohol may be present.

Quitting the drink has not led to the two of them enjoying any more free time with one another, more's the pity. In fact, what with #DryHard taking up a lot of the scant free time they do have when not at work, the Temples are spending even less time together as a couple these days.

Given that, and given how rare this opportunity is, both Kate and Scott have made an effort this evening. Scott's wearing his nicest suit, and Kate has dragged out the dress she wore to the wedding last year. The vomit came out fine on a hot wash.

PinkyPud *hasn't* dressed up. He's wearing a black *Call of Duty* hoodie and green skinny jeans. His hair is orange and blond. Pinky's head puts you rather in mind of a boiled orange sweet. The rest of him looks like a clown on dress-down Thursday.

He's every inch the successful social media millennial.

'Wow! Hi, guys!' he exclaims with pleasure, in exactly the kind of voice you'd expect from a millionaire YouTube vlogger. There's a rampant but ever so slightly fake-sounding enthusiasm to it that could become really grating after a while.

PinkyPud comes across the restaurant floor towards the Temples as they stand just inside the double glass doors.

'So good to have you here!' he says, grabbing Scott's hand and shaking it, then embracing Kate and giving her a kiss on the cheek. This display of overfamiliarity stuns both of them. PinkyPud then looks over the top of Holly's camera lens. 'Hey, you're Holly, right?'

'Er, yes!' Holly says, her disembodied voice raised so it can be heard over the murmur of punters eating crunchy insects.

PinkyPud moves around to one side of the camera, and everything goes very wobbly for a moment as he gives Holly a long embrace as well. The camera alights on Scott and Kate for one second, showing an extremely disconcerted look on their faces.

'It's so good to meet you finally,' PinkyPud's muffled voice is heard to say.

By the length of the embrace that's still going on, this much is obvious.

Eventually, the hero of exciting YouTube vloggers everywhere pulls himself away from Holly, and she manages to hold the camera up again. It's shaking quite a lot now.

'Welcome to Control, Alt, Del-Eat!' PinkyPud says, arms thrown open. 'We've got a great table for you guys. Follow me!'

Their ebullient host marches off in the direction of the centre of the restaurant, with his assistants in tow.

'I guess we'd better follow then,' Scott says, still looking a trifle disconcerted. That hug really did go on for a *very* long time.

'Yeah! Come on, you two! Let's eat!' Holly orders. One arm appears from the side of the shot, pulling at Kate's coat sleeve.

'Okay, Hols, calm yourself,' Kate tells her, looking straight into the lens. 'And let's just have a minute without that thing on, shall we?'

'Aw, Mum.'

'Please just turn it off for a while, Holly,' Scott says in a fatherly tone. 'PinkyPud's minion over there is recording everything as well. You won't miss much.'

Without further argument for once, Holly turns the camera off, allowing the Temples the luxury of sitting down at a dinner table without a video camera recording their every move.

They don't get to eat their starters without it being recorded, though, which means everyone on YouTube will soon get to see Scott trying to eat an ostrich egg omelette, while Kate worries at a plate of deep-fried shark bites.

PinkyPud has laid on a very special menu for his two older dinner guests, so the choice to have something a little less adventurous has been taken away from them.

Of course, he's also made sure there are non-alcoholic drinks on offer. All of them are served in very clearly branded Control, Alt, Del-Eat bottles.

You'd be forgiven for thinking this whole set-up was one big advertisement for his restaurant . . .

Holly gets to eat and drink what she wants, however. She's not the centre of attention here tonight.

Both Temples look increasingly uncomfortable as they finish their starters and wait for the main dishes to arrive. There's only so long you can take being stared at by a camera lens, a millionaire YouTube vlogger and at least 75 per cent of the other restaurant guests without beginning to feel like an exhibit in the zoo.

It's Kate who decides to speak up.

'Um, guys . . . this is all very nice, but is there any chance we can have a little time without everyone paying so much attention to us?' She looks at PinkyPud. 'I know you want to record us, Mr Pud, but could we have a few minutes just to ourselves, do you think?'

For the briefest of brief moments, PinkyPud looks exceptionally chagrined at this request, but it's gone from his face almost before it appeared, to be replaced by an effusive smile. 'Of course! We'll get your main dishes served up, and the two of us will go eat upstairs, leaving you in a bit of peace.'

Scott looks a bit startled. 'You and Holly?'

'Of course!' PinkyPud exclaims. 'We can have a nice chat while you guys eat.'

'Sounds great to me!' Holly proclaims, the camera shaking a little again.

'Oh . . . okay,' Kate says, looking at her daughter with barely concealed alarm.

A couple of minutes later, the main dishes do indeed turn up. Scott has a kangaroo burger with aioli and thick-cut Venezuelan chips, and Kate is served a wild-boar steak and Caribbean risotto. Quite what makes the chips particularly Venezuelan and the risotto specifically Caribbean may never come to light, because at this point PinkyPud makes good on his promise and pulls himself and Holly away from the table.

Scott and Kate look a little worried as they leave. For people who didn't want to be recorded while they ate, they certainly don't seem happy about their daughter leaving the table.

If you wanted a bird's-eye view of Scott and Kate eating their first meal out together in months, then it's your lucky day.

Holly really is dedicated to her job as chronicler-in-chief, and when she sees that her parents' table is easily viewable from the mezzanine level of the restaurant, she can't resist filming them from on high.

While Holly's camera watches Scott and Kate eat, PinkyPud strikes up a conversation with their star-struck daughter.

'You're doing a great job with this hashtag Dry Hard thing, Holly,' he says, voice smooth as silk.

'Thanks, PinkyPud!'

'Call me Jasper. That's my real name.'

'Okay . . . Jasper.'

'It's a shame you've not been in the clips more yourself though.'

'You think?'

'Oh yeah. You're incredibly photogenic.'

Holly doesn't manage a reply to this, but you can imagine the expression on her face, can't you? A mixture of embarrassment, surprise and happiness.

'Leave your parents for a bit and come talk to me,' PinkyPud tells her. 'I really want to hear about how you got all of this started . . . and tell you how I think we can move it forward.'

The camera shakes a little once again. 'Okay. I might leave it recording, though, so I've got some stuff to edit in before I upload the clip tomorrow,' Holly replies.

'Sure, sure, no problem, Holly. You do that.'

There's a definite *slimy* tone in Jasper's voice now, which isn't something anybody wants to hear.

Sadly, the two people who *should* be hearing it – and hustling their daughter away from it as fast as possible – are currently a good thirty feet away, pushing strange food around their plates.

As Holly goes off to chat to PinkyPud, her parents continue to eat – in apparent silence. All around them people are talking, laughing, *drinking* and having a lot of fun. Not Scott and Kate though. They look like they're at a wake.

In fact, as the camera continues to record them for another half an hour, we see them barely communicate.

Maybe it's the pressure of being the centre of attention.

Maybe it's the concern over what their daughter is doing with PinkyPud.

Or maybe . . . there's something else going on here.

There certainly appears to be something *missing*. A very important thing that would have accompanied any other meal they had out together before this year.

PinkyPud may have laid on as much free Control, Alt, Del-Eat elderflower lemonade and cherry-flavoured Coke as he liked, but none of it is a substitute for what Scott and Kate are used to on occasions such as this.

The thing that used to make the night go with a bang.

The thing that's probably making all those other diners around them laugh loudly.

As the Temples finish their main courses, they look like two people who might as well be strangers. It's like watching a couple on a first date. A bad one, at that.

It's hard to decide what's more uncomfortable – the unheard conversation happening between Jasper Peabody and Holly Temple somewhere up on the mezzanine, or the complete *lack* of conversation between Scott and Kate Temple down on the restaurant floor.

Finally Holly returns and picks the phone back up.

'So, we'll meet up next month when I'm back from Cannes then?' PinkyPud says, as Holly starts to walk towards the stairs leading down to her parents.

'Yeah! That'd be great!' she replies. There's a level of eagerness in her voice that would make her mother and father cringe.

'Excellent!' PinkyPud exclaims, popping into the camera frame and giving everyone a big thumbs up.

Holly giggles. It's the giggle of a girl who's just been flattered to within an inch of her life.

'Let's see how your folks are doing,' the Pudster suggests, leading Holly over to their table.

'How's the food, guys?' he asks as he reaches them.

Kate and Scott do that very British thing that involves a lot of fake smiles, accompanied by a look of mild torment in the eyes.

'Oh, it's great!' Scott says.

'Absolutely!' Kate agrees.

'Fantastic!' PinkyPud crows with pleasure. 'Let's get the desserts out then!'

Scott and Kate attempt to look pleased about this. They're only marginally successful.

The rest of the meal continues the advertisement for Control, Alt, Del-Eat.

PinkyPud waxes lyrical about how he started the business, how successful it's been, how much time and trouble he takes to source the alternative foodstuffs on the menu. It's one big ego-stroking exercise for the twenty-year-old vlogger, which causes much eye-glazing and sighing from the Temple Twosome.

PinkyPud then moves on to lots of questions about Dry Hard, and how Scott and Kate think the whole thing is going.

The answers he receives are strained and unimaginative, as if the two people concerned have forgotten the art of conversation. There's an unspoken air of discomfort between them that is quite tangible – if you can notice it over PinkyPud's constant cheerful oration, that is.

By the time the Temples have finished their after-dinner coffee, and risen to leave, they both look extremely tired, as if a great weight has suddenly descended on them.

At the restaurant exit, PinkyPud capers around for a few moments with his goodbyes. Not just to all three Temples, but to all the followers of #DryHard, who he thanks for watching. As well he might, given that they've all just sat through an extended advert for his business in the guise of another update on their favourite teetotal couple.

By the time the Temples clamber into the taxi laid on for them by Control, Alt, Del-Eat, the silence between Scott and Kate has become almost deafening. So much so that Holly comments on it as the cab pulls away.

'What's up with you two? Didn't you have a nice time?'

Kate looks into the camera. 'It was fine.'

'Yeah . . . fine,' Scott agrees.

'Really? Then why are you both so quiet?'

Kate shakes her head. 'It's nothing, Holly. We just . . . just feel quite tired.'

'Yeah . . . tired,' Scott parrots, looking out of the window, apparently lost in thought.

'Er . . . okay. Maybe I'll just stop recording for now then,' Holly says, sounding concerned.

Her parents look at her and nod slowly, thoughtful expressions on their faces.

The following morning, back in Holly's bedroom – and she's not hyper-excited any more. She looks glum. *Extremely* glum.

The hair is being twiddled to such an extent it might burst into flames at any moment.

'What's the matter with them?' she asks, in the manner of someone who knows she is getting no answers. 'I thought they'd be really upbeat after the free meal last night, but ever since we got home, they've been almost silent. It's really bloody weird. I stopped watching *The Walking Dead* because it got boring, but apparently I have my own version of it right here in my house.' Holly chews on a fingernail. 'What is going on with them? Was it the food? Was there something in the Venezuelan chips?' Hair twiddle. 'Or is it Dry Hard? Is the whole thing getting too much for them? They seemed to be alright with it before last night. What's changed?'

Holly shifts on the bed and looks up at the ceiling for a moment, drawing in a deep breath. 'I thought we all had a great time. Jaspe—sorry, *PinkyPud* was really friendly.' She pauses and waves at the camera. 'Hi, Pinky!' she says with a smile before continuing her point. '. . . and nothing embarrassing happened to either of them for once, so what the hell has gone wrong?'

Poor Holly. She was unfortunately far too busy being wooed by Jasper to notice how her parents were behaving. This is something she's just realised as well, by the look on her face.

'Maybe I should go back through the video footage I captured of them eating,' she says as she flicks the camera off. 'That might clear things up a bit.'

When the camera is recording again, Holly has been crying.

'Oh God. They . . . they could barely look at each other!' she says, wiping a tear away from one eye. 'They looked so . . . so *lost*.' She chews again on her fingernail, which has become quite ragged. 'Why are they like that? Is it because . . . because they *couldn't have a bloody drink?*'

Holly whispers this last part. Not because she's afraid of her parents overhearing her, but because to say it too loud just makes the concept all the more awful to contemplate.

#DryHard may have done an extremely thorough job in motivating the Temple Twosome to stay off the booze, but it may also have highlighted something very worrying – that without the booze *there is no* Temple Twosome.

Before, when the drink was still flowing, Scott and Kate always enjoyed their time together – what little there was of it. They made the most of those oh-so-rare occasions when they could let their hair down.

But now?

Now that the booze has dried up?

Well, that ability to enjoy each other's company has apparently gone the way of the dodo!

Alcohol was making their lives worse in so many ways, but could it be that in one important respect it was making it *better*?

That it was the thing – whisper it – *the thing that kept them together?*

That should make absolutely no sense whatsoever . . . but when did human beings ever make that much sense, eh?

It's becoming quite clear that giving up drinking is not simply a matter of quitting an addictive substance; it's also about completely changing the way you live your life.

Not all for the better, apparently.

Could this whole thing have been a massive mistake?

PART FOUR
WEAK

CHAPTER TEN

KATE FALLS OFF THE WAGON

'*Unexpected item in bagging area.*'

'No, there isn't.'

'*Unexpected item in bagging area.*'

'No, there bloody isn't. I've moved it. Look!'

'*Unexpected item in bagging area.*'

'It's not there any more! I've moved it back!'

'*Unexpected item in bagging area.*'

'It's just a fucking cucumber! And it's gone! Look at it! Here it is in my hand, you silly bitch!'

'*Unexpected item in bagging area.*'

'I swear to God, if you don't shut up, I'm going to empty this bottle of olive oil all over your circuits.'

'*Unexpected item in bagging area.*'

'No! No! I just picked the olive oil up to show you what I was going to do to you! Here, I'll put it back! Everything is fine!'

'*Unexpected item in bagging area.*'

'Fuck off!'

'Is there a problem, madam?' a rather bored member of staff says to me as she sidles up.

'What? No! Er, I mean yes. This thing won't stop saying—'

'*Unexpected item in bagging area.*'

'Ah. You've probably not scanned the item properly.'

'Yes, I did! It's just the cucumber I bought for my lunch. I put it on the scale, chose it on the screen and it went *bink.*'

'The cucumber?'

'No, not the bloody cucumber. The machine!'

'It went *bink*?'

'Yes! It went *bink*, and then I put the cucumber in my bag, but then the machine went—'

'*Unexpected item in bagging area.*'

'Exactly!'

'I'm very sorry, madam. This is one of our old machines that hasn't been replaced yet. It's a bit wonky. Perhaps you'd like to come over to a regular checkout?'

'No! No, I wouldn't actually! I just want to buy my bloody shopping here at this machine and go home. That's all I bloody want! But I can't because the fucking thing keeps going—'

'*Unexpected item in bagging area.*'

'Shut up! Shut up, you bastard! Aaaaarggghhhh!'

I'm not in a good way at the moment.

No, this is something of an understatement. I am about as far away from being in 'a good way' as it's possible to be and still be breathing.

Usually, a malfunctioning automated checkout would not drive me to such behaviour in public. I am not, by nature, the type of person to cause 'a scene'. Not when I'm sober anyway.

And boy, am I sober.

Really, really fucking *sober*.

And I have been now for bloody *months*.

Up until July, I would probably have told you that this was a good thing. A *very good thing indeed*. After all, alcohol was ruining my life, wasn't it? It was causing me no end of misery, and it was absolutely the right thing to cast it from my life, so I could march off into a glorious new sober dawn. Everyone and his wife on YouTube and social media certainly seemed to think so. I've had *thousands* of people tell me how proud they are of me, and how pleased they are that I've managed to work myself free of the shackles of the evil alcoholic beverage.

Yes indeed, it was all supposed to be going so very, very well.

And I genuinely felt that it was for a while, to be honest.

But then Scott and I went to that stupid restaurant and everything fell apart.

Do you have any idea how *excruciating* it is to realise you have nothing to talk about to the person you're supposed to be closest to in the world? That there's nothing that you want to say to them, and there's nothing they want to say to you?

Scott and I both thought a nice meal out would be a great way for us to spend a little quality time together somewhere posh – even if it did include having the whole thing recorded. When Holly went off with PinkyPud, leaving the two of us alone, I thought the night could begin properly. Scott and I used to have so much fun when we went out for a meal together.

Used to.

But now it appears that we have nothing in common, and zero chemistry.

We both tried to initiate conversation, but each time it dribbled out with a few half-hearted comments about the Venezuelan chips, and what exactly constitutes a Caribbean risotto.

We decided it was probably the mango.

And that was it. For an interminable half an hour, my husband of twenty years and I could think of nothing to say to one another that didn't involve a South American country or a tropical fruit.

Where once sparkling conversation and loud giggles were the order of the day, flat silence and the occasional dull burp have taken their place.

And as the minutes ticked by, the reason for this lack of spark between us dawned on me. It also dawned on Scott at more or less the same time. I could tell from the way he looked forlornly at the bar every few minutes.

In the months we've both been sober, I have never wanted a drink more than I did right at that moment.

Oh sure, I've had wobbles before then. That's to be expected. But I had Holly and her hashtag to keep me on the straight and narrow, and offer me the encouragement I needed.

And I was never really *desperate* for a drink. Not even after a hard, stressful day at work.

It would have been *nice*, don't get me wrong, but I really felt like I'd turned a corner, and had reached a point where I was coping fine without it.

But sitting at that table, with the remains of my wild boar and Caribbean mango risotto in front of me, and my husband sat across from me looking as miserable and lost as I felt, I would have cheerfully throttled my own mother for a small glass of red wine.

I would probably have punched my grandmother for a large one.

Because it was at that moment that I realised giving up the booze may not be entirely a good thing *at all*.

Because in one very particular way, it may be the worst thing I've ever done.

Because it's made me realise that without a drink in our hands, Scott and I are *nothing* together. There's just *nothing there any more*.

Oh, God help me.

I didn't have a drink that night, of course. How could I? Even with such a horrible realisation, I could hardly jump off the wagon right there in the restaurant.

And I didn't have a drink when we got home either. Or the next day. Or the day after that.

I had all those lovely people on social media to please, didn't I? Not to mention my daughter, with her burgeoning career as a YouTube vlogger.

So, no alcohol passed my lips. Because #DryHard is apparently more important than my ability to hold a decent conversation with my husband.

He didn't drink either, for much the same reason.

And we didn't talk about the night at the restaurant. Of course we didn't. We both independently put it down to the stress of being recorded by both Holly and PinkyPud, and moved on with our clean and sober lives. We'd spent years making excuses for our behaviour while drunk, why wouldn't we do the same when sober?

Except I didn't move on at all. Not one little bit. Every night when I closed my eyes, and listened to Scott breathing next to me, I flashed back to that restaurant table, and the gulf of silence that existed between us.

A gulf that has never really gone away in the intervening weeks between then and now.

We don't talk now. About anything. Where once I could rely on Scott to be there to help me through the pressures of work, and of life in general, now I have no one. He is supposed to be my support mechanism, but he's not any more. And I'm not his either.

You have no idea what it's like to need to hear someone's warm, reassuring voice, only to be met with cold silence.

'*Unexpected item in bagging area.*'
    'Shut up! Please shut up!'
    '*Unexpected item in bagging area.*'
    'Be quiet!'
    '*Unexpected item in bagging area.*'

Unexpected breakdown in marriage area.

I don't want to be crying at a broken self-service machine. It wasn't on my list of things to do today – on the one day this week that I haven't had to go into fucking work.

Nevertheless, here I am, at 12.30 p.m. on a drizzling Sunday in August, crying like an idiot because this machine won't recognise my cucumber.

Perhaps I should have bought a mango instead.

'That's it!' I scream, drawing even more attention from the small crowd of fellow shoppers around me. 'I can't do it any more!'

'Do what?' the completely confused shop girl asks me, stepping back slightly.

I splay my arms wide. 'This! This!' I screech, looking around and gesticulating wildly, as if that will help the poor girl glean what afflicts me.

'As I said, you can go through a regular checkout, madam,' she says, completely misunderstanding me, for completely understandable reasons.

I look at her for a moment.

And in that moment, something *snaps*.

'Ah, to hell with it!' I cry, and stalk off towards the alcohol section at the back of the store, leaving all my shopping – unexpected or otherwise – in the bagging area, and unpaid for.

I grab myself a bottle of red wine when I get to the best aisle in the supermarket. It's not one of the cheap ones either. No. If I'm going to give in to my base instincts and fall off the wagon, it's going to be thanks to the twelve quid good stuff.

Clutching the bottle of Pinot Noir like it's my firstborn, I go over to a manned cash till that's as far away from the self-service section as possible. When I hand over the cash for the wine, I have to take a moment to silence a small and irritating voice inside me that's pleading with me not to do it.

This I can ignore, because I still remember the thick silence that sat between Scott and me in Control, Alt, Del-Eat.

With the wine paid for, I storm out to my car, and pull out of the car park at some speed. All I want to do is get home and crack this bottle open. Scott is round his friend's house helping him fix his car, and Holly is off with Amber up in town, so an empty house awaits me, my Pinot Noir and the death of my willpower.

I'd like to tell you that as I drive, an internal torment begins within me. That I wrestle with my conscience over the decision I'm making. That it's hard for me to just throw away all the progress I've made up to this point.

It fucking isn't though.

It's *easy*.

So pathetically, simply, excruciatingly *easy*.

I should be worrying about the fallout from doing this. I should be concerned that I'm about to let down my husband, my daughter, the legion of followers we've gained on social media and, perhaps most importantly, myself.

None of this is the case, however, because all I can think about is the sound the cork will make as it pops out of the bottle, and the way the light in the kitchen will glint off the wine as it pours into the pristine wine glass, which even now sits ready for me in the cupboard back at home, willing me on.

My hands are shaking as I open the front door. I am a woman completely consumed.

I nearly drop the large wine glass as I snatch it out of the cupboard. The cork does satisfactorily pop from the bottle, but there's no light glinting off the pouring wine, as it's grey and miserable outside.

I've been feeling grey and miserable inside for the past few weeks.

Time to bloody rectify that.

The first gulp is heaven. The second gulp makes the first seem like drinking horse piss by comparison. The third is everything I've wanted in life. The fourth . . . the fourth is just a gulp of red wine, to be honest with you. Even a woman as starved as me can't prolong the ecstasy much past the first three swallows.

By the time the glass is empty, I'm already feeling a dreadfully pleasant sense of equilibrium. A *levelling out*, you might say.

I fully intend to stop at this one glass. It's done the job I needed it to. It's brought me down off the edge of the cliff. I don't need to have any more. I'll be fine now, for the rest of the day. I can just pour the rest of the wine down the sink, wash the glass, and no one will be any the wiser that I've—

Ho ho! What's this?

Another full glass has appeared in front of me!

And I don't even remember pouring it!

Well, I'd probably better drink it then. My subconscious is clearly pointing out to me that one glass is not sufficient to achieve the kind of complete equilibrium I so cravenly desire. I'd better not make it angry with me, otherwise it might start rebelling and make me do stupid things I don't want to.

Like drink two large glasses of wine when you're supposed to be teetotal?

Be quiet, small, annoying voice! You have no power here!

The second glass goes down just as well as the first. By the time I start to pour a third, I'm well on the way to being properly drunk. After all, this is the first alcohol to pass my lips in *months*. I have become a total lightweight.

I've drunk a good half of the third glass before the crushing horror of what I've done here overwhelms me.

Gone is the tight, horrible feeling of frustration and emptiness that the malfunctioning self-service machine sparked off. In its place is shame. Huge Himalayan *mountains'* worth of shame, covered in the sheep of self-loathing, and the yaks of disgrace.

You have to be pretty bloody drunk to think up something like a yak of disgrace, let me tell you.

Oh God . . . I'm *drunk*!

Oh shit, oh shit, oh shit. I'm fucking *druuuuunk*.

I hold up the now empty bottle of Pinot Noir, checking the alcohol content. Surely this must be some incredibly strong wine that I've never tried before? I know I haven't had a drink in a while, and I haven't had any lunch, but two and a half glasses shouldn't make me *this* pissed.

Nope, it's the usual 13 per cent. Nothing out of the ordinary here. Fuuuuuck. I'm in *trouble*.

The sheep of self-loathing and the yaks of disgrace are joined by the Sherpas of terror, as I assess my situation. I spend a good few minutes contemplating how long it's going to be before Scott and Holly return home, and whether I can sober up before they do.

Then I think about tiny Sherpas of terror, riding around on large yaks of disgrace for a bit, which is *hilarious*, let me tell you. I mean, what would a yak of disgrace actually look like? It'd probably have its head down a lot, which would make it easy to see all the rocks under-foot, but would probably mean it banged into a lot of the larger ones.

And what colour would it be?

Ooh!

It'd be *blue*. A big, blue yak of disgrace, carrying around a Sherpa of terror . . . who would be dressed in black and carrying a pitchfork.

And the yak . . . and if the yak was feeling disgrace, it'd have to look like it, wouldn't it? It would have to have a . . . wait for it . . . a *sheepish* look on its face.

No! Wait! A *yakkish* look on its face.

Yeah, that makes more sense, doesn't it?

After all, the sheep of self-loathing would have to look *sheepish*. Of course they would! Now, what colour do you think a sheep of self-loathing would be? Maybe red? A nice pink shade to complement the yak—

Shut up, you silly cow! Holly and Scott will be home soon! You have to sober yourself up!

I shoot out of the kitchen chair like someone's just stuck forty thou-sand volts through me. As I do, I knock over the wine glass, which hits the kitchen tiles and shatters, spraying the rest of the wine everywhere.

'Oh fucking Christ!' I scream, as much in shock as in horror.

I spend a moment leaning against the sink, trying to get my heart rate to slow down a bit.

And I then take stock.

The way I see it, I have a swiftly diminishing amount of time in which to clean up the mess left by the wine glass – which won't be easy, because the kitchen now smells like a bloody winery. Why did I have to pick a Pinot with such a strong aroma?

I then have to try my hardest to sober up. How I'm going to do this, I have no idea. I feel comprehensively bladdered right now, which is ridiculous, as I've only had two and a half large glasses. I could drink two and half large glasses standing on my head before. In fact, I think I literally *did* drink a glass of wine standing on my head once, for a bet.

First, though, I must clean. And clean well!

Have you ever attempted to do a little light housework while pissed? I don't recommend it.

The first problem is what I'm going to clean up the wine and shattered glass with. In our cleaning cupboard there are all manner of suitable things I could employ to do this. Sadly, though, they are all at the *back* of the cleaning cupboard, and therefore might as well be on another continent to my drink-addled brain.

At the front is one of those Pledge duster things. You know, the thing that looks like someone's inserted a green handle into a fluffy white gerbil.

This is absolutely *not* the right implement with which to clean up broken glass and liquid, so of course I put it into action straight away.

This results in two things.

A soaking wet duster that'll have to go in the bin, and several small cuts to my left hand from trying to pick glass out of the duster's wine-sodden material.

The next things that my grubby mitts get a dubious purchase on is a tin of WD40 and a jumbo car sponge. These must be Scott's.

Ha! They are now *mine*!

The WD40 isn't very helpful. There's only so much glass you can poke around on the floor with a tin of WD40 before it becomes readily apparent that it's not up to the job.

The car sponge, however, works like *gangbusters*.

Okay, I tear the damn thing to pieces, and receive several more cuts to my left hand, but in no time at all (actually thirty-five minutes) I have the wine off the floor and in the sink.

And in the toaster.

And over the kettle, the slow cooker, the normal cooker, the coffee machine, the microwave – and the downstairs toilet when I realised I needed a pee, and took the wine-soaked sponge in there with me, for reasons I will never work out until the day I die.

This is not going well.

Finally, my hands grab something out of the cleaning cupboard that'll get the job done properly. A pair of old gardening gloves and some antibacterial wipes.

Look, I have no idea why a kitchen cleaning cupboard contains WD40 and gardening gloves either. It's just something that happens. The same way you designate a drawer exclusively for all the takeaway menus, and it ends up full of batteries, paperclips, wedding invitations, foreign coins . . . and *no* takeaway menus.

The gardening gloves prevent further injury, and the antibacterial wipes allow me to get rid of all traces of the wine from the various places around the kitchen I've managed to spread it.

After a mere hour and a quarter, I have managed to clean up one broken wine glass and a relatively small amount of red wine.

Okay, in the process I've ruined a duster, a car sponge, a pair of gardening gloves and my left hand, but we'll still call it a win.

I then spend another ten minutes attempting to plaster the cuts on my left hand. We haven't got any small plasters, though, just the large ones that normally never get used, because nobody ever injures themselves enough to need them.

This results in my hand looking like it's suffered third-degree burns. I can barely move my fingers under all that sticky beige plastic.

At least the kitchen looks sparkling clean, though, eh?

Spoiler: The kitchen does *not* look sparkling clean. There are smears of red wine and even redder blood still all over the place. Small slivers of glass trapped between the floor tile grout will be a hazard for months to come, and the stench of wine is still palpable. Never, ever do housework when you're drunk. The place is likely to end up looking worse than it did before you started.

Okay, so now I have to try to sober up – extremely quickly.

I've never had to sober up extremely quickly before.

What methods exist for such a task?

I know, let's have a look on Google. That'll tell me.

I pull out my phone and balance it precariously on my sticky left hand. Having punched 'sober up quickly' into the search engine, I am rewarded with several solutions that all seem like they might do the trick.

Drinking black coffee.

Taking a cold shower.

Getting your face slapped.

Yes indeed, these all seem like the kinds of things that would sober you up quickly, don't they? I've certainly seen them all used in movies!

This is the kind of logic that only seems plausible when you've had a skinful. Any sensible, clear-headed person knows that the chances of finding any actually useful information just by googling a single question are slim to none.

Also, basing your opinions on what happens in *movies* is not going to get you very far.

Drinking coffee, taking a cold shower or getting your face slapped do not help sober you up in the slightest.

I'd know all this if I was in any fit state to think about it for more than a few fleeting moments. But as it stands, I'm drunk enough to think these three methods will work.

But have I got time to do them all, that's the question. It's now getting on for 3 p.m., and Holly and Scott will be coming home at some point in the very near future.

Aha!

I know how to speed things up a bit!

I'll try all three things at once! That should do the trick, and will no doubt increase my chances of achieving successful sobriety before my loved ones come in through the front door!

Yes, folks. I'm actually going to take a shower, drink coffee and slap myself in the face all at the same time.

I should be taken away to a nice padded cell where I can't do myself any harm.

I put the kettle on, and while I wait for the water to boil, I put two heaped teaspoons of coffee in a mug with one hand, while slapping my cheek with the other.

I say slapping, but given that I'm doing it with my plastered left hand, it's more like cack-handed punching than slapping. Happily, though, I do at one point manage to pick my own nose with my pinky finger, so I really did learn something from all that Krav Maga.

With the coffee made, I head upstairs, scalding my lips on the hot beverage as I do so. In the bathroom I fire up the shower and quickly strip out of my wine and blood-soaked clothes.

I then clamber into the shower and stand shivering under the cold water, with my shaking coffee cup in my right hand, and the hastily applied plasters covering my left starting to peel off in the damp conditions.

There has never been such a sorry sight. A bedraggled, wasted, forty-something woman trying to sip hot coffee and punch herself in the face repeatedly under a twelve-year-old power shower.

I spend ten minutes doing this.

By the time I'm done, I'm freezing cold, have consumed all the coffee – burning my lips and tongue even more in the process – have ruined all the cute curls I put in my hair this morning with my most expensive set of tongs, and have turned both my left hand and left cheek into a sticky, gummed-up mess. There's so much gooey white adhesive on my face it looks like I've allowed Spider-Man to have an accident all over me.

I am also still drunk, of course.

Oh!

Was that the sound of the front door slamming shut?

Well, of course it was!

Panic hits me hard and fast, sending my heartbeat skyrocketing. This burst of adrenaline is actually just what the doctor ordered, as it clears my head enough for me to just about function.

I turn off the shower and clamber out.

From downstairs I hear Scott's voice. 'Kate? Are you in?'

I take a deep breath. 'Yes! I'm in! I'm just in the shower!'

I hear his footsteps on the stairs. 'The shower? In the middle of the afternoon?'

'Yes! I felt . . . felt really hot!'

It's about eighteen degrees outside, so that excuse really isn't good enough, but my brain has no capacity for anything more creative right now.

'Oh . . . okay. Would you like a cup of tea?'

My heartbeat increase even more. He can't go into the kitchen!

No, no, it's fine. You've done a good job cleaning up, Kate. He'll be none the wiser.

'Yes, okay. That'd be lovely,' I tell him, leaning against the bathroom door, and hoping I sound relatively straight.

There's a brief pause. 'Are you okay, sweetheart? You sound a little strange.'

'I'm fine . . . honnersly!'

Oh shit. That didn't sound sober *at all.*

'Pardon?' Scott sounds like he's right outside the door now.

'Hon – honers – *honestly!*'

'You don't sound fine, Kate. What's going on?'

Oh Christ. Oh fuck. Oh shit. What do I do? What do I tell him? I can't just pretend I'm fine any more!

Think of something, you dim-witted cow!

'I've got the shits,' I blurt out.

'What?!'

Yes . . . what indeed, you drunken clot.

'The shits! Really bad ones.'

'Really?'

'Yes! And . . . and my period! It's a really, really heavy one!'

Oh *fucking hell.* That's truly gilding the bloody lily, isn't it? Either terrible excuse would probably have been enough, but no – I have to throw them both out there, like a total fool. I should just tell him I've come down with the Ebola virus while I'm at it, and have done.

'Oh Jesus,' Scott exclaims. 'That sounds horrible, sweetheart. Look, I'll go make you a nice hot drink. You just come out whenever you're ready.'

'Er . . . okay.'

I hear the front door slam shut again downstairs. 'Mum? Dad?' I hear Holly shout.

'We're upstairs!' her father calls down to her. 'Your mum's not feeling very well.'

'Oh no!' Holly exclaims, and also comes up the stairs.

Fuck me. Normally I'd be very appreciative of all this familial attention, but right now I wish they'd both just piss off and leave me alone to my fictional diarrhoea and menstruation.

'Are you okay, Mum?' Holly says from outside the door.

'Yes, yes. I just need a few mowmins to sort myself out.'

'Mowmins?'

'Moments! A few *moments*!'

Both of them seem to accept this with good grace, and tell me they'll see me downstairs when I feel up to coming out.

With the sounds of my family going downstairs fading away, I sit on the toilet and contemplate how long I should stay in here before venturing back downstairs.

I mean, how much time would someone need to cope with the galloping poos? I'd like to stay here three or four hours, until I know I'm sober again, but they might get a bit suspicious, and I can't be doing with another doorway-based conversation with either of them.

I elect to give it fifteen minutes.

That would be enough time for someone to clean themselves up and refresh any sanitary products they might need to, surely.

I get dressed again, and by the time I've done this, I'm actually starting to feel a little less drunk, which is a very good thing. Maybe if I'm clever and careful enough, I can get through this with neither of them suspecting anything!

Taking a few deep, long breaths, I emerge from the bathroom in what I hope is a serene state.

Look, you've been here before, I'm sure.

At one time or another we've all had to pretend we're not drunk – usually in our teenage years, and coming home from a party early enough for the parents to still be awake.

Okay, you might not have had a bleeding left hand, a face covered in sticky white adhesive, burned lips and tongue, and hair that looks like you've been through a spin cycle, but you've all been in my position before, and can no doubt fully appreciate the awkwardness of the situation.

My husband and daughter cannot know that I've been drinking. They just can't.

I am hoping to Christ that my efforts to straighten up have been successful, and that my hastily constructed web of lies about why I've been in the shower is convincing.

I walk into the kitchen, thinking that I'm moving with the grace and élan of a person who is completely unfamiliar with alcoholic consumption.

What I actually look like is someone who's shit themselves and is trying not to let any more slip out – which is actually not such a bad thing, considering the lie I've just told.

Let's hope it helps with my subterfuge, eh?

'You've been drinking,' Scott says in the flattest of flat voices as I enter the kitchen.

Holly looks at me daggers.

How? How can they know?! I've been so careful! I've been so convincing! I've cleaned! I've showered! I've—

. . . turned the kitchen into a bomb site, that's what I've done.

I've sobered up just enough to see how poor my cleaning efforts actually were. The kitchen still stinks of wine. There are bits of glass in nearly every corner. There's blood smeared over the sink taps. There are several half-opened plasters scattered across one of the countertops, while another is covered in coffee granules.

'Um . . .' I say, and trail off.

The two of them say nothing, preferring to let me baste in the juices of my gigantic shame.

I then choose to say exactly the wrong thing.

'I haven't been drinkin'! I *swear!*'

Silence.

'Honnesly! I've . . . I've . . . I've had the poos. And a period.'

'Really, Kate?' Scott says, brow furrowed. 'You haven't had a drink?'

'No!'

'Then how do you explain this?' Scott lifts up the empty Pinot Noir bottle and places it carefully on the kitchen table.

Oh shit. I'd forgotten all about the wine bottle.

This is something of a rookie mistake, when you get right down to it.

The sheep of self-loathing, the yaks of disgrace and the Sherpas of terror are now all performing a conga line around the mountains of shame, like their lives depended on it.

'I . . . I . . . I didn't . . .'

The combined looks of confused anger are too much to bear.

'It . . . I . . .'

Oh God, what the hell do I say?

I stand there oscillating between shame and frustration for a few moments, before I hold my arms open wide and scream the first thing that comes into my head.

'It said there was an unexpected item in the bagging area . . . *and there fucking wasn't!*' The last bit comes out in a primeval, low-pitched growl that feels completely right and proper.

'What the hell are you on about, Mum?' Holly asks, totally perplexed.

'My cucumber, Holly! My cucumber was unexpected!'

This really isn't mounting much of a cohesive defence, but I'm having trouble making much sense – for what should be obvious reasons.

Scott and Holly look at each other, and then back at me. I'm sure one of them is about to pull their phone out and google 'how to get a loved one sectioned'.

I'd better start to make some sense fast.

'It all just got too much!' I cry, the words tumbling from my mouth. 'I was standing there, and the damn machine wouldn't give me my cucumber, and then I started thinking about that meal, and about how we just sat there in silence, and something . . . something just *broke* inside me. I couldn't help myself.'

Holly is still confused, but Scott's expression is telling me he understands just fine.

I give him a pitiable look. 'I'm sorry. I just haven't been able to get it out of my head. How it felt like there was nothing . . . nothing *there* any more.'

He runs a hand down his face and gives me the briefest of brief nods. 'Yeah,' he eventually says, very quietly.

'What do you mean, Mum?' Holly says, her voice now laced with an edge of panic. 'What do you mean there was nothing there any more? Do you mean between you and Dad?'

I look at her helplessly.

'But . . . but you *love* each other!' Holly exclaims. 'That's all that matters, right? Of course there's something still there!'

I wish I could say the right words that would take that dismayed look away.

'This whole no drinking thing has been hard on us, Hols,' Scott says to her. 'In ways we weren't expecting. It always helped us . . . helped us get on well with one another.' He looks quite pathetic. 'And maybe without it, we're . . . we're not the same people, with the same feelings.'

Now our daughter looks angry. 'Are you actually saying that you don't love each other any more just because you can't have a fucking *drink*?'

I wince hard at this. Teenagers have a way of oversimplifying complicated problems, but maybe Holly has actually just speared right into the heart of the matter.

'No! Of course not!' Scott says hurriedly. A little too hurriedly, for my liking. 'It's just that not drinking has forced us to . . . see some issues with our relationship that we obviously have to work on.' There's a hectic strain of denial in his voice and in his body language that says as much as the words coming out of his mouth.

Holly rises to her feet. 'You're both crazy! It's just bloody *alcohol*! It's not who you are!'

And with that, she storms out of the kitchen, in a magnificent teenage huff that she has every right to unleash on us.

We *are* both crazy. She's absolutely right.

Because how can two people who have been married for so long discover that their relationship may be based on nothing more than fermented sugar?

I look to Scott for some kind of support at this point, hoping he's thinking much the same as me, but instead he looks like he wants to bite my head off.

'Well done,' he says sullenly.

'What?! What do you mean *well done*?'

'Holly's really upset now, because you couldn't resist a bottle of Pinot.' He looks aghast. 'And after we've been doing so well for so long!'

My hands ball into fists. Or at least my right hand balls into a fist. My left just squelches a bit and starts to bleed again. 'That's not why she's upset, Scott! She's upset because we've pretty much told her our marriage is fucked because we can't get wasted any more!'

His arms fold tightly across his chest. 'You look pretty wasted to me.'

'Because of what happened at that restaurant!' I cry with frustration. 'Because of what's happening *to us*!'

The look of pompous indignation on his face makes me want to send the sheep, yaks and Sherpas on a swift and painful attack run. 'Well, I've managed to not drink, even though things aren't great, Kate. Why couldn't you? Getting shitfaced on cheap wine isn't the way to solve this.'

'It wasn't *cheap*!' I screech, defending something that really doesn't need defending.

'Whatever! You've let us down though. How is Holly meant to carry on with her YouTubing now?'

'Oh, for the love of God, who cares about bloody YouTube!!'

'I do! I do!'

I whirl round to see that my daughter has reappeared, at just the wrong moment. 'I didn't mean . . . I – I wasn't . . .' I stammer.

Holly seethes at me silently for a second, before spinning round and storming away.

I turn back to Scott, who is still giving me that self-righteous look that I want to slap so hard it makes my right hand hurt as much as the left.

This is that point in an argument where one of two things can happen. You can either take a few deep breaths and back away, or start to throw insults about that guarantee the damn thing will go on for hours.

I am tired. I am hurt. I am emotionally drained.

I am still pretty bloody *drunk*.

I just don't have the energy for a full-blown fight right now. And I don't want the only passionate and meaningful communication I've had with my husband in weeks to be a bloody row.

'I'm going to have a bath,' I tell him.

'But you only just had a shower.'

'Yes. And now I'm going to have a bath as well.'

'Why?'

Oh, for crying out loud. What the hell am I supposed to say to him?

I elect for the surreal. 'Because I bought cucumber when I probably should have bought mango, Scott, that's why.'

'What?'

I leave him sitting there in a puddle of confusion and self-righteousness, and make my way back upstairs. As I pass Holly's room, I can hear her talking into that bloody iPhone again.

The bath I draw is deep, hot and womblike.

In the two hours I spend in there, I manage to scrub away the sheep, yaks and Sherpas enough to see the Himalayan wood for the trees for the first time today.

Yes, I fell off the wagon spectacularly, but I'm not about to beat myself up about it *too much*, because it was for a very good reason.

My life might be falling apart in front of my very eyes, you see.

If there's a good reason for breaking a vow of sobriety, that must be it.

When I get out of the bath, I will attempt to apologise to both my family members for allowing myself to have a drink today. Hopefully they will accept that apology and we can move on.

The problem is, I now have no idea what we'll be moving on *to* . . .

CHAPTER ELEVEN

SCOTT FALLS INTO A TRAP

Well, fuck it.

If she's going to have a bloody drink, then I am too.

The glass One-Armed Jeff holds out to me is full of three of my favourite things: large ice cubes, a generous measure of tonic water and a double measure of Camberwell Distillery's finest gin – the pretentiously entitled 'Seventh Wonder' – which derives its name from the fact that the gin is distilled a ridiculous *seven* times.

It's a bloody lovely gin, though, there's no doubt about that. A strong juniper taste, but with hints of Lebanese mint and Persian lime, that tingles on the tongue and feels smooth as it slides down the throat.

I lick my lips . . . and take the glass in my hand.

Two weeks have passed since I discovered that Kate had fallen off the wagon and consumed nearly a whole bottle of Pinot Noir, before half-destroying the kitchen.

In the end, her explanation for why she did this was fair enough, even if I wasn't prepared to acknowledge it at the time.

I've been feeling that strange sense of being unmoored from my life, the same way she has. I can't pretend I wasn't disappointed that she'd had a drink, though, not after all this time. I was also disappointed that she didn't try to speak to me about it. Maybe I could have talked her out of it. But then, the whole reason why she bought that bloody bottle of wine was because we've not been communicating properly.

That stupid meal really has got under both our skins, like some kind of burrowing insect. Not one you'd want to fry and eat.

The night out at PinkyPud's bizarre restaurant has become indicative of something that we've apparently lost from our relationship.

Kate and I have always had an easy-going marriage. Arguments were few and far between, and none ever went unresolved overnight.

We've managed to raise a well-adjusted and intelligent daughter together – which must say something good about our relationship – and no matter how stressful things have got in our lives, we've always been there for each other.

Our marriage is built on very strong foundations. We work well together, we live well together, we play well together. We are meant to *be* together.

. . . at least, that's how I *used* to think.

Now, though, I'm deathly afraid that the foundations of our marriage are actually pretty damn weak – and made out of empty gin and wine bottles.

I can't remember a time when alcohol wasn't a significant part of our lives.

Even before drinking became a crutch to help us with stress, I can easily recall both Kate and me loving our booze, as far back as our first few dates.

When I think of the fun times we've had, almost all of them came with a glass held in my hand.

Alcohol has been a part of our relationship from the get-go, and even became a defining aspect of it.

No wonder we feel lost with one another, now we've cut it out of our lives.

It's like we're *strangers*.

It certainly felt that way when I passed Kate on the stairs this morning on my way to work. I gave her a half-hearted smile, which she returned with even less enthusiasm. The phrase 'ships that pass in the night' isn't even appropriate here. It's more like ships sailing on different oceans.

At the front door, Holly comes over to me and points at my tie. 'You might want to straighten that a bit, Dad,' she tells me.

I look down. The knot does look extremely skew-whiff, it has to be said. 'Why the sudden interest in how I look, young lady?' I ask her.

She contrives an air of innocence. 'Oh, no reason, Dad. Just want you to look smart for work, that's all.'

My eyes narrow. 'What's going on, Holly? Why do you care what I look like for work?'

'Oh God, Dad. It's *nothing*. I just thought your tie could do with being a bit straighter.' She looks up the stairs. 'How are you and Mum this morning?'

The change of subject nearly gives me whiplash, but I don't have the time to question my daughter on this further. If she's being cagey about something, then it'll just have to stay in the cage until she's ready to let it out. 'We're . . . we're fine, sweetheart,' I lie to her.

She gives me a look. 'Really? I haven't heard you say much to each other in the past few days.'

'It's difficult, Hols. But we'll sort it out . . . one way or another.'

I don't quite yet know what I mean by 'one way or another', but I'm horribly aware that something deep down in my subconscious certainly does, and will make it clear to the rest of me at the appropriate time.

Holly forces a smile. 'Yeah. I'm sure you will. And I think Mum is a bit better now. She promised me she wasn't going to drink again anyway.'

This comes as no surprise.

With Kate's permission, Holly uploaded a video to YouTube detailing how her mother had relapsed. I didn't want her to do this, but Kate was the one to say yes to it. People react to shame in different ways, and Kate's the type of person who doesn't like to bury her mistakes.

The reaction on social media was not what I'd expected. There were some people who were critical, but most just wanted to offer their support to Kate, and tell her not to be too hard on herself. Zooby even got in touch to suggest a few new ways to leach out the fresh toxins that she'd ingested. All of them sounded painful, and possibly life-altering.

I get the impression that as the months have gone on, we've lost a lot of the gawkers and trolls we picked up in the first few weeks of Holly's hashtag experiment. Her viewing figures and subscription rates have certainly dropped off a bit. Now I think we're just being followed by people with a genuine interest in seeing how we do. The ones who have built up an affinity for our situation, and want to see how it plays out.

That's social media and the internet for you. It's all about the instant gratification for a vast swathe of the online population. Once the novelty of something wears off, it's on to the next big viral sensation. The casuals probably got sick of watching our progress the minute somebody posted a new clip of a kitten in a bonnet, riding on a Roomba.

The people who have stuck with it obviously want to see us succeed in our efforts, by and large – hence the words of encouragement to Kate after her relapse.

I get the impression that a lot of people have been in her place. We're not all addicted to alcohol, but I don't think there are many of us without an addiction to *something* in this world. And to err is human, as we all know. I think we'd all be massive hypocrites if we spent our time heavily criticising others for backsliding. We've all done it. Some of us more than once.

The one thing that hasn't been mentioned in any of the recent videos posted using #DryHard is the apparent gulf that's grown between my wife and me thanks to being sober. And I'll fight tooth and nail to keep it unmentioned. Our followers don't need to know the negative effect that being teetotal is having on our marriage. That won't help them – or us – in the slightest. #DryHard is supposed to be a positive thing, after all.

There's a nagging feeling at the back of my mind that being dishonest about this process isn't a positive thing either, but I just can't stand the idea of my marital issues being broadcast across the internet.

Even more of my marital issues, I mean.

'Have a good day at work, Dad,' Holly tells me, snapping me out of my reverie. 'Hope it's an *interesting* one for you.'

Holly smiles in a way that I can only describe as 'creepy'. It's not nice having to describe a smile from your daughter as creepy, but that's how it looks. Something is going on here, and—

Oh shit!

It's eight thirty! I'd better get going! Charlton has decided that he's dead set against tardiness these days, and I can't be doing with another tirade from him.

I kiss Holly on the cheek and rush out of the front door. It's only when I'm in the car and driving that I realise I never tried to say goodbye to Kate. This causes the cold feeling that I've been carrying around in my chest for the past two weeks to drop a degree or two more.

I manage to make it into work with about twenty seconds to spare. Thinking this means I'm going to be spared another Camberwell rollicking, I relax a bit into my seat and go through my morning emails.

There aren't many of these – which is a worrying sign. Things have not been going all that well at Camberwell Distillery recently. Charlton's bizarre escapades with new and revolting gin flavourings over the past few years have really put us on the back foot. Gin is the most popular alcoholic drink in the UK these days. You wouldn't know it from working around here.

Charlton's stupidity is all that's to blame for our lack of current good fortune. The actual *normal* gin we make is rather fabulous. One-Armed Jeff is some kind of distillation sorcerer, and creates the kind of gin that you'd want to settle down and have kids with, if you could. It's incredibly frustrating that his efforts – along with mine and those of the rest of the staff – are constantly hamstrung by Captain Lard Balloon, and his overweening sense of self-importance.

Speaking of whom.

'Temple!' I hear him scream across the office. It's not a large office – barely room for eight desks, but he screams nonetheless.

I rise from my seat, as the eyes of my fellow workers fall upon me with pity. There's also some relief there, though, as it means that they have been spared the fat idiot's ire for at least the very near future.

'Good luck, chief,' Matt says from behind his computer screen.

I give him a flat smile, and make my way over to the large and unnecessarily ostentatious office that Charlton occupies.

'What can I do for you, sir?' I ask timidly as I walk in.

'Sit down, Temple! Got some good news!' he barks.

I relax a little. If Charlton has good news, then I'm likely to be spared his red-faced wrath for the moment.

My boss leans forward in his seat. 'Excellent news, Temple! You can keep your job!'

What?!

'What?!'

'I said, you can keep your job!' Charlton grins at me broadly, his words left hanging in the air like wet laundry.

'My job?'

'Yes, my boy! I'm *not* going to sack you!' He seems delighted about this turn of events.

'But . . . but I didn't know you were going to, sir!' I point out in plaintive fashion. I've had no indication from anyone that my job was under threat. None whatsoever.

Charlton's brow knits. 'Didn't you?'

'No!'

The brow stays furrowed for a second before being replaced by that idiotic smile again. 'Well, nothing to worry about then! Because you're *not* getting sacked!'

'Wh . . . ha . . . eh . . . ah . . .'

I mean, *fuck me* – is it any wonder I'm speechless? What exactly is he expecting from me here? Bloody *gratitude*?

Charlton looks at me indulgently and holds up a hand. 'It's okay, Temple, I can see you're lost for words with happiness.' I'm lost for words with something, alright. 'Your job is safe and secure.' He pauses to burp expansively before carrying on. Charlton always enjoys a full English before work. You can generally smell the bacon on his breath until about 3 p.m. 'Of course, you'll have to take a very small pay cut.'

'I'll have to do *what*?'

Charlton holds two fingers a centimetre apart. 'Small pay cut, Temple. *Tiny*, really.'

'A *pay cut*?'

'Yes, my boy! Everyone in the office is having to. It's not just you.' He gives me a confidential smile. 'But I wanted you to know first, as my top man!'

'Everyone?'

'Yes!' He sits back in his large leather chair. 'Up here, I mean. All you pencil-pushing types. The boys downstairs in the distillery already work for peanuts. Damn shame.' He shakes his head. 'It's difficult times we're having, Temple! We're all having to make sacrifices, you know!'

My hands ball into fists tight enough to draw blood from my palms.

Last week Charlton returned from a fortnight in the Maldives on an island called Wimbufushi. I looked up how much a fortnight costs there. It was more than our ad buyer, Marion, earns in a year.

Charlton also bought a new Jaguar last month. That could have paid for the much needed renovations to the distillery. All eight of us here in the office are still sharing one toilet, and the lads in the distillery are still using a Portaloo, since their toilet backfired, nearly turning One-Armed Jeff into No-Armed Jeff.

The man sitting opposite me is a cunt.

I feel rage start to boil up from my deepest regions.

How dare this fat idiot cut my wages, when he's frittering away money like there's no tomorrow? How dare he!

Quit then, you fool! Leave this bloody place! Show some backbone!

'Are you okay, Temple?'

'Hngngngh.'

'Temple?'

'Y – y – yes, sir. I'm . . . I'm *fine*.'

'Really? You look a little peaky.'

'No . . . no . . . just a bit tired, that's all.'

Charlton guffaws. There aren't many people left in this world that can guffaw, but Charlton Camberwell is certainly one of them. 'I thought all this sober living was supposed to give you bags of energy, my man! I'd start drinking again, if I were you. Much better for you!'

The colossal amount of willpower I'm employing to ensure that I *stay* employed is Herculean. All I want to do is jump across this table and insert my fist into Charlton's gob. And not in a sexy way.

'Can I . . . can I go back to my desk now, sir?' I ask in a strained voice. 'I have rather a lot to be getting on with.'

'What? Ah . . . yes, okay, Temple. Back you go. I'm glad we had the chance to have this little chat. Don't say anything to the rest of them, until I put my email out before lunch, there's a good boy.'

'No, sir, I won't.'

I rise from the seat, every muscle in my body tense and hurting.

Charlton snaps his fingers. 'Oh! And another thing . . . got some young fool coming by this afternoon to look over the distillery. Says he might want to invest. Might get you to talk to him at some point.'

'Okay, sir. That's fine, sir.'

I haven't actually heard a word Charlton has just said, as I'm still reeling from 'there's a good boy'. If I didn't feel emasculated, frustrated and enraged enough by this man already, he's just used language on me more suited to an overexcitable Springer Spaniel.

Hold it together, Temple. *Hold. It. Together.*

I stalk back to my desk, jaw clenched so hard that sharp, stabbing pains rocket through my head.

I sit down in a cloud of impotent fury, and stare at the computer screen blankly.

I continue to do this for a good two hours, unable to get any work done at all, such is my tumultuous state of mind.

When Charlton's email about wage cuts comes around the office, everyone else gets a taste of how I've been feeling since nine o'clock. By the time it hits 12.30 p.m., you can taste the combination of anger and anxiety in the air.

So much so that I have to get out – and get out *fast*.

I can barely look at poor Marion's tear-stained face as I hurry out of the office, and I ignore Matt when he calls after me.

I don't really know where I'm going, I just know I have to leave.

'Scott! What's up, my lad? You look mad as all hell and back!' One-Armed Jeff says to me as I pass him along the corridor leading to the distillery floor.

Jeff is easily one of the most laid-back human beings you are ever likely to meet. So would you be, if you spent most of your days in a permanent alcoholic fug of exquisitely prepared gin.

It may be the alcoholic fug that cost Jeff his left arm back in the 1980s, but that's neither here nor there at this stage.

He's the oldest, and probably wisest, person who works for Camberwell Distillery, and the only indispensable person on Charlton's payroll. Permanently dressed in a dark-blue boiler suit, and sporting a bushy grey beard that only adds to his mystique, Jeff looks like the company janitor, but is the sole source of this distillery's success over the years. Success that lasted until the moment Charlton came to power.

Jeff is usually an ocean of calm and tranquillity around here. There are worse people to offload your problems on to.

With my fists still clenched, I tell Jeff all about what happened in the office this morning.

His face darkens. 'Oh boy. I had a feeling something like that was coming. You can always tell when the idiot is about to do something stupid. He goes even redder than usual.' He looks me up and down. 'I think it might be a good idea for you to come and sit with me for a bit, young Scott.'

'Really?'

'Yes. You look like a man who's about to explode. And I don't like explosions of any kind around the stills, thanks.' He gives me a kind look. 'Especially when they involve people I like.'

God bless you, One-Armed Jeff. You are a saint.

'Okay,' I agree, and allow Jeff to lead me to the dark little cubbyhole he refers to as his office at the back of the distillery floor.

The first sip of the gin Jeff hands me is everything I want, and everything I need.

It shouldn't be. It really, really shouldn't.

This is *not* the answer to my problems, and will in fact only add to them, but if my wife's breaking point was an annoying robot voice, then mine is the only too human voice of Charlton bastard Camberwell.

I spend the rest of my lunch hour knocking back the gin with our chief distiller, matching him drink for drink.

This is an enormous mistake, as One-Armed Jeff has a tolerance for gin that is *legendary*. Someone swears they once saw him down a litre bottle of Gordon's for a bet, with no adverse effects whatsoever.

There's every chance Jeff is at least three parts pure gin now, given how long he's been working around it. When he dies, there will be no funeral, just a pickling ceremony, where they pop him in a giant jar.

Needless to say, I do not return to my desk when my lunch hour has concluded.

Fuck Charlon Camberwell an' this stoopid job!

'Shouldn't you be getting back?' One-Armed Jeff asks me, as I down the dregs of my fifth gin and tonic. He sounds as sober as the day he was born.

I don't.

'Nah! Fuck 'em! Iss . . . iss . . . *fine*, Jeff. Nobody cares if 'm at my desk or not.'

This statement is proved incontrovertibly inaccurate about half an hour later, when I hear Matt hurrying around the distillery floor, calling my name.

'Wha's the matter?' I shout after him, as he rushes past One-Armed Jeff's cubbyhole of ginny loveliness.

Matt turns swiftly on the ball of one foot. 'There you are! Why are you down here? Charlton wants to see you! Something about a special guest coming to the distillery today. He wants *you* alongside them!'

In the dim recesses of the parts of my brain that are still functioning, I suddenly remember Charlton saying something about an investor coming here today. I think he wanted me to talk to him, for some reason or other.

'Oh yeah. I . . . I remem'er,' I tell Matt, belching as I do.

Matt looks shocked. 'Are you *pissed?*'

I stare at him for a moment. 'Yes, Matthew,' I intone in a grave voice. 'I am indeed, as you say, pissed.'

His eyes go wide. 'Oh Christ, Temple! I thought you were teetotal these days?'

'I am!' I tell him, puffing my chest out with pride. '. . . mos'ly.'

'Well, you'd better sober up a bit now, mate. You've got work to do!'

'Pfft! It'll be *perfectly okay*, Matthew. I'm proba'ly better at talking when I've had a few anyway.'

This is not the right attitude to have at this particular moment.

I should be in fear of my job and my life right now. But if alcohol does anything to me, it gives me a confidence that is entirely unwarranted. I am convinced I can get through this meeting quite handsomely, just like I was convinced I could handle a fireworks display.

'Come on,' I tell Matt, handing my glass to One-Armed Jeff. 'Let's go meet this bloke with all the cash.'

Jeff gives me a worried look, before slowly pulling the door to his cubbyhole closed. This should be a worrying sign, as Jeff never closes his cubbyhole door. Sadly, I'm already zigzagging back through the distillery to my office, so I don't see him do it.

'Hello, everyone!' I exclaim to the other six members of our tiny office as I walk in. Charlton is standing at Marion's desk, probably about to berate her for crying on the job.

'Ah! There you bloody well are, Temple! Where the hell have you been?'

'Conductin' an inspection of the distillery floor, sir!' I assure him. 'Had a good chat wi' One-Armed Jeff about the la'est batch!'

'Good man!' Charlton roars.

'I know!' I roar back.

'Come into my office, my boy. Got a couple of people I'd like you to meet. The lad is some kind of entrepreneur who might want to throw us a little cash – and we never say no to a little cash around here!'

'Of course not, sir! That Jaguar is't gonna run on fairy farts and happy thoughts now, is it?!'

This takes Charlton back a bit. 'No, I suppose . . . suppose not.'

I wrap an arm around his portly shoulder as best as I can. I can't quite get it all the way because I'm not Mr Tickle. 'Come on, boss, let's go see what this fella wants!'

And with that, I lead him over to his office. The man actually comes along quite happily. I get the impression that Charlton isn't used to anyone else being full of bluster and bullshit around him, and it's rather thrown him off a bit.

Ha! Good for me, that's what I say!

I am a stronger and more capable man when I've had a few drinks.

I have no idea why I thought I'd be better off without booze in my life.

This is the man I want to be! *This* is the man who has no problem talking to his wife, and showing her a good time! This is the man who knows exactly what's what, when's when and where's where.

What the *hell* was I thinking?

'We coul' give them a tour of the disilerry, Charlton!' I tell him, in a brash but slurry voice. 'They'd love to see the shop floor, 'm sure, and the gardens look lovely this time o' year!'

'Yes, they do, don't they!'

I've never known Charlton to be so agreeable!

Maybe if I stay pissed, I can talk him around to not cutting my pay.

'And then we can give 'em a taste of what we make here!' I say, throwing open Charlton's office door. 'They've gotta have a swig of the good stuff, before they—'

My blood runs cold.

My skin blanches white.

My heart starts to hammer.

My soul, such as it is, crawls into a bombproof shelter at the back of my body and hunkers down.

In one of the chairs opposite Charlton's antique desk is PinkyPud.

In the other is my daughter, Holly. She's holding her iPhone and is recording *everything*.

'What the ever-loving fuck?!' I blurt out clearly, extreme shock making me stone-cold sober for a split second.

'Hi, Dad!' Holly calls out from behind her phone. 'Try not to swear too much!' she says, pointing at the camera.

'Hey, Mr Temple!' PinkyPud joins in. 'Surprise!'

'S – s – surprise?' I stammer.

'Yeah! Holly and I thought it'd be *cool* to surprise you at work for the fans out there,' Jasper Peabody informs me. 'Get a day in the life of Scott Temple at his job, so to speak. People *love* that you're clean and sober, even though you work in a place like this. We thought it'd be cool to show how you cope with it!'

Badly, Jasper. I cope with it very, *very* badly.

Holly looks at me from over the camera. 'Is it okay, Dad? We didn't think you'd mind, but . . .'

She can see how fucking terrified I look. I just hope she can't see how drunk I am.

'Well, as long as you edit out anythin' I say or do that, you know, looks bad,' I mutter, trying to sound light, but feeling extremely heavy.

'Can't do that, Dad. We're streaming this live!' Holly tells me, inexplicably with a smile on her face.

'*Live?!*'

'Oh yeah! You're probably being watched by *millions* of people, right now, Scott,' PinkyPud tells me. 'Give them all a wave.'

It should be impossible for the camera lens on an iPhone to grow from a few millimetres across to the size of a dustbin lid, but that's precisely what's now happening.

I hold up a hand that feels like it's been dipped in liquid nitrogen. 'Hi,' I say with a grimace, as I try to make my fingers wiggle a little bit.

'Isn't it *great*, Temple?' Charlton says to me with delight. 'Jasper here called a few days ago about this lark. Said you'd be well up for it! And he also said he'd make sure that I, and my fine distillery, got loads of exposure! Can't argue with that, now can we?'

I think we can all argue that Charlton Camberwell being exposed is the last thing the universe needs, but that is neither here nor there at the moment.

'And a healthy investment, Mr Camberwell,' PinkyPud says indulgently. He looks back at me. 'I've been wanting to get into the gin game for a while now, Scott. Most popular drink in the country. My feed is full of people going on about it these days.'

This is hell. Pure, unadulterated hell.

Things couldn't be any worse if my old headmaster walked through the door, accompanied by the girl who rejected me when I asked her to the school disco, my doctor wanting to perform a rectal exam, and Piers Morgan.

'Mr Camberwell says you can give us a tour of the place, Dad!' Holly says excitedly.

'Does he?'

'Yes, Temple!' Charlton exclaims. 'You know this place like the back of your hand. Take your daughter and her friend around. Show them how well this place functions. Make Jasper here see that any investment in the company *would be a great idea*.' The look Charlton gives me as he says all this is full of meaning . . . and not a little menace.

'Okay,' I squeak.

I receive a large and painful clap on the back as a response. 'That's the ticket! On you go then! Show them around, and then we'll all come back here for a nice drink.' He pokes me confidentially in the ribs. 'Softies for you and your kid, though, of course! Aha ha ha ha ha!'

'Of course!' I agree. 'Because I'm no' a drinker any more, am I?' I shake my head vigorously as I say this, making the entire world spin for a moment.

PinkyPud and Holly both stand up.

For a second I'm terrified that my daughter will come over and try to give me a hug. If she does this, she'll definitely smell the alcohol on my breath, and I'll be fucked. Luckily, though, her desire to capture every glorious moment of this impending farce overrides her daughterly instincts, and she remains a good five feet away from me as we exit Charlton's office.

'Don't worry about me, Dad!' she says. 'Just walk along with Pinks. That's what the audience will want to see.'

Pinks?

She's calling him *Pinks* now?

'She's a great girl, huh?' PinkyPud confides in me, as we cross the small office floor. 'A *great* girl.' That same indulgent smile spreads across his face, and in that instant I know that all this little streak of piss really wants to do is shag my seventeen-year-old daughter. Exploiting my attempts to live a sober lifestyle is probably just a secondary consideration.

'Go on, Dad! Tell Pinks where we are!'

I stare down the barrel of her lens for a moment, full of instantly generated rage. It's impotent rage as well, of course, because it's not like I can do anything about my sudden revelation, is it? I can't just punch Jasper in the face for wanting to put his PinkyPud in my daughter. I'd lose my job, my audience, my daughter's trust and any pretence of appearing sober if I did.

So instead I grit my teeth (again) . . . and start to tell PinkyPud all about what we do all day here in the office.

I get through this quite well, all things considered. Okay, I speak slowly and over-pronounce my words a lot, but you could easily put this down to feeling scared about being live on camera, rather than being trolled. There's a difficult moment when it takes me three attempts to say the word 'administration', but other than that, I get through this first ordeal relatively unscathed.

I figure the best thing I can do is get them both to the distillery floor as quickly as possible, because that's the interesting part of the whole operation, and the smell of gin being made should cover up the fact that I stink of the stuff myself. Looking at a load of big bulbous copper tanks and lots of twiddly pipes and tubes is always more fun than watching someone try to make Windows 10 function properly.

'Wow!' PinkyPud says, as I take them on to the distillery floor. 'That looks exactly how I'd imagined! Only bigger!'

That's generally what most people say when they see all the distilling equipment for the first time. Camberwell's has been here for two hundred years or so, and is a very old-school operation. Some of the equipment is decades old, and maintained scrupulously by One-Armed Jeff and his small team of squinting assistants.

The distillery is a cavalcade of fascinating and intricately wrought copperwork. Huge, bulbous tanks, thin columns, pipes heading off at all different angles, shiny chrome taps and big, beefy analogue dial displays everywhere, which look like they've been pulled from the nearest antique U-boat.

If Willy Wonka decided to diversify away from chocolate and into juniper berries, this is probably what he'd build.

Holly is agog as she films all this. And I have to wonder why I've never brought her here before. Then I remember who I work for, and that answers the question for me. Holly is a precious, precious thing, and needs to be kept away from people like Charlton Camberwell for as long as possible.

'So, tell us about this place, Scott! How does it all work?' PinkyPud asks me, expertly playing up to the camera.

The little snotbag is fast becoming my second least favourite person in the world, but you can't fault his presentation skills.

'This is where we ma'e the gin,' I say, desperately trying to sound straight.

PinkyPud's eyes narrow. 'Yes, we know that, Scott, but *how* is it made, that's what everyone at home wants to know!'

'Is it?'

'Of course. Like I said before, gin is very, *very* popular . . . with *my audience.*'

I may be sozzled on five gins, but I can still read between the lines pretty well.

Old Pinkster here is obviously working an angle that he thinks can make him some more money. I'm not sure what that angle is, but it probably isn't one that'd be beneficial to me, or Camberwell's Distillery.

'Right . . . fair enough,' I say, and turn away from him to call One-Armed Jeff over, in a voice that's probably way too loud.

'Dad!' Holly exclaims in horror. 'You can't call somebody that!'

I look perplexed. 'Why not? Tha's his name!'

'It's not *right*, Dad. He should be called something less abusive.'

My brow furrows. Abusive? If we don't call One-Armed Jeff *One-Armed Jeff*, he's the one who gets abusive. Somebody once recommended he get a prosthetic arm to 'make him look more normal'. The usually placid One-Armed Jeff was not so placid that day, I can tell you.

He's always seemed quite proud of the injury, to be honest with you. Like it's a badge of his commitment to the production of the finest gin. 'I'd give my left arm to make gin like Jeff' goes the famous and oft-repeated joke – sometimes even when he's in earshot. Always makes him laugh, that one.

There's nothing in the world that fazes One-Armed Jeff.

Aside from video cameras, it appears.

'What's that?' he says in a suspicious tone, as he spots what my daughter is holding. I haven't even managed to introduce him properly yet.

'It's just a little camera, Jeff. You know that YouTube video thing I've been doing?'

'Yeah?'

In fact, I very much doubt Jeff grasps the whole #DryHard thing. To him, technology peaked in the nineteenth century with the invention of the gin still. He made positive noises when I tried to explain it to him, though, so hopefully some of it might have sunk in.

'Well, my daughter here is jus' filming us live for it, to show all of the lovely, lovely peo'le who follow us how you make your lovely, lovely gin,' I explain, saying the word 'lovely' at least three times too many.

Jeff's face drops. 'This is being recorded live, *right now*?'

'Yep.'

'To lots of people?'

'Yep.'

'Including the police?'

'*What?*'

Jeff takes a step back. 'I'm not doing it! You handle it, Scott!' he exclaims, and instantly scuttles off behind one of the massive copper tanks.

'Oh,' I say, quite lost for words, and rocking back and forth on my heels a little. It seems Jeff may have had some shadiness in his past that I wasn't aware of. I fear this may have to be a story for another day though. I have more immediate concerns, like what the fuck I'm supposed to do now.

'Never mind!' PinkyPud says. 'I'm sure you can tell us about everything anyway, can't you, Scott?'

He gives me a clap on the back very reminiscent of one of Charlton's.

I stare at him.

'Isn't that *right*, *Scott*?' he asks.

'Y – yes?' I hazard.

I do know quite a lot about the gin distillation process actually – when I'm sober, that is. You don't work in a place like this for as long as I have without picking things up. But those five magnificent gins are utterly befuddling my brain. How much I'll get right about it all now is anybody's guess.

'Great!' PinkyPud exclaims. 'So glad that you're doing this, Scott!' He leans forward. 'And so great to see how well you're doing *at being sober*,' he says with a sly smile. 'Really looking forward to you explaining all this stuff to us as a *teetotaller* working for a gin company!'

He *knows*.

The little bastard knows I'm drunk.

'Yeah,' is about all I can manage.

What's his angle here?

What's he playing at?

'So!' PinkyPud says in a loud voice, sweeping a hand towards one of the stills. 'What does all this do?'

Breathing deep, I try to compose myself and sound like I know what I'm talking about.

'That, Pinky, is wha' we call the *gin still*.'

'Great. What's that bit?'

'Er . . . tha's the . . . the . . . catalyser.'

'Cool! And that bit?'

'Um . . . tha's a condenser.'

'Excellent! What's that long thing with the holes in it?'

Oh fuck.

What *is* the long thing with the holes in it? Begins with R. R something. Definitely an *R*.

R . . . R . . . R . . .

'Tha's the rectum column!' I say proudly.

'The what?'

'No! No! Not *rectum*. Defini'ly *not* rectum.' I think for a moment. 'Rectif . . . the rectifabul . . . the rectifigulation column. Yeah. Tha's it. The rectifigulationary column.'

'And what does that do?'

'It *rectifigulates*,' I tell him, confident that I've explained things extremely clearly.

'Okay. What about that?'

The questions are quick-fire, and no doubt designed to first put me on my toes, and then knock me soundly off them. I'm afraid it's working like a charm.

'Which bit?'

'*That bit*, Scott!' PinkyPud snaps. 'That long steel barrel with the dial at the top. You can see that okay, can't you, Scott? You haven't got any issues seeing that clearly, have you?'

'No! Of course not!'

I *can* see it, I just can't remember what it's bloody *called*.

For some reason, all I can think of is the word 'phlegm' in relation to it.

But why would phlegm have anything to do with making gin? I don't remember One-Armed Jeff ever hocking a wad of spit into the machine at any point.

'So, what's it *called*, Scott?' PinkyPud presses me, no doubt waiting for that moment when I completely fall apart.

I'll have to take a stab at it.

'I's called the phlegmaticator,' I tell him.

'The phelgmaticator?'

'Yes! The phlegmaticatoror.'

'Is it now . . .' PinkyPud says, stroking his chin. 'Are you sure you don't mean the *dephlegmator*, Scott? The thing designed to partially condense the vapour stream?'

Oh, you little bastard! You little *sneaky* bastard!

'Yes, Pinky. Tha's exactly what I mean,' I reply, the incoherent rage from earlier in the day returning with interest. It makes a heady combination with the drunkenness, let me tell you.

'You don't seem to be very *clear* on all of this, Scott,' PinkyPud points out. 'Are you having some problems today?'

I step back. 'No. No. I'm fine, Pinky. Jus' fine.'

'Dad?' Holly says from over the camera. I gaze at her. She looks both shocked and suspicious.

'Really?' PinkyPud continues. 'Only to me you look a little out of sorts. A *lot* out of sorts, actually.' He stares into the camera lens, giving everyone at home a meaningful look. 'In fact, if I didn't know better, I'd say that you were quite . . . quite . . .'

'Drunk,' Holly finishes for him, in a small voice.

That look of realisation and disappointment on my daughter's face will haunt me for the rest of my life.

I step towards her. 'Hols, I can explain, please!'

'*Can you*, Scott?' PinkyPud exclaims. 'Can you explain to all these fine people why you appear to be drunk as a skunk at work, when you're supposed to be clean and sober?'

'Shut your mouth, Jasper,' I spit at him.

'Oh, well that's *charming*!' he says, folding his arms and contriving to look hurt. 'It's not me who's let everyone down, Scott! It's not *me* who's let Holly down!' He shrugs theatrically. 'Who is she supposed to *trust* now, Scott? Who can she turn to, now both you and your wife have let her down by drinking again?'

Right, that's it, I'm going to beat him to a fucking pulp.

'Dad! No!' I hear Holly scream, as I pull back an arm and clench my fist.

Great, so now I'm live on YouTube, drunk as a bastard, and about to plant a punch on one of the most popular vloggers in the country. I couldn't look more like the villain right now if you dressed me all in black and gave me a red lightsabre.

I have been expertly manipulated here by someone who is obviously very, very good at it. I always wondered how PinkyPud built up the following he has, and now I guess I have my answer. He can read people like a book, and is clearly far more intelligent than he lets on in all those videos of him eating pizza and skateboarding.

And the worst thing is, he's bloody *right*. I *have* let my daughter down.

I'm to blame for this stupid, stupid situation I find myself in. Me, and me alone.

I was weak.

I was foolish.

And now I'm *screwed*.

What the hell do I do? With all these people watching me? With my daughter watching me? What possible solution is there for this predicament?

How about running away?

What?

Just . . . just run away, mate.

You can't be serious, brain.

Yeah. Go on. Do it. Things can't get any worse.

No. I suppose they can't really, can they?

Nah. Everything's fucked, *so we might as well run like the clappers.*

Hmmm. Seems a little immature, though, doesn't it?

I dunno. Maybe. We are very pissed, though, so it's probably perfectly acceptable, under the circumstances.

Ah, gotcha. You make a fine argument, brain.

Thanks.

Righty ho then. Running away it is.

Great!

Get ready!

In three . . . two . . . one . . .

CHAPTER TWELVE

HOLLY FALLS FOR THE WRONG GUY

Holly Temple – being the budding professional vlogger that she truly is – makes sure to capture her father's rapid egress from the distillery floor, even as she calls after him and tries to hold back her embarrassed tears.

It's quite something to watch a man in his mid-forties, who hasn't exercised in years, flapping his way out through the back exit of a gin distillery, rebounding off a couple of complicated-looking copper contraptions as he does so. It's like watching a pinball dressed in an off-the-peg M&S suit having a nervous breakdown.

You can only imagine the looks on the faces of all those people watching this unfold on their computers and tablets. All those followers were looking forward to finding out how their favourite gin is put together – only to see their equally favourite teetotaller completely fall apart.

God knows what the Dry Hard hashtag will be buzzing with on social media over the next few days.

They won't all be talking about the gin distillation process, that's for fucking sure.

And PinkyPud isn't even trying to conceal that sly smile as he looks at the camera.

Everything has fallen into place for him, without a doubt.

Jasper clocked the fact that Scott was drunk the second he walked into Charlton Camberwell's office. And Jasper Peabody is a man-child who can think on his feet. What he thought would just be a marginally interesting YouTube live broadcast suddenly had the makings of a bloody *classic*.

He only agreed to the stupid idea to keep Holly sweet, and wasn't expecting it to be anything actually *worthwhile*.

But once they got there and he saw the state Holly's father was in, he knew that all he had to do was provoke Scott Temple a bit, and surely the drunken fool would do the rest.

And he didn't disappoint!

This shit is *bound* to go viral.

Scott and Kate Temple are comedy *gold* when they've had a few, and that's proved to be the case here again today.

A man who's supposed to be on the straight and narrow having a breakdown so apocalyptic that it causes him to actually *run away*? Perfect! Absolutely *perfect*!

And all of it streamed *exclusively* on PinkyPud's YouTube channel.

Much better for the video to be only on his feed, he'd told Holly – because it'd mean more exposure and more views. That way, the clip would earn more money, which Pinks would – of course – share out to Holly in a fair and decent manner.

Ha!

And she was so star-struck and awed by his attentions that she let him get away with it.

Bad times.

Bad times indeed.

If Holly has managed to just about hold it together enough to keep filming her father's rapid descent into apparent lunacy, then PinkyPud is positively vibrating with happy energy as he addresses all the people watching.

'Well! There you go, guys! Not much more to say at this stage, is there? It looks like it's not only Kate who's fallen spectacularly off the wagon! What do you think though? Are *you* disappointed in Scott? Are you *angry* with him? Or can you sympathise with the guy?' PinkyPud seems less enthusiastic about this final choice, it has to be said. 'Please leave your comments below, letting us know how you feel! And don't forget to subscribe to this channel, *my* channel, right here!' He's slid effortlessly into sales mode now. 'And how about taking a visit to my merchandise shop? Where you can buy your #DryHard and PinkyPud T-shirts right now! We've got some new ones in this week, with some of your favourite Dry Hard slogans on them, like "Release the Kraken!" and "Oh God! My Fucking Plums!" Just twenty-five pounds each!' He points at the camera. 'Stay tuned for more in the next few days! See ya!'

PinkyPud looks meaningfully over the camera lens at Holly, who obviously takes the hint as the video ends on Jasper's endlessly irritating, smug face.

From all that excitement, it's back to just Holly and her camera, in her bedroom, alone.

Again.

These videos of hers really have taken on the air of a confessional over the weeks and months, even though they've been subsequently posted to YouTube.

If the audience have been enthused by watching Scott and Kate's attempts to go without drink, then surely they've been just as interested in following how Holly has coped with the whole thing.

After all, she's of a similar age to a lot of the people watching, who all have parents, and lives that are no doubt full of their own trials and tribulations.

Maybe seeing what Holly is going through, and how she's coping with it, is some kind of comfort to them.

If the older viewers out there can sympathise with Scott and Kate, then the younger ones can put themselves in Holly's shoes with no problems whatsoever.

Not that they'll be seeing *this* particular video any time soon. No – this one will stay in the memory bank of Holly's iPhone and never see the light of day, for reasons which are about to become very obvious.

'I think . . . I think I'm falling for him,' Holly says in a whisper, as she twiddles with her hair. 'He's just so . . . so *great*. And I think he might like me too.' She mutters this in an even quieter voice. 'He wants to take me out next week into the city. There's a launch party happening for the new game by ShadowPlaya, and Jasper says he can get us in! He says he and ShadowPlaya are best friends!' Her eyes go wide. 'I love ShadowPlaya's games!'

Holly then suddenly looks incredibly shy. The bold young woman has reverted to being a little girl in a split second. It's an expression that would tug at Scott Temple's heartstrings. 'I think I love Jasper too,' she says in a barely audible voice.

This is clearly a girl so enamoured that she can't see the wood for the trees. Or the Pinky for the Pud.

It'd be easy for others to see what a conniving little sod Jasper is, but then they're not full of teenage hormones, and angry at their parents.

Because make no mistake – Holly Temple is *very* angry with the people that sired her, and that makes for a dangerous state of mind to be in when a good-looking young man with a strong line in personal manipulation comes calling.

You'd be angry too if you'd just spent the last three weeks trying to claw back some goodwill from the people following the #DryHard experiment.

Holly has made her parents record fulsome apology videos, and spent a great deal of time showing just how sorry they are on camera, to make sure that no more subscribers leave what is starting to feel like a sinking ship.

Holly has watched with horror and dismay as the subscriber and view counts have plummeted recently, something she entirely blames on her parents' lack of willpower.

The truth – as in all things – is a little more complicated though. Yes indeed, some people have given up on the Temples, thanks to their respective relapses, but if you had to pin down a reason for a vast majority of the losses, then you can look no further than Jasper Peabody.

The live broadcast of Scott's shameful display at the gin distillery was only the first of the #DryHard videos to be exclusively played on PinkyPud's channel, instead of on *The TempleGurl*.

His aggressive and fast takeover of the whole thing, including his insistence that Holly's videos are played on his YouTube channel, have put *thousands* off.

The public are *not* fools.

They can tell when something genuine has been hijacked in the name of profit.

Of course, Holly can't see that. For her, Pinks is somebody who can do no wrong.

No, for her, it's all her parents' fault.

Why can't they just be better?!

Why couldn't they just stay sober?!

Why do they always let her down?!

All this remains unspoken on the particular video Holly's recording now. She seems comfortable confessing her love for PinkyPud into her non-judgemental camera lens (and it says a lot about the girl that she'd rather do this to a phone camera than a best friend), but she's still not able to voice the hurt and betrayal she feels about her mother and father, despite the fact that this clip will never see the light of day.

This is a girl who is veering wildly between two extreme emotional states.

On the one hand, she's falling in love with a new man in her life, and on the other she's falling *out* of love with the people who are supposed to be closest to her.

What a sorry state of affairs.

Time to jump to a video game launch party before things get any worse.

This is *awful*.

Awful if you're over the age of twenty-five, that is.

Look at all those energetic young people down there. Look at them bounce. Look at them jiggle. Look at them shake.

It's enough to make you want to go and have a nice lie-down on their behalf.

And the music is at least twenty decibels too loud. Definitely. It's so loud you can barely even think.

Holly Temple isn't thinking much.

She's too busy having a *great* time at ShadowPlaya's big launch party. The release of the DJ's newest dance game is an event that no self-respecting social-media-savvy teenager would want to miss. For here, there be *celebrities*. Celebrities of every hue, denomination and sexual preference.

You won't have a clue who any of them are if you aren't as social media savvy as Holly, of course. None of them have ever turned up on *The One Show* or *Celebrity Big Brother*. No, these are the stars of the modern era. The stars of the internet. The stars of the *stream*.

Look! There's SuperDigger! And over there! That's LilMissPartyHo, isn't it? Oh wow! Is that really BooshTail talking with The_Strange_Dolphin? Yes! Yes, it is!

So cool!

Holly records all this with a non-stop whirling camera lens that never stays still for a second. And it's all going out live across the web, to anyone who happens to be watching. Because these days, a party just doesn't exist unless it's broadcast online.

It's only when PinkyPud comes over to her, where she's standing at a railing looking down on the dance floor below, that she manages to bring the lens into focus on one person for more than a few moments.

'Are you having a good time?' PinkyPud roars over the sounds coming from ShadowPlaya's extensive amplifier stack on the floor below.

'Yeah! It's fantastic!' Holly replies with a giggle.

'Great! I've got you a drink!'

PinkyPud holds out a tall glass full of clear liquid towards Holly.

He continues to hold it out when she doesn't take it.

Suddenly, the camera has become very still.

PinkyPud shakes the glass slightly, slopping some of the contents on to his hand. 'Here! Take it!'

'I . . . I don't know, Pinks,' Holly says, her voice having lost all its enthusiasm.

'Why not?' he replies, brow creasing.

This response says everything about Jasper Peabody's appreciation of how Holly Temple's life has been in recent months and years. He is literally holding the very thing that's caused her so much pain and distress, and he doesn't even realise it.

Well, of course he doesn't. For him, alcohol is just another part of his crazy, wild and carefree lifestyle. Just like the wrap of cocaine he has secreted in his back pocket for later.

'I just don't think I should,' Holly tells him, backing away from the drink.

'Why the hell not?!'

'Well . . . because of my mum and dad!'

'But they're not *here*, Holly!' PinkyPud tells her, completely misunderstanding what she's trying to tell him. 'It's perfectly okay! You can have a drink!'

PinkyPud continues to hold the glass out, so close that the camera lens can make out the bubbles forming against the ice cubes.

And every single person watching this unfold is surely willing her to push the glass away. Pleading with her to say *no*. Hoping against hope that she'll have the strength of character to deny PinkyPud. To go with her best instincts.

Not just because they know how badly things go when a Temple has a drink in their hands, but because if she does take that glass, then he'll have her completely, won't he?

Holly will have taken the final step into the world of a man who will probably cast her aside just as soon as he's done with her.

Don't take the glass, Holly, just *don't take it*.

Don't take the—

Oh shit.

PART FIVE
STRONG

CHAPTER THIRTEEN

KATE AND HER INNER CHILD

'I want to see a marriage guidance counsellor.'

'You want to do what?!'

'You heard me, Scott. I want us to go and see a marriage guidance counsellor. Will you come with me or not?'

I cross my arms and look at my husband with an expression that I hope tells him he'd better answer in the affirmative.

Scott looks around him. 'And you thought the best time to bring this up would be *now?*'

'Yes. Why wouldn't I?'

Scott looks incredulous. 'Because we're standing next to the cucumbers in the vegetable aisle?' He points down at the rack of cucumbers to underline this.

'I know where we are, Scott.'

He rubs his eyes. 'And you felt that this would be the best time and location to bring this matter up, did you?'

'Yes.'

'Because cucumbers are a visual reminder of the problems our marriage is having?'

I think back to my meltdown at the self-service machine that even now lurks a scant few metres away. 'In a roundabout way, yes.'

'Right, well. Good to know, I suppose.' He squints slightly. 'What happens if I don't agree to this by the time we get to the tinned food aisle? Will you throw a tin of Green Giant sweetcorn at my head?'

'Quite possibly.'

'Well . . . I guess I'd better say *yes* then. I will come to the marriage guidance counsellor with you.'

'Thank you.'

'Now, perhaps we should move out of the way a little. This woman appears to want to actually purchase cucumbers, rather than come up with ways to save her marriage.'

'My marriage is perfectly fine, thank you so very much!' the woman in question tells Scott in a slightly offended voice. 'And I want the courgette, not the cucumber!'

'We all want the courgette and not the cucumber, love,' I tell her, shuffling out of the way. 'But life really just isn't fair sometimes.'

This is greeted with the level of confusion and bafflement I was frankly expecting.

Scott and I move away from the lady, to allow her to continue her shopping – and her life – unmolested. Her marriage is perfectly fine, and I'm sure she wants to keep it that way. She doesn't need to hear any more about how mine is fast disappearing down the swanny.

The space that's opened up between Scott and me has become a *gulf*.

This shopping trip is the first time we've done anything together in *weeks*. It's a sad state of affairs when the only reason you have to spend time with your husband is because all the home delivery slots were booked up until Friday, and you need something for tea today.

Not only are we separated by our mutual realisation that alcohol is the fuel that powered our marriage, we also now have an undercurrent of resentment towards one another, thanks to us both getting caught drunk.

Scott was angry with me for doing it, and then I was even more angry at him when he turned around and did *exactly the same thing* – only captured in a glorious live-stream.

You can imagine the argument that ensued between us after he came home that night, can't you? He was barely out of the taxi before I was on him.

And can you blame me? After looking down his nose at *me* falling prey to a moment of weakness?

Since that night, things have been colder than the frozen food aisle we're currently strolling down. I had to force him off the couch to accompany me on this shopping excursion, and the only reason I did that was because I need him to help me carry all the bags.

We've barely spoken otherwise – and had no physical contact whatsoever.

I can hardly remember what sex actually *is* at this point. I think it has something to do with rubbing yourself up and down against another person for a few minutes until one of you turns red and falls over – but don't quote me on that.

Our sex life used to be *fantastic*. Inhibition-free, energetic and *memorable*.

That all came to a grinding halt when we quit drinking though. Ridiculous!

I thought being teetotal was supposed to be *good* for you! Okay, my skin feels a lot better, I've lost a good half stone, my sinuses have cleared up and I have more energy almost all the time . . . but at what cost? What's the point in looking good if you *feel* like crap?

I want my life back. I want my husband back. I want my *sexy time* back.

But it's quite clear that I can't do that just by cracking open a bottle of wine again. Because I know deep down that doing so won't help me *at all.* Getting pissed is not the answer – even though there is a part of me still screaming that it is. The problems Scott and I are having now are bad, but would things actually be any better if we were drinking? We were spiralling out of control at the end of last year. Our jobs were being threatened, our relationship with Holly wasn't good, and all that sex I keep reminiscing about? Well, if I'm honest with myself, I know damn well that had dried up long before the alcohol did.

I'm doing what any addict does – looking at the time before quitting as being some rose-tinted wonderland, when in reality it was probably comprehensively *awful.*

What I wasn't expecting was for the landscape to still be awful *after* quitting.

That wasn't in the leaflet.

By this time, I thought we'd be living happy, booze-free lives. Instead, my marriage is on the rocks, and my daughter is slipping away from me even faster than before.

Aaaargh!

It's the legendary no-win situation, and I have no idea what to do!

. . . other than go and see a marriage guidance counsellor, in what I cheerfully accept is something of a last-ditch attempt to claw things back.

I figure Scott must feel the same way, which is why he's agreed to go with me.

We manage to get around the rest of the shop discussing the idea like sane, rational adults for the most part. There's a wobbly moment in the cleaning aisle when Scott starts to put up objections, and I feel the compulsion to throw a lavender Air Wick at him, but by the time we reach the checkout, he's fully onboard.

'We can't sort this mess out ourselves, so why not let somebody else have a go?' are his last, sage words on the matter as we drive out of the car park.

***

A week later and we're standing outside a large Victorian building on the outskirts of London. The hour-long drive up here was conducted mostly in silence, and that silence continues as we both contemplate what we're about to do.

'I'm nervous, for some reason,' I say, twiddling my hair.

'Me too,' Scott replies in a cautious tone, before he steps up to the door and presses the buzzer next to the name of the marriage guidance counsellor we've come to see.

I found this woman after a great deal of research online. It gave me something to do in the evenings, instead of talking to my husband.

She advertises herself as a counsellor who specialises in couples with addiction problems, which sounded perfect to me.

Her name is Greta von Holst, which is the kind of Germanic name you can have huge confidence in, isn't it? This is the name of someone who has got their *shit together*. Somebody called Greta von Holst has never timidly asked directions from a police officer, or been afraid to speak her mind at a public meeting. No, for Greta von Holst, life is all about seizing the moment in her big German hands, and being 100 per cent sure of herself, no matter what the situation. She's probably built like a shot-putter, and will wrangle the Temples into better shape in no time whatsoever!

This is absolutely the *right* person for us to come to!

***

This is absolutely the *wrong* person for us to come to!

Greta von Holst is not a bloody shot-putting German with big hands and a loud commanding voice. No, Greta von Holst is a softly spoken, dark-haired Dutch woman, who is bloody *gorgeous*. She actually bears something of a resemblance to Annabelle Mastriano, my one-time nightmarish client at Stratagem PR, only without the towering ego and snide expression.

Greta's general demeanour is one of cool, calm confidence. No doubt borne of the fact she looks and moves like a gazelle among hippos.

My marriage is *over*.

Whatever wisdom Greta may be able to impart here today will be lost on my husband, because his brain has frozen. Hell, mine is having trouble functioning properly, such is this woman's obvious beauty. How the hell can she be a marriage guidance counsellor? Surely every man who comes in here falls in love with her so hard that any chance of salvaging his relationship with his wife is doomed to failure.

'I'm very pleased to meet you both,' Greta says, offering us a seat on a very comfortable-looking grey couch. The office space it sits in is stylishly modern. It's rather like walking into one of the more expensive pages in the Ikea catalogue. About the only thing wrong with it is the fact it's quite cold in here. She could really do with turning the air con down a bit.

'Thank you,' I say, taking a seat.

'Mnmnmn,' Scott adds, helpfully.

It's probably the white suit she's wearing. It's elegant in all the right places and tight in all the others.

'I read your email with interest, Kate,' Greta tells me, as she sits in a chair opposite us. 'Thank you for being so detailed about your current situation. It really is quite unusual for someone to be so open before they've actually met me.'

I shrug. 'We've been watched on YouTube by thousands of people this whole year, Ms von Holst. We've long since become accustomed to complete strangers sharing in every aspect of our lives. We're open about pretty much everything these days – including the shameful stuff.'

'Well, that is good!' Greta replies, smiling the smile of someone who really should be in a famous oil painting somewhere. 'But there is nothing for you to feel shame about. What you're feeling is perfectly understandable, and perfectly natural.'

'Is it?' I say with incredulity.

'Yes, Kate. All my clients in a similar position to you feel much as you do. When a couple gives up a joint addiction, it can be very hard to find something to replace it with.'

'Really?'

'Absolutely. You are not alone.'

I could cry. I could honestly *cry* – right here in this beautifully appointed office.

Greta then goes on to talk to us for the next few minutes about her extensive qualifications, and then details how she's helped other couples with marital problems that stem from addictions.

Last month, she worked with two people who were almost ruined by the husband's gambling, and a year ago, she brought a couple back together who were almost destroyed by their cocaine addictions.

All this starts to give me great hope that Greta can help us.

I'm not sure if Scott feels the same way, because Greta's legs make a soft swishing noise every time she crosses them. This is making him very hard to read. And probably making him very hard.

It'd be the first time in *ages*, so maybe it's not such a bad thing.

'Your technique must be very good,' I say as Greta finishes her anecdotes about Mr and Mrs Cocaine-Fiend, who are very happy together now that their marriage has been healed – along with their deviated septums.

Greta smiles. 'I like to think so. It's a little unorthodox, but has proved extremely effective.'

I sit back in my chair. 'Okay then, we'd be very pleased if you could help us in the same way. Wouldn't we, Scott?'

'Mnmnmnm.'

'I said . . . *wouldn't we, Scott?*'

'Yes! Absolutely,' he says, and then massively overcompensates. 'Abso-*frickin'*-lutely!'

Good God.

'Excellent!' Greta rises from her chair. 'If you'd both like to go and get changed next door, we can begin.'

I blink a couple of times. 'I'm sorry, *what?*'

Greta holds out a hand towards a side door. 'In there, please. It's an important part of my therapy technique. I use role play to get to the heart of the psychological difficulties that lead to both the addiction and the subsequent estrangement. It's very effective. The costumes are a necessary part of the process.'

'You want us to wear *costumes?*' Scott says.

'Yes.' Greta looks at us softly. 'I know it may seem a little strange, but trust me, it will help you both. A lot of my clients find they very much enjoy wearing them once they get used to it!'

'Do they?' I say, puffing out my cheeks. I knew this was going too well.

'They do!' Greta once again points at the door. 'Please, go and get changed and we can begin. There's no need to take your clothes off, just put the outfits on over them.'

I'm about to ask another question, but Scott is already making his way over to the door. There's a slumped resignation about him as he goes. His shoulders are down and there's a long-suffering expression on his face as he passes me.

'Are you alright?' I whisper, catching up to him as he gets to the door.

'What? Oh . . . yeah, I'm fine.'

'You're not more curious about what's going on here? You're not worried about what she wants us to do?'

He gives me a hangdog expression. 'Kate, in the last year I've nearly blown myself up, had sex with a Christmas tree on YouTube, been molested by a horny kraken and watched my daughter fall in love with someone called PinkyPud. There is quite literally nothing behind this door that could be any *worse.*'

It's quite incredible just how wrong my husband can be, when he puts his mind to it.

'I'm dressed like a fucking baby,' Scott says, staring at me.

And there's no denying it. He really is dressed like a fucking baby.

Unfortunately, so am I.

Scott has just climbed into an adult-sized onesie in an attractive powder blue, and I am now firmly ensconced in an equally ridiculous pink onesie.

Both of them are extensively fluffy.

Soul-*crushingly* fluffy.

Brain-*meltingly* fluffy.

No wonder she keeps the temperature in her office so cool.

'I mean, the thing is,' Scott says, shaking his head, 'it's not even like *this* is that out of the ordinary. For some, this would feel like the height of embarrassment, but for us? It's just *Wednesday*.'

'It's Thursday, Scott.'

'Whatever.'

I look down at myself. 'You might have reached a stage where this kind of thing doesn't faze you that much, but I'm not sure I have.'

'You've forgotten your bow.'

'My what?'

'Your bow. It goes in your hair. Here.' Scott picks the bow up and hands it to me.

'No. I'm not wearing that.'

'But it's part of *her process*.'

'It's part of her failing grip on reality,' I retort. Scott laughs at this.

I think this is the first time I've heard him do that in weeks. In fact, this exchange over how ridiculous we both look is probably the most animated conversation we've had in a long time.

I snatch the bow out of his hand. 'Oh, for crying out loud,' I say, clasping it to my hair. 'How do I look?'

'Like a woman in her forties wearing a pink onesie, with a big bow in her hair.'

'How are you doing in there?' Greta calls from beyond the door.

Suddenly, I become convinced that this is one giant hoax. That beyond the door, Greta is standing there trying her best to stifle laughter, while someone else stands by with a video camera, ready to capture us in all our glory when we come out.

. . . it's PinkyPud!

Bloody PinkyPud – the arsehole who is slowly seducing my poor, vulnerable teenaged daughter – has set this whole thing up to make us look as bad as possible!

From what Scott has told me about what happened at Camberwell's, it's just the sort of thing he would do.

For weeks now, I've had to watch as he wormed his way into my impressionable daughter's affections. And there was nothing I could do about it.

On the surface, Jasper the Grasper has been the apparent well-behaved friend and ally, with only the most honourable of intentions. He hasn't done anything to make Holly suspicious of his motives. And he's worked Scott and me a treat – managing to paint us in the worst possible light.

What's really galling about it is we've let him do it. We've *helped* him do it.

If I were Holly, who would I trust right now? The kind young man who is offering her a career and a lifestyle that any teenage girl would crave? Or her two weak-willed parents, who can't even keep a promise to stop getting drunk and stop making her life miserable?

It's enough to make you chew your own foot off.

'We're fine!' I call out to Greta. 'Nearly ready!'

'Don't forget the bibs!' she reminds us.

I try to detect the sound of muffled laughter, but can't hear any. There's every chance she's serious about this.

Scott holds up the two bibs he discovers on the arm of the small couch that our onesies were laid out on. One bib is blue with 'Special Boy' written on it. The other is pink with 'Gorgeous Girl' written on it.

Disturbingly, they're big enough to comfortably fit round our necks. Somebody has made these deliberately for adult use.

Shudder.

'I am, apparently, a special boy,' Scott says. He looks upwards. 'I've always felt like a decidedly average person, by and large. It's nice to discover that I am, in fact, special.'

'This is fucking ridiculous by any conceivable measure,' I reply, ignoring his attempt at humour.

'It is, isn't it? Shall we go back out there?'

'You first,' I say in a flat voice.

Scott does as he's told, and the Special Boy leads us out of the small changing room.

Outside, there are no cameras, just Greta standing there with a satisfied look on her face. 'Good. Well done. Embracing the process is the first step.'

'I wouldn't exactly say I feel like I've embraced anything as yet,' I tell her.

Greta smiles. 'All in due time, Kate.' She walks back to her seat and sits down. The couch that Scott and I were on has been moved back against the wall. 'Come and sit down on the floor, and I'll explain what this is all about.'

'On the floor?'

Greta nods. 'Oh yes.'

Once again, Scott slouches with resignation and plonks himself down in front of her on the plush cream carpet. Damn him and his newly found fatalistic streak!

I follow suit (because what else am I going to do?) and await what I hope will be a decent explanation of why I'm being forced to act like an infant.

I'm not sure the explanation Greta gives is decent enough, but let's see what you think.

Apparently, all human beings are actually three people, Greta tells us. The *id*, the *ego* and the *superego*.

The ego is the person we are in the world. You know, the one that shouts at malfunctioning self-service machines and enjoys a nice tractor ride.

The superego is the person we'd all like to be. Or, someone who doesn't shout at self-service machines, and can resist tractors with no problem whatsoever.

The id is the childlike person inside all of us. The one who fucking *loves* tractors.

The only way for Scott and me to truly come to terms with having given up the drink – and find our way back to one another – is to embrace and acknowledge the id inside of us and, in the process, discover what it's fucking problem actually is.

To do this, we have to dress up, and act, like babies.

This all sounds like so much unbelievable blather to me, but she's the one with all the certificates on the wall, so I guess she might know more about this than I do.

'And how is all that supposed to help our marriage?' Scott asks her.

'By tapping into your inner child, you can uncover why there's this distance between you, Scott.'

'But I remember being a child,' he replies. 'I was a right twat. My mum used to tear her hair out.'

'Ah, so were you an *angry* child, would you say?' Greta suggests, dropping into full-blown therapist mode.

'I wouldn't say angry so much. I just used to eat a lot of mud, and poo myself when I didn't get my own way.'

'I used to flick dog poo at my sister, Jennifer,' I add, feeling as if I should contribute something. 'I always aimed for her hair. Then I could call her "Poohead" all day, which made me very happy.'

'Very interesting, Kate,' Greta says, making a few notes in a pad that's appeared from nowhere. 'So, you are both quite wilful children.'

'*Were* quite wilful,' I correct.

'Not at the moment, Kate,' Greta says. 'The reason I've made you put on those outfits is so you can communicate with your id. So you can throw away your adult inhibitions and become one with your inner self.'

'I'm still not sure I want to become one with my inner self,' Scott says. 'At least not in public with the curtains open.'

'Now, now, Scott,' Greta admonishes, wagging her pen at him. 'Don't be such a naughty boy.'

'I'm sorry?'

'Stop being a naughty boy, otherwise Mummy will have to put you in the naughty corner.'

Scott looks like someone's just shoved a carrot up his bottom.

There are men who would probably find this the height of sexual arousal – having a beautiful, raven-haired European woman in a tight white suit tell them off for being a naughty boy – but Scott is not one of those men, thank God. If he was, we'd be members of the Conservative Party.

Sexually, he's a meat and potatoes kind of guy. *My* meat and potatoes, to be exact.

'That's my *husband* you're talking to,' I say to Greta in an ominous voice, hoping she gets the hint without me having to be more explicit.

'Only speak when you're spoken to, young lady!' Greta snaps, and I'm instantly transported back to my mother's kitchen table, where she would always sit me when I'd been bad and needed a good telling-off. That happened a lot after I'd flicked poo at Jennifer, as I recall.

Scott stifles a giggle, drawing Greta's attention back to him.

'Right! Into the naughty corner with you, Scott!' she orders, pointing fiercely at one corner of the room.

'You've got to be kidding me,' he says in a dismayed voice.

'Do as you're told!' Greta snaps at him.

Scott sits there in shocked silence for a moment, before rolling his eyes. 'Oh, good fucking grief,' he says under his breath. 'We should have just bought a fucking courgette and had done with it.'

He gets up and walks over to the corner of the room.

'Turn round!' Greta orders.

Giving me a look that speaks volumes – I will get the blame for all this for some time to come, I fear – Scott turns round and looks at the wall.

'Now, Kate, be a good girl and tell me why you love drinking more than you love Scott,' Greta asks me.

'What?'

'Don't say what, say pardon!' she barks.

'Pardon!' I cry, now fully under whatever spell this strange woman is weaving. It's very hard to ignore that tone of voice, you know. Greta is an expert at it.

'I said, please tell me why you love drinking alcohol more than you love Scott.'

I'm horrified by this. 'I don't!'

'Don't you? But you told me that your marriage is failing because you don't drink any more. Booze was the thing that brought you together, and marriages are built on love, so I can only assume that you love booze more than Scott, if the marriage is failing now the alcohol is gone.'

I stare at her dumbfounded.

Did any of that make sense? *Any* of it?

'I don't know what you mean,' I tell her, pulling at the neck of the onesie. I'm suddenly feeling very hot.

'I mean, Scott is a very naughty boy because he loves alcohol, and why would you love a naughty boy, Kate?'

I hold my hands up. 'I literally have no idea what you're talking about.'

'Are you a naughty girl?'

'What?'

'Say pardon!'

'Pardon!'

'Are you *a naughty girl*, Kate?'

'No . . . I don't think so.'

'Then why did you marry Scott?'

'Stop blaming Scott for all of this!' I roar.

'Yes, please stop blaming me for all of this,' Scott says plaintively, turning round.

'Face the wall!' Greta screams at him.

'Jesus!' Scott exclaims, but immediately does as he's told.

Greta leans forward in her chair, looking down at me. 'Why did you marry him, Kate?' she asks.

'Because . . . because I loved him!' I say, really wishing she'd come to some kind of point.

'But you love *drinking* more, yes? Drinking is the thing that brings you together? The thing that kept you both going? And without it, you're nothing together, Kate, isn't that right?'

I shake my head in total dismay and thump my clenched fists on the soft carpet. 'I don't know! I just don't know!' I look at her. 'Yes! I think so! That's how we both feel!'

Greta's head snaps round to Scott. 'Is that right, you naughty little boy? Is that how you feel too?'

'Probably!' Scott says, still facing the wall. 'Yes!'

'You feel *distant* from Kate, don't you?'

'Yes!'

'Because the booze was the thing that kept you together?'

'Yes!'

'Come back here, Scott,' Greta orders. My onesie-clad husband spins round and scuttles back over, looking for all the world like a very naughty little boy.

We're both caught in Greta von Holst's extremely bizarre world now. She's almost bloody hypnotic.

'Both of you are very, very naughty!' Greta chides, wagging her finger at us. Unbelievably, this makes me feel deeply ashamed. I feel as if I should flick some dog poo at Scott, just to round things off properly.

'Why?' Scott pleads.

'You're naughty little babies, who are crying because you've had your favourite thing taken away! Do you know what I'm talking about?' She glowers at us. 'What have you had taken away?' Greta demands.

'Our dignity?' I pipe up.

'No! Bad Kate!' Greta screeches, now glaring at me like I've just funnelled a ton of dog poo over an entire nursery school full of children. 'What do babies love having?' she asks us. 'What do babies hate not getting? What do they hate having taken away from them?'

'Nap time?' Scott guesses.

'Not that!' Greta tells him.

'Er . . . a mobile thing?' he guesses. 'Like, one of those things from Fisher-Price? They squeak a lot?'

'No! Try again!'

'Apple sauce?' Scott hazards once more. 'Holly loved the stuff as I recall, and—'

'No, Scott! No!' Greta screeches.

'A bottle,' I say in a tight voice. 'You're talking about a *bottle*.'

Greta looks at me, her face instantly softening.

Good grief. That's what all this idiocy was about. Greta von Holst has made Scott and me dress and act like babies, just to make that one simple point.

'And what do babies do when they don't get their bottle, Kate?' she asks me.

'They cry,' I reply, voice still flat and tight. I can see exactly where this is going now.

'Why do they cry?'

'Because they're angry.'

'Who are they angry at?'

'The person that took the bottle away.'

'And who took your bottle away, Kate?'

I'm silent for a moment. I don't want to say it, but I know I have to. 'Scott. Scott took my bottle away.'

Greta looks at my husband. 'And who took your bottle away, Scott?'

He looks at me forlornly. 'Kate did. At least . . . that's what it *feels* like.' He covers his eyes with one hand. 'That's crazy though. Really, really crazy. We agreed to quit together.'

'You did indeed,' Greta says. 'And the adult in you knows that. But the child in you *doesn't*. It doesn't care that quitting the drink was the best thing for you both. It doesn't care that it was the right thing to do. It just cares that it's had its bottle taken away from it, and will blame whoever is nearest.' She gestures to us both. 'And you said it yourselves, your marriage had alcohol as its cornerstone, so who else are you going to blame, but each other?'

'That just sounds so *silly*,' I tell her, feeling the most embarrassed I've been since we walked into this office.

Greta shrugs. 'Children don't care about silly, Kate. They care about what they want. Your mind deep down doesn't care whether something sounds rational or not, believe me. It just wants what it wants, and to hell with being sensible about it.'

Scott looks at her – for all the world like a lost little boy looking up at his mother for guidance. 'I still don't entirely understand, Greta.'

She pauses in thought for a moment. 'Think of it this way . . . you may have put down the glass in your hand, Scott. But neither of you has put down the glass in your *mind*. That childlike part of you has refused to let go of the bottle. And until it does that, the gulf you feel between you will continue to be there.'

I pick at the onesie. 'So, all of this was really just to show us how childish we've been?'

Greta shakes her head. 'No. To show you that we're all still children, deep down inside. And that unless we understand and accept that, getting over an addiction can be impossible.'

A silence descends on the room.

It is a thoughtful, reflective silence.

Then I look at my husband . . . and see him properly for the first time in months. There he sits, with his thinning hair all skew-whiff, wearing a powder-blue onesie and a bib that tells the entire world he is a special boy.

Oh God . . . but he *is* a special boy though.

My lips curl up at the edges. He looks so funny, sitting there dressed like a baby. I see his eyes flick up to the top of my head at the bow perched there. His lips are also curling.

A sudden and gigantic wave of hilarity rushes through me, and I start to laugh. Scott joins me, unable to dam his emotions any more than I can.

In a few seconds we're both reduced to howling, crying, shaking balls of laughter.

Even Greta finds herself joining in, though she's far more reserved. Let's face it, this probably isn't the first time she's watched people rolling around on her floor wearing onesies. It's probably all part of her 'process'.

A few minutes pass before Scott and I can get ourselves under control again.

I feel absolutely *drained*, but in a very therapeutic way. I won't say a weight has been lifted from my shoulders – but maybe an invisible bottle has been taken out of my hand.

'If you'd both like to get out of those outfits, we can have a cup of tea and discuss what progress we've made today,' Greta says, smiling indulgently at us. She knows she's made a breakthrough here.

'Well, fuck me, that was something else, wasn't it?' Scott says, as we divest ourselves of the onesies back in the small side room.

'I'll say. How do you feel?'

'Knackered. But also like I'm finally getting a handle on all this stuff. How about you?'

'The same, I think.'

He cocks his head to one side. 'And . . . do you think she's right? Do you think we've been angry at one another all this time, and didn't even realise it?'

I nod my head slowly. 'I don't know, sweetheart. But it *feels* right, doesn't it?'

Scott thinks for a moment, then nods. 'Yeah. I guess it does.'

'I'll tell you one thing though – I certainly don't feel angry at you now.'

He smiles. 'Me neither.'

Scott drops the onesie on the couch behind him, and I throw mine over there too. We're adults again. And boy, does it feel good.

Scott reaches out a rather tentative hand, which I take, equally tentatively. He gives me a warm smile and squeezes my hand affectionately.

It's probably going to take more than just ten minutes dressed in a onesie for us to work through all this, but I'd say we've certainly made a very good start.

'Are you guys okay?' Greta calls from the other side of the door.

'Yeah! We're fine!' I reply, and for once I think I probably mean it.

'I can't decide whether she's a genius or a lunatic,' Scott whispers.

I chuckle. 'Me neither. Mind you, she has the body of a goddess, so even if she is a lunatic, she can get away with it.'

Scott contrives to look innocent. 'Really? I can't say I'd noticed.'

'There's still some dribble on your chin,' I point out.

'We'd better go back out there, otherwise she'll start to think we're up to something.'

I waggle my eyebrows suggestively, but choose not to reply. I think the ice is somewhat thawing between us, but we're still a way off from those kinds of shenanigans.

Scott reluctantly lets go of my hand, and we make our way back into Greta's office, this time feeling quite good about ourselves, thanks to both the recent breakthrough and the distinct lack of onesie.

The rest of the session is conducted in a more prosaic fashion. Scott and I sit on the couch and nod sagely as Greta tries to explain everything that's gone on in more detail.

It takes her a good forty minutes to do this, with occasional interjections from us both, but what it all boils down to is that we have to stop blaming each other for not drinking any more, and start leaning on each other more for support instead. Communication is the key to this, apparently. Scott and I have to be open and clear about how we're feeling on a day-to-day basis. That should begin to mend the strange and scary rift that has grown between us.

'There are no guarantees, of course,' Greta says, as the session concludes. 'But you'll certainly stand a better chance of finding your way through this together, now you have a better idea of why you've grown so far apart.'

Damn, I don't think I can take much more of this wisdom.

Greta's starting to sound like a Dutch version of Yoda with a modelling contract. I think I'd better leave this office before I start to develop an inferiority complex. Also, all I can now picture is Yoda wearing lipstick and a negligee, which is disturbing on more levels than I care to mention.

Greta bids us a fond farewell, and returns to her office, no doubt to count all the money we've just thrown at her. Still, I'm starting to think it was money well spent.

'Yeah, I'd say so,' Scott agrees, as we drive home. 'It all got a bit weird there for a while, but I get the impression she makes it weird deliberately.'

'Why though?'

He shrugs. 'I guess because you're so worried about looking stupid, you forget to be worried about what brought you there in the first place. Maybe that helps you see exactly what the problem is.'

This is an extremely *profound* thing for my husband to say. Possibly the most profound thing I've *ever* heard him say – certainly since that time we were in Scotland when Holly was six, and she asked him in a timid voice if the Loch Ness monster was evil, and he replied, 'No evil monsters in there, sweetie. Mother Nature is too clever to worry about silly things like evil.'

I snake my hand into Scott's, where it rests on his thigh. This time I am not quite so tentative.

'It was worth it then. Going to see her,' I say to him.

'Yes. It was.'

I shudder. 'But I don't think I ever want to wear a onesie again. That was too embarrassing.'

'Really? I thought you looked like you quite enjoyed it. In fact, I thought you might want to keep it.'

'*Really?*' I reply in horror. 'What makes you say *that?*'

He briefly looks over at me and his eyes flick up to the top of my head. 'You've still got the bow in your hair.'

When we walk through the front door, I am still berating Scott for allowing me to walk out of Greta's office with the bow still atop my head. I do it in a happy, laughing manner though. I really do feel quite a lot better than I did this morning.

My happy mood turns to puzzlement as we enter the kitchen and find Holly's iPhone on the kitchen table.

Next to it is a piece of paper with the words 'play the video' written on it.

'What's going on here?' Scott says, looking at the note.

'I don't know.' I look at my watch. 'She should be home by now though.'

'Did you tell her where we were going today?'

'No. I thought it best to keep it between us. You know . . . just in case.' I leave that hanging in the air, knowing that I don't really need to say any more.

Scott nods. 'Right decision. I didn't say anything to her either. She just thinks we've both been at work.'

'So, what's all this about?' I say, looking at the iPhone, with a degree of unease entering my voice.

'Let's watch this video and find out.'

Holly has left the phone unlocked, and with the video set to run on the screen. Scott presses play, and we watch with mounting horror as our daughter tells us of her plans.

She's sitting in her bedroom, in the same position she's used in all her YouTube videos when she's been doing a bit of diarising. The hair is already being twiddled furiously, which is never a good sign.

'Mum, Dad, please don't be angry at me,' she says, 'but I've made an important decision that I really need you to accept.'

'Oh fuck,' Scott says, in a hushed voice.

'I thought that . . . I thought that when you two quit drinking, things would get better. I really did,' Holly says. If she pulls on that hair any harder she's likely to leave herself with a bald patch. 'But they're *not* better. In fact, if anything, they're *worse*.'

I swallow hard. It's difficult to disagree with her.

'You're not talking to each other, and the atmosphere in the house is *terrible*.'

There are tears in her eyes, and that means there are tears in mine too. We've let her down so very badly over all this.

'I can't . . . I can't take it any more.'

'Uh oh,' Scott breathes, having decided he knows what's coming. It's the same damn thing I know is coming too.

'I've decided that for a while, it'd be best if I moved out. Went and stayed with somebody else while you guys sort your . . . your problems out.'

Please say it's Amber.

Please say it's Amber.

Please say it's Amber.

'Pinks said I can stay at his place.'

'Fuck!' Scott snaps.

'And I'm going to do that. I don't know how long for. But I don't want to come back while you two are . . . are . . . well, you know.'

Yes, I do know, Holly. I know damn well what you're driving at.

I also know that you staying with bloody PinkyPud is the worst decision you could have possibly made. But it's a decision I can entirely understand you making, under the circumstances.

'Pinks is *lovely*. I'm sure he'll take care of me very well.'

'Yeah, I'm sure he fucking will,' Scott whispers, through gritted teeth.

'Please don't try to find me,' Holly continues. 'I'm not going to say where Pinks lives, and I'm leaving my phone behind.' She's trying to hold back her tears. 'I need this time alone. I need this time without you. I love you both so much, but . . . but I can't keep seeing you the way you are. I'm the one who stopped you drinking, which I know was the right thing to do. But now you're both so *quiet* all the time. Both so . . . so *sad*.'

'Oh Christ, she's blaming herself for this,' I say in a horrified voice.

'And I know there's nothing I can do about it,' Holly goes on, 'so I just need to be away for a little while.'

And then my daughter says the one thing she must know is never going to happen.

'Please don't worry about me,' she says. 'I'll be absolutely fine. Pinks has told me I can stay with him as long as I like.' Holly is interrupted by the sound of a car horn. She looks up. 'That'll be him now!' There's excitement in both her voice and her face now. She looks back at the camera. 'Please take the time while I'm away to see if you can sort things out between you.'

Aaaargh! Why didn't we tell her we were going to see Greta? We might have avoided all this!

'I love you both very much, and will see you very soon.' And with that my poor, confused and lost little girl leans forward and shuts the camera off, leaving her father and me staring at a black screen.

Scott slowly puts the phone down on the kitchen table and then does something I've never seen him do before. He stamps his foot hard on the kitchen tiles. I don't know whether it's because he was wearing a onesie less than two hours ago, but I think maybe his inner child hasn't quite returned to the depths of his subconscious yet.

'I'm going to kill him! I'm going to wring his scrawny fucking neck!' Scott starts to make a twisting motion with his fists. 'I'm going to find that little shitbag and break him in half!'

'Calm down, Scott! We have to think clearly about this!'

'Oh, I'm thinking clearly, Kate. I'm thinking clearly about how I'm going to pummel his smug little millionaire face so hard he won't be able to appear on YouTube for weeks, just in case he makes his subscribers throw up!' Scott is shouting now. Understandably so. He also starts to kick the kitchen table leg, which isn't really fair, as it's completely blameless in all this.

'This isn't helping us, Scott!' I tell him.

He looks at me with rage in his eyes. 'I want my bloody daughter back!' he roars.

'So do I! But I have no idea how to find her, and you throwing a tantrum isn't going to help us think of a way any faster!'

This brings him up short. Scott is never a man prone to extreme anger – not on the surface anyway.

'What the hell are we going to do?' he asks me, grabbing the phone again.

I shake my head. 'I don't know. But we'd better think of something *fast*. Who knows what that odious little sod might be doing to our poor little girl!'

Scott's face blanches. 'He'll *do things* to her, Kate,' he says in a small, dismayed voice. 'I don't want him to *do things* to her. I used to be his age. I know what boys like to do. I did them to you . . .'

Four times in one day, on one memorable occasion.

'If he touches her,' Scott growls, 'I'll . . . I'll . . .'

'Wring his scrawny fucking neck?'

'Yes! I'll wring his scrawny fucking neck!'

'And I'll help you, but we have to find him first.' I take the phone from him. 'She left this with us, knowing we'd track her if she took it with her.' I bite my lip. 'Where do you think somebody like PinkyPud would live?'

'I have no idea, Kate,' he replies. 'These silly sods all live in weird places. There's some guy in California who does vegan recipes on YouTube and lives in a hollowed-out tree.'

'Really?'

'Yes. He calls himself Veego Beego Bongo. *Veego Beego Bongo.*' The look of disgust is palpable. 'These are the kinds of people we're dealing with here! We have to find Holly!'

'Yes! I know, Scott, but I have no—' I stop myself, having just had a brilliant idea.

'What? Have you thought of something?'

I hold up Holly's iPhone. 'Oh yes, Scott. I've thought of something alright.' I start stabbing the phone's screen, finding all Holly's social media apps. 'The people of the internet have got enough out of us recently, it's time we got something *out of them.*'

'What do you mean?'

I waggle the phone at him. 'Time to put the bastards to work, Scott. Time for them to help us find our daughter, before it's too late!'

CHAPTER FOURTEEN

SCOTT AND THE RESCUE MISSION

All most people on the internet are really after is a cause they can get behind. Something they can support. Something they can *be a part of.*

It doesn't even need to be a *worthy* cause.

Spend a few constructive minutes on one of the petition sites that are dotted around cyberspace, and you'll find all manner of rather strange causes that people will happily throw their support – and their money – behind.

Several thousand people want to force McDonald's to provide at least three ketchup sachets for free with every order. Another several thousand think sporks should be instantly banned for being too dangerous. I assume there's a fair amount of crossover between these two.

An awful lot of people want S Club 7 brought back, for no identifiably sane reasons, and many, many more want to force Boris Johnson to change his name to Blondie Jellybrains McTwattyface – which is one I seriously considered giving five quid to, if I'm being honest.

Ask the fair people of the internet to help you find your wayward and upset daughter, and you will be guaranteed a plethora of suggestions, helpful information and directions in no time at all.

You will also be guaranteed to receive comments like 'She's up my arse', 'Where did you last leave her?', 'What kind of fucking terrible parents are you?', and most memorably 'Holly has become one with The Great Flying Spaghetti Monster. She has been taken up to exist among his heavenly noodley appendages. Ramen!'

But then this is the internet, so what the hell else was I expecting?

Happily, we received a great many more useful responses when we posted a video using the Dry Hard hashtag, explaining what the situation was – but leaving out a majority of the details. Nobody needs to know what nefarious plans Jasper Peabody might have for my innocent daughter, and I'm also aware that libel and slander laws still exist on social media, so we were careful to keep things pretty non-specific.

Not that we needed to worry about getting into much detail. People were more than happy to help out, even though we didn't tell them more than that we had lost contact with our daughter, we knew she was with that popular vlogger called PinkyPud, and we were worried about her.

Most people didn't have a clue where the little bastard lived, of course. They just wished us well with the search – but some *did*, and we started to get private messages with increasingly precise directions. One guy called JammoBaggins (don't any of these people just want to use a nice normal name?) actually gave us PinkyPud's specific address, having been to his house last month for a business meeting.

It doesn't sound like the meeting went all that well, hence his apparent willingness to give the guy's address to two complete strangers.

PinkyPud lives in a penthouse in a brand-new apartment block in the city. I would have expected nothing less. It probably cost more than I've made in my entire time at Camberwell's.

'We've got him!' I crow triumphantly, as I scrawl down the address on a notepad. 'All we have to do is get round there, knock on his door and pull Holly out when he answers it.'

'She won't like that.'

My eyes narrow. 'I don't care if she never speaks to me again. I don't want her spending the night in that spunk trumpet's flat. We'll just go round there, grab her and leave. Hopefully without too much fuss.'

Kate looks at something on the laptop screen and her eyes widen. 'It might not be that easy, Scott.'

'Why?'

She swivels the laptop around to show me. 'He's having a party tonight. Look at his Twitter feed.'

Sure enough, there's a tweet right there from PinkyPud that says: Yo! Tonite's da nite! ShadowPlaya in da house, and we ready to get lit! Another lege party at the Pinkster's crib! We'll be rockin' dat shit til them birds are a-singing! #PinkyPud #ShadowPlaya #PartyPud

What an absolute cunt.

'It doesn't matter,' I tell my wife. 'We're going anyway. There's no way I'm letting Holly stay there, especially if there's a party going on. Who knows what she'll be exposed to.'

'Nothing good.'

'No. Definitely nothing good.' He grimaces. 'But something *pinky* and *puddy*, if we don't stop it.'

Kate stands up. 'I'll get the car keys.'

I stand up too. 'I'll get my cricket bat.'

She gives me a look. 'You're joking.'

I deflate a bit. 'Yes. I guess I am. Holly has a drunk for a father, she doesn't need a convicted criminal as well.'

'Wise words.'

'Sometimes my brain actually kicks into gear and spits them out. It's usually totally at random.'

Kate rolls her eyes, and then marches out of the kitchen with me in tow.

There's a vibrancy and purpose to both of us now that I have to confess I'm very much enjoying. Okay, this is a fairly fraught situation – and who knows how my daughter is going to react when we turn up at PinkyPud's expensive doorstep – but having something constructive and positive to do alongside my wife of twenty years is filling me with drive and determination.

We're together.

For the first time in a long time.

Together.

And there's not a glass of gin or a bottle of wine in sight.

'That is an extremely tall apartment block,' I say, as we climb out of the car and look up. And up.

'Yeah, it is,' Kate says, in the voice of someone who knows they're about to go up to the very top of it.

'Looks quite secure as well,' I add, looking through the smoked panes of triple-thick ground-floor glass at the woman sitting behind the reception desk inside the vast, gleaming foyer. Next to her is a large security guard, with a nice line in overdeveloped arm muscles.

In our rush to get our daughter back, I hadn't really considered that it might be difficult to even get to PinkyPud's front door, let alone drag Holly out through it.

'How do we get in?' Kate says, obviously thinking much the same thing. 'This is the kind of building that rich people live in. I can't see them letting in any old Tom, Dick or Harry.'

'You're probably right. How about we pretend to be party guests? That should get us in, shouldn't it?'

Kate looks at me. 'You think we can pass for guests at a party thrown by a multimillionaire, twenty-something YouTube vlogger?'

'Yeah, why not?'

Kate's expression flattens. 'Who is ShadowPlaya, Scott?'

'No idea.'

'No, me neither. We couldn't pass for people going to this shindig any more than we could pass for guests of honour at the annual shot-putting convention.'

'You think they have an annual shot-putting convention?'

She gives me a withering look. 'I have no idea, but hopefully you get my point.'

I nod my head. 'Yeah. I do.'

'We just don't have a good reason to be going up there, and they'll know that,' Kate says, indicating the woman at the desk and her beefy friend.

'Shit,' I exclaim, and think for a moment. 'Maybe we could just tell the truth?'

'Hmmm. I don't think it'd do much good. It's not like Holly's up there against her will, and I'm sure those two wouldn't do anything to jeopardise their jobs. I imagine Jasper the Grasper would probably make sure they got fired if they let us in to steal away his newest prize. He strikes me as that kind of person.'

I wince at Kate's blunt but accurate description of how PinkyPud probably thinks of our daughter.

'We have to get in there!' I spit, clenching my fists.

'Yes, I know. But there's no way. There's literally no reason for us to go in there. Why would PinkyPud have anyone as old as us at his party?'

I snap my fingers. 'That's it!'

'What?'

'We're old!'

'Yes. There's no need to rub it in.'

'No, no, no. We can *use* that.'

'How?'

I yank the car keys out of my pocket. 'Just . . . just give me a second.'

I run around to the rear of the car and open the boot. I pick up a rather battered case and return to my wife.

'What's that?' she asks.

'Our way in!' I tell her, putting the case on the bonnet and opening it. Inside are about thirty tiny bottles of Camberwell's gin, all of them bright orange.

'That's a lot of gin, Scott,' Kate says, looking at me suspiciously. 'Why is it in your car?'

'Don't fret, I haven't been drinking. This has been in here for months. It's the taster kit I was supposed to be taking around to distributors for that godawful Gin Fawkes that Charlton came up with a year ago. The whole idea got shit-canned before I had to go around with it, and it's languished in here ever since. I was going to chuck it all away, but I'm bloody glad I didn't.'

'Why?'

I smile at her enthusiastically. 'Because PinkyPud is taking a delivery of his favourite new gin this evening, Kate! To make his party go with a bang!'

I hold up a couple of bottles of the offensive liquid and wave them back and forth.

'Oh, good grief,' she says, putting her head in her hands.

'Come on! Have a little faith! All we have to do is walk in there, convince those two that we're expected and then get up to the penthouse.'

Kate shakes her head. 'It'll never work. We won't be convincing in the *slightest*. They'll see through us in *seconds*. Neither of us is ballsy enough to pull this kind of thing off, Scott.'

She's probably right.

Neither of us is ballsy enough, nor brash enough, to make this hare-brained scheme a success.

But I know a man who is.

'Evening you!' I bellow at the receptionist, in the most accurate impression of Charlton Camberwell I can muster. The poor girl blinks at me a couple of times and recoils a bit. This is what everyone does when they meet Charlton, so I must be doing a pretty good job.

'Come on, woman! Keep up!' I bark at Kate as we cross the marble-floored atrium and approach the desk.

'Can . . . can I help you, sir?' says the receptionist in a pleasant Eastern European accent. The security guard looks down at me under a pair of magnificent bushy black eyebrows. This makes Scott Temple quail a little, but has no appreciable effect on Charlton Camberwell.

'Of course you bloody well can, my good woman! You can let me and my assistant here up to young Peabody's place, so we can give him all this lovely gin!'

I slam the case down on the reception counter and open it, to reveal the sticky orange ghastliness inside.

'Er . . . er . . . I wasn't aware Mr Peabody had any more deliveries coming today. All the catering staff came hours ago,' she tells me, peering at the gin with a severe degree of uncertainty.

I bluster for a few seconds. Charlton always gives good bluster. 'I'm not catering staff, my good woman!'

'So who are you?' the security guard intervenes in a deep, rumbling voice. I notice that his name tag tells me his name is Jamal. Jamal looks like he bench-presses small Middle Eastern countries in his spare time.

I stare at him for a moment. I hadn't counted on being asked my name.

Then I stick a hand into the lining of the carry case and pull out a rather crumpled business card. Business cards can be very useful things. Only people who are officially supposed to be somewhere carry business cards.

If I have one, I *must* be telling the truth.

This is what I dearly hope my new friends will believe anyway.

I hand the card over to the receptionist. 'There! Have that! My name is Mr Temple and I am a very, *very* senior person at a very important gin distillery – one Mr Peabody is investing money in. He specifically asked me to bring him this very special gin this evening, and you are making me late!'

The receptionist suddenly looks a bit worried. Good. If she thinks she'll be in trouble if she doesn't let us through, it might get us past this first hurdle.

But then she picks up a phone.

'Don't do that!' I screech. The Charltonesque bluster has been replaced by Templesque terror.

'Why not?' Jamal asks.

'Because . . .'

Oh fuck me, I don't have a *because*.

'Because Mr Peabody wants to surprise his guests with this fabulous new gin flavour!' Kate says in a hurry.

I stare at her in mild awe. My wife is exceptional at coming through in a crisis.

'That's right!' I bellow, remembering to channel my boss again. 'It's bloody great stuff, and I'm sure he wouldn't want anyone knowing about it until he gets to give it out himself!' I then think of the kicker. 'He told me he wanted to YouTube it! Said it'd make a great thing for his subscribers!' My brow knits in mock anger. 'You wouldn't want to spoil Mr Peabody's YouTubey surprise, now would you?'

The receptionist looks terrified, and puts the phone back down. 'No,' she squawks.

Even Jamal looks a bit sick. Old PinkyPud clearly does have the kind of reputation around here that Kate predicted.

'Make your way to the lift at the end,' the receptionist says, pointing at a row of four lifts to her right. 'That'll take you directly to Mr Peabody's residence.'

Hooray!

'You'll need to punch the access code into the keypad before it'll take you anywhere though. I'm sure Mr Peabody would have told you it.'

Boo!

'Of course he bloody well did!' I lie magnificently, and gather up the carry case. 'Thank you for your co-operation!' I tell them both. 'It will be carefully noted!'

I grab Kate's arm and start to yank her towards the far lift.

'You've gone bloody mad,' she says, with a fraught look on her face.

'Possibly!' I agree.

We reach the lift and I stab the button a couple of times. When the doors open we step inside and I finally let go of Charlton Camberwell. Pretending to be him has been hard on both my nerves and my jaw muscles.

'Now what, genius?' Kate asks as we step inside, pointing at the keypad.

'I have no idea,' I reply, looking at it forlornly.

We, of course, have no clue what the access code to PinkyPud's apartment is. Why would we?

'We're fucked,' I mutter. I hold up the case. 'This was all for nothing. Any minute now, Jamal is going to come over here and see we haven't gone anywhere, and throw us out. We're totally fucked.'

'JammoBaggins!'

'*What?*'

'JammoBaggins, Scott!' Kate exclaims excitedly.

'What are you on about?'

'*JammoBaggins!*'

I back myself against the lift wall. 'Stop screaming JammoBaggins, you're scaring me!'

She lets out a gasp of frustration, and delves into my coat pocket, pulling out Holly's phone, and half the lining with it. 'JammoBaggins will know the code! He's been here, remember! I'll send him a message and hopefully he'll reply.' Kate starts to type on the phone's screen as she says this.

'Oh. That's a great idea,' I tell her.

'Yes, sometimes my brain kicks into gear and spits them out. It's usually totally at random,' she says, working away at the phone like a thing possessed. 'There! It's sent. Let's just hope he sees it before Jamal gets over here and—'

'Gets over here and what?' says Jamal, as he comes to stand in the open lift doorway. For such a hefty bugger he can move like a cat.

'Hello, Jamal!' I screech in a high-pitched voice. The Charlton impression has deserted me, and I am back to being plain old Scott again.

'Why are you still down here?' he says, eyebrows creasing like shifting continental plates.

'We're preparing ourselves,' Kate tells him. 'Mr Peabody can be difficult to deal with sometimes, and we want . . . want to be in the right frame of mind.'

What a magnificently *silly* excuse.

Jamal's eyebrows uncrease, preventing any further earthquakes. 'Yeah. He is a bit of a twat, isn't he?' he says slowly, lips curling at both ends.

What a magnificently *brilliant* excuse.

'Just don't try to sound too clever,' Jamal adds. 'He doesn't like that. I sense he's a person who inherently suffers from low self-esteem, and compensates by putting down those with less power than him.'

Kate and I stare at Jamal with our mouths open.

Jamal chuckles. 'And I suffer from people making an assessment of my intellectual prowess simply by judging me on my physical appearance.'

'Do you?' I squeak.

'Yes. I do.'

The phone beeps in Kate's hand.

'Well, we must be off,' she tells Jamal, sneaking a look at the phone screen to see the incoming message, and then leaning forward to punch the code into the keypad.

'Have a good night,' Jamal says, as the doors close on his gigantic frame.

'We will!' Kate and I exclaim at the same time.

Once we're going up, we both release explosive breaths.

'I can't believe that actually worked,' I say, dumbfounded.

'I can't believe Jamal's stuck in a security guard's job,' Kate adds.

I swallow hard. 'That was the easy bit. Now we've got to get Holly out of there.'

The lift pings to a stop and the doors open on a broad, glossy marble hallway being rocked by loud, thumping dance music.

There's only one front door up here in the hallway, and it's right in front of us.

The lair of the PinkyPud lies beyond.

We step out of the lift and gird our loins as best we can.

'Do we knock?' I wonder, as we cross the small space between lift and front door.

'There's a buzzer here,' Kate points out. 'I guess we should press it.'

'Go ahead,' I tell her, unconsciously raising the carry case full of gin up in front of me.

She presses the buzzer and we hear the sound of a strident doorbell over the loud thump, thump of the music.

The door flies open incredibly fast, almost making us jump out of our shoes. At the door stands a tall, skinny-looking individual, wearing a large black baseball cap, a *Minecraft* T-shirt and a pair of blue jeans that are more rip than jean.

'Yeah?' he says, his eyes darting between us.

'Where's PinkyPud?' I spit, forgetting my manners. I'm not in the mood for pretence any more. I want my daughter, and I want to get out of here.

Mr Minecraft looks at me blankly. 'Dunno. He's here somewhere. Are you the guys with the blow?'

'The what?'

'The blow, mate. The scazz. The heeby jeeby.'

I have no idea what he's fucking on about.

'You know,' he says, nodding his head. 'The Granny Wanker's Ashes.'

Aaah . . .

I'm on safer ground here, I feel.

I hold up the carry case. 'Right here, pal. All the Granny Wanker's Ashes you can stick up your nose.'

His narrow face brightens considerably, and he steps aside. 'You'd better come in then! Pinky's somewhere out in the pool area, I think.'

Kate and I dart into the apartment and survey the scene.

It's basically Sodom and Gomorrah in here, only with more expensive interior design, and millennial entitlement.

The apartment is a giant open-plan tribute to twenty-first-century excess. The walls are shining white and covered in pieces of artwork that all look awful, but probably cost the earth. The furniture is almost exclusively black and chrome, and the flooring is all highly polished, gleaming parquet.

The apartment is full of people, none of whom look old enough to be here, to my eyes anyway. All of them are dressed in ways I truly don't understand, and virtually all of them are doing something with a mobile phone. If they're not texting, they're taking selfies. If they're not doing that, they're playing a video game. It's all rather disheartening, to tell the truth.

The entire west wall of the place is constructed of glass bi-fold doors that lead out on to a massive veranda, which contains a large swimming pool, full of brightly coloured inflatables, and equally brightly coloured girls and boys in various stages of undress.

There's a bar at the back of the huge open-plan living area, behind which is a short black gentleman in neon-green dungarees and a neon-blue trilby hat, standing at a set of what we used to call 'disco decks'. I assume this is the legendary ShadowPlaya.

Standing next to him, hooting and hollering at the crowd of people dancing in front of them . . . is the bastard PinkyPud.

There is no sign of Holly.

My heart plummets as my anger rises. She shouldn't be in a place like this. She just shouldn't. I have to protect my little girl!

'Here. Have this,' I say, holding out the case of gin to a passing millennial in a long black coat, who is playing on his phone, and has a suspicious dusting of white powder under his nose.

'What is it?' he says.

'It's a new drink, mate. It's expensive and stupid. You'll love it. Pass it around to everyone.'

He nods and smiles 'Alright, man! Too cool!'

Yeah? Let's see how your bowels feel about it in the morning, pal.

'We need to go and talk to him,' Kate says, pointing to where PinkyPud is now crowd-surfing.

'Yes. Let's do that,' I agree, eyes narrowing.

We walk over to where our quarry is being carefully lowered to the floor. Nobody wants to drop the host on his head, apparently, just in case he ruins their lives by vlogging about it the next day.

He has a broad, dumb grin on his face that's probably fuelled by whatever designer drug he thinks is the coolest this week.

The grin disappears once he sees my wife and me.

'What are you doing here?! How did you find this place?!' he shouts angrily over the loud, adrenaline-inducing music.

'Where's Holly?' I shout back.

PinkyPud's face clouds even more. 'Not telling you! She doesn't want to see you!' He grabs a passing millennial. 'Go get the bloody security guard, SlappyDaps! These two shouldn't be in here!'

SlappyDaps (his real name is probably Kevin, by the looks of him) stares at Kate and me for the briefest of moments, before nodding at PinkyPud. He then scuttles off towards the front door, clamping his ShadowPlaya baseball cap on his head to stop it flying off in the rush.

I fear Jamal will be returning to block our view of the world very soon.

Time to get our skates on.

'Tell us where our daughter is, *right now!*' Kate orders. 'Or we'll call the police!'

PinkyPud sneers. 'Call them! Holly's here of her own free will!'

'Yeah? So are all the drugs your little friends are taking, Jasper!' I say to him. 'If I call the coppers and tell them you've kidnapped our daughter, they'll be down here faster than you can say Granny Wanker's Ashes!' I poke him in his scrawny chest. 'Do you think they'll let you record something for YouTube from your prison cell?'

PinkyPud's face goes very pale.

Ha!

Underneath that party-hard, vlog-hard exterior, there is still a kid who's barely out of his teens, and is no doubt terrified of the prospect of a police raid. I'm confident he's seen the light of day and will tell us where Holly is without any more—

Bloody hell!

The little bastard's making a run for it!

I stand and watch somewhat dumbfounded as PinkyPud takes to his heels, pushing through the crowd of partygoers, in the direction of the veranda.

'So that's what that looks like,' I mutter to myself.

'Come on, Scott!' Kate cries. 'We have to get him to tell us where Holly is!'

Kate takes off after PinkyPud, and I follow her, doing my best to dodge several enthusiastic young people as they pogo around on

PinkyPud's parquet flooring to whatever that din coming out of the amplifiers is.

The Pink One makes it out on to his veranda, and turns to see us both in hot pursuit. He shrieks in surprise, and starts to run around the edge of the swimming pool, close to the railing of the expansive terrace.

Kate follows him, but I decide to shift my trajectory and run around the other side of the pool, hoping to capture Pinky like a rat in a trap.

My plan proves a partial success when Kate and I close in on Jasper at the corner of the veranda, giving him nowhere to go. Some of the partygoers around the pool scatter in every direction, while the rest look on in amazement at what's apparently happening to their host. Inevitably, the camera phones start to come out to record all this for posterity.

'Where is Holly?!' I shout at PinkyPud.

'Not telling!' he pouts.

Pinky appears to have regressed a decade in his panic.

'Yes, you are, young man!' Kate yells at him, advancing further.

'No! No, I'm not! Leave me alone!' PinkyPud screams, and jumps away from us, right at the pool.

I reflexively reach out a hand to stop him, grabbing on to the back of his T-shirt as he sails past me. This unbalances me, and I topple over, following PinkyPud into the swimming pool.

I hadn't planned on a nice relaxing dip this evening, to be honest with you.

Pinky comes spluttering to the surface, with me right behind him. Our heads smack into the bottom of a girl floating around on a rubber ring. She goes flying, and Pinky and I get our heads wedged in the centre of the inflatable ring.

We're now close enough to kiss.

'Aaaargh! Leave me alone!' he screams and splutters right into my face.

'Where's Holly, you rancid little turd!' I scream right back at him.

Then somebody hits me with an inflatable banana. Which is probably par for the course at this stage.

'Get off our Pinky!' the girl whose bottom I've just inadvertently assaulted cries, hitting me on the head again. 'Leave Pinky alone!'

'Stop it!' I squeal at her, as the Pudster ducks underwater and away from me.

I do the same thing, and then swim towards him, the chlorine burning my eyes. I blurrily watch as Jasper climbs out of the pool, and I follow suit – right into the waiting clutches of Jamal the security guard.

'Let go of me!' I order, forgetting just how large my captor is.

'Calm down, gin man!' he tells me, squeezing my arm. It's not a terribly painful squeeze, but it has all the hallmarks of a squeeze that could become *exceptionally* painful, should the squeezer decide such escalation is necessary.

I instantly stop struggling. I am not by nature a violent man. Nor am I one that has seen the inside of a gym in twenty years. If I try to fight Jamal, I will just end up embarrassing us both.

My wife, on the other hand, has no such qualms.

She has been grabbed from behind by SlappyDaps, and is not happy about it in the slightest.

'Let go of me, you prick!' she demands.

'Nah! You ain't getting away!' SlappyDaps snaps, holding Kate by the upper arms.

PinkyPud, soaking wet and now apoplectic, starts to jump up and down on the spot, throwing the kind of tantrum that I'd have sent him to bed for, had I the misfortune to be his parent. 'Don't let them go! Don't you fucking let them go!' he orders Jamal and Slappy. 'I'm going to sue you bastards for trespass!'

'Yeah! Trespass!' SlappyDaps crows, and tightens his grip on Kate's arms.

A visible wince of pain crosses her face.

SlappyDaps leans his head in uncomfortably close to Kate's ear. 'I'm gonna make you regret coming up here,' he says in a low, disturbing voice.

I'm about to try to break free of Jamal's clutches to help her, when something rather incredible happens.

Kate's look of pain is instantly replaced by one of incandescent fury.

I am transported back to that day Holly and I watched her attempting Krav Maga, and the moment when my wife was held in a similar position by her friend Ester. The instructor showed Kate how to get out of this particular hold in a manner both shocking and awfully violent.

In a flash, I see SlappyDaps's immediate future laid out in front of me.

'Er, you might want to let her go, because—'

Too late.

Kate scrapes her right heel down SlappyDaps's shin, ending this manoeuvre by stamping on his foot.

He screams in agony and instantly lets her go. Kate is now free, but is also mad as a crate of badgers, so poor old Slappy isn't just going to get off with a broken toe. Kate does something strange and complicated with her elbow at this point, which ends with her hand windmilling around into SlappyDaps's face.

I'm not sure she meant to pick his nose for him, but that's jolly well what happens.

Slappy shrieks in pain, and – as seems to be the fashion these days – runs away. Or rather, he stumbles painfully away, given the blows my wife has just struck to his leg and foot.

Kate stares at everyone surrounding us. 'Anybody else?' she offers, fists clenching and eyes narrowing.

I've never been so proud or horny in my life.

PinkyPud isn't impressed though. He's still having a tantrum. 'Get out! Get out of here now!' he yells, spraying water everywhere.

'Not until you tell us where Holly is!' I yell back at him, doing an equally good job of spraying the contents of his pool around the place.

'Where is my daughter, Jasper?' Kate says, in the kind of gruff tone usually reserved for black-clad vigilantes on a mission to clean up their city.

'Right here,' a voice says from beside us.

Holly looks like she's been crying. She's also wearing a pair of denim shorts that are *far too short for her*, thank you very much. And how much make-up has she got on? A hell of a lot. I'm not happy with the ShadowPlaya T-shirt she's got on either. It's been cut to expose an awfully large amount of midriff.

'Holly!' Kate cries and takes a step towards her child.

Holly then does something that breaks my heart. She steps backwards, away from her mother.

'Please leave,' she tells us in a small voice.

'No! You've got to come with us!' I splutter, trying to unsuccessfully free myself from Jamal's clutches. 'You shouldn't be here, Hols!'

'Why not?' she asks, chin thrust forward defiantly.

'Because he's a lying little shit, who only wants one thing,' Kate tells her, looking daggers at the subject of her ire.

'He cares about me,' Holly argues.

'No, he doesn't!' Kate snaps. 'He only wants one thing from you, sweetheart. Please believe me!'

'Your mum's right, Hols,' I say, trying to remain as calm as possible under the circumstances. 'Please come home with us. Don't trust this guy.'

She looks at me, tears at the corners of her eyes. 'And I'm supposed to trust you two instead, am I?'

'Of course! We're your parents and we love you!'

'Not enough to stay sober when you said you would!' she cries unhappily.

'I know! And we're very sorry!' I wail.

'We were stupid,' Kate tells her. 'And we were *weak*, and we let you down. But it won't happen again, we *promise* you.'

Holly looks angry now. 'You promised me before! Why should I believe you now?!'

'Because we got some help, kiddo,' I tell her. 'This Dutch woman made us dress up like babies.'

'What the fuck?' Jamal exclaims, looking down at me in horror.

'It wasn't like that,' I tell him, shaking my head briefly.

'Please just leave,' Holly says. 'I don't want to do this any more.'

'Yes! Yes! Bloody *leave*!' PinkyPud agrees. 'Holly doesn't want you here! She doesn't trust you!' He goes over and places one squelchy arm around her. 'She trusts *me*!'

Kate steps towards her again. 'But we *love you*, Hols. Please don't do this.'

Holly looks at her mother for an instant, before the tears start to flow down her face. She turns and runs back inside, in a direction that will take her past the dance floor and into the depths of the rest of PinkyPud's huge apartment.

The entire party watches her go. Mostly from behind a phone camera lens.

'Okay. Time for you to leave, gin man,' Jamal then orders.

'Alright,' I say in a deflated voice.

'Scott?' Kate says, looking at me aghast.

'She's not going anywhere with us tonight, sweetheart,' I tell her, looking over at Jasper the Grasper. 'He's won.'

'Yeah! Damn right!' he sniggers at me.

I wish I could punch that smug look off his face, but Jamal is propelling me back towards the front door before I have a chance.

Kate follows alongside me. She pulls Holly's phone out of her jeans pocket. 'I'm going to tweet about this! I'm going to tell everyone about it! He won't get away with it!'

'Don't bother,' I say, as we get to the hallway leading to the front door.

'Yeah! Don't bother!' PinkyPud agrees, from where he's capering along behind Jamal's ample frame. 'She doesn't want you around, and nobody will believe you anyway!' He throws his arms open. 'People fucking *love* me, you idiots!'

I hate to admit it, but he's right. People *do* love him. *And* trust him.

Certainly more than they trust two old fools who can't stay sober anyway.

Mr Minecraft is still at the front door, and throws it open as we get there. Jamal pushes me out through the door into the foyer, with Kate just behind.

PinkyPud now appears to have dropped into 100 per cent gloating mode, and isn't going to let us leave here without giving us his best bad-guy monologue. As Jamal calls for the lift to take us back to ground-floor level, Jasper starts to strut up and down like a peacock.

'Ha! You think you can come up here and make me look bad?? I am Pinky *fucking* Pud,' he spits, stabbing his chest with one thumb. 'Nobody makes *me* look bad!' He points back into the apartment. 'All of those fucking idiots lap up whatever I do. I've got them all twisted right round my little finger – including your stupid daughter! She'll do whatever I say! I stole your fucking Dry Hard thing away from her, didn't I??'

I lunge at him hard, but Jamal again grabs me by the arm, stopping me from getting too close. Kate doesn't budge.

'And when you two are gone,' PinkyPud continues, 'I'm going to go back inside, get your beautiful little Holly good and loaded – and have some *proper* fun with her once the party is over!'

Once again I try to break him in two, and once again Jamal prevents me. Kate appears to have been stunned into complete immobility at what this odious little runt is saying.

'And she'll fucking *love me*, whatever I do,' Jasper sneers. 'Because I can make or break her on YouTube. I can make or break any of those *wankers*.'

The lift goes ping.

'Now, get the fuck out of my building, and never, ever come back,' he concludes. 'But remember to subscribe to my channel, so you can see your daughter from time to time.'

Jamal pushes me into the lift, blocking my view of PinkyPud. 'Real sorry about this, man,' he tells me.

'It's not your fault, Jamal,' I reply. 'You can't help being employed by a cunt.'

He smiles at this, making sure PinkyPud doesn't see. Kate calmly comes and stands next to me in the lift.

What the hell is going on with her?

The lift doors close on Jamal standing impassively, with Jasper next to him, leering like a Bond villain.

As soon at the lift starts to descend, I hammer the wall in frustration. 'Motherfucker! I am coming back here with my *fucking* cricket bat, Kate! I swear to God!!'

Kate then does something completely unexpected. She smiles at me. 'Calm down, husband of mine. Everything is going to be fine.'

I look at her in shuddering disbelief. 'How can you say that?? You heard him! You heard Holly! How exactly is everything going to be alright??'

She holds up Holly's iPhone. 'Because I just recorded everything he said on this.'

I stare at the phone.

I stare at my wife's smug expression.

I stare at the phone again.

Finally, I stare at my wife, who has never looked quite as beautiful as she does right now.

'I love you,' I tell her, in a rushed breath.

'Yeah. I know,' she replies, nodding briefly.

I take the deepest of deep breaths and feel my whole body relaxing. We've *got him*.

We've got him bang to rights.

I take Kate's hand. 'You know. I think it's about time we uploaded a brand-new video to YouTube, don't you?' I say to her.

She nods again. 'Oh yes.'

'Under the Dry Hard hashtag?'

'Oh yes.'

'How long do you think it'll be before people see it?'

Kate smiles an evil smile. 'Oh, not very long at all, Scott. You know what these young people are like. All got their heads buried in their phones, haven't they?'

'They have, Kate. They really have.'

My wife hands the phone to me. 'You do it. You're better at the technical stuff.'

I take the phone and open up the YouTube app. I'm no expert, but by the time we hit the ground floor and the lift doors open, I have managed to get the video ready to upload. I've also dripped a great deal of water on to the floor of the lift. The cleaners will hate me in the morning.

By the time we get back to the car, I've stopped dripping quite as much – #DryFast – and the video clip is ready to go.

In the clip's description I type the following: PinkyPud shows his TRUE colours! This one is for you Holly, and everyone who thinks Jasper is a good guy. Time to see the REAL PinkyPud! #DryHard #TrueColours #VillainMonologue #PartyPud #ShadowPlaya

I show Kate what I've written. 'Harsh . . . but entirely fair,' she says.

I complete the description, knowing full well that using all those hashtags will mean the clip starts to get seen pretty damn quickly.

Then I hold out the phone to Kate with the app open on the upload button.

'You do it, sweetheart,' I tell her.

'Really?'

'Sure. You were smart enough to record the footage. You should be the one to let the world see it!'

She smiles, takes the phone, takes a deep breath and thumbs the upload button.

We then watch with delight as the clip goes live.

It's not the clearest or best video ever made, of course. Kate is holding the phone down and trying to angle it up, and therefore it captures PinkyPud's legs as much as it does his face. But the audio is *crystal* clear. Every word he says is perfectly audible and understandable. It'll do the job we want it to, with any luck.

About half an hour passes as we wait in the car for further developments. The heater dries my clothes out enough for me to start feeling slightly comfortable again – though the upholstery is going to need a bloody good airing tomorrow.

YouTube has exploded.

Those following #DryHard are the first to see PinkyPud's rant, but as they begin to share it to everyone they know, the video starts to spread like . . . well, just like a *virus*. The view count begins to rocket. Within minutes, *thousands* have seen it.

'I wonder what's going on up there?' Kate ponders, looking out of the windscreen and up to the top of the apartment block PinkyPud calls home.

'I don't know, sweetheart,' I reply. 'But I bet it won't get streamed on PinkyPud's YouTube channel any time soon.'

'Probably not.'

'You think Holly will see the clip?'

'I don't see how she couldn't. Every bugger up there had a mobile phone.'

After about forty-five minutes, the first people start to appear from the building's main exit. The exodus is slow to begin with, but the trickle soon turns into a flood. I suppose you can only fit so many people into a lift, and it probably takes quite a while to get down all those stairs.

Kate and I watch as a parade of disenfranchised and disappointed young people come flooding past us. All of them have their faces buried in their phones, of course. And all of them look suitably shocked and angry.

'Well, this is going *very well*,' I say, as Mr Minecraft bowls past us, a huge scowl on his face, which is illuminated nicely by his phone screen.

'Scott! Look!' Kate exclaims, pointing at the main entrance.

It's Holly. My daughter has made it out. She's standing in the foyer, looking lost and confused.

Kate and I are out of the car like a shot and hurrying over to her, dodging disgruntled millennials as we go.

She sees us as we run through the main doors, and immediately bursts into tears.

'Mum! Dad! I'm so sorry!' she wails as we reach her and throw our arms around her. 'How could I have been so *stupid*??'

'Oh God, you weren't stupid, Hols!' I tell her, tears starting to flow from my eyes too. 'We're the stupid ones. If we hadn't let you down, you wouldn't have gone to him. It's our fault, and we'll never stop making it up to you, we promise!'

'Really?' she says, wiping the tears away.

'Of course, sweetie!' Kate cries, hugging Holly even tighter. 'Things *will* be different, we promise!'

'You bastards! You utter bastards!'

We all swing round to see PinkyPud lurch out of the lift, with my carry case in his hands. He delves into it and starts to throw orange gin bottles at us in a fit of absolute pique. His aim is terrible and they all miss completely.

'You've *ruined* me! You've ruined my fucking life!' he howls, continuing to lob the tiny gin bottles at us.

He runs out of ammunition as he gets closer, however, and starts to bawl his eyes out instead.

It's all rather a pathetic sight to behold.

I couldn't be happier.

Holly then steps forward. 'You tried to turn me against my parents, you bastard,' she says to him. 'You lied to me. You *manipulated* me.'

He gives her a pitiable look. 'I didn't mean it!' he squeals.

'Did you mean it when you said you were going to have some *proper fun* with me tonight after the party?' Holly asks, through gritted teeth.

'I'm sorry! I'm sorry!'

'Was *this* the kind of proper fun you meant?' she says, and knees him right in the balls.

PinkyPud drops as hard as the subscriber count on his YouTube channel is no doubt doing as we speak.

Jamal, who has been lurking by the lift this entire time, is doubled up with laughter.

Holly turns and walks slowly back over to us.

'Mum, Dad – can we get out of here, please?'

'Of course we can,' Kate tells her. And we do just that.

All three of us.

Together.

CHAPTER FIFTEEN

HOLLY AND THE FUTURE

Welcome, for the final time, to the bedroom of a decidedly *un*average eighteen-year-old.

It's as untidy as it's ever been, of course. The clothes are still spread in heaps around the place, and the make-up is still scattered across the dressing table. The iPad still teeters precariously on the edge of the bedside cabinet, with that tiny silver Christmas tree sat next to it again.

But today, this teenage bedroom is very different from normal, because today, the teenager that owns it has happily allowed her parents inside.

This is virtually unheard of in Western society, and probably marks some kind of watershed moment for everyone.

Scott Temple is sitting on one side of his daughter, Kate Temple on the other.

All three are looking at the video camera lens with goofy smiles on their faces.

'Is it recording?' Scott says from one side of his mouth.

'Yep,' Holly tells him.

'So, who's going to talk first?' Kate asks, her smile turning slightly fixed.

Holly looks at both of them, before rolling her eyes and looking back at the camera. 'Hello, everyone,' she says, and waves. Her parents follow suit. 'Welcome to another video we're putting together for Dry Hard.'

'Yes . . . welcome!' Scott parrots enthusiastically.

'Yeah. Wel – welcome!' Kate also parrots, stumbling a bit over her words.

There is not a career in television presenting in either of their futures.

'We all wanted to be in this particular video,' Holly continues, 'because we want to tell you what we're going to be doing, going forward.'

'We've made some . . . *changes,*' Kate interjects.

'I've quit my fucking job!' Scott exclaims loudly, staring down the barrel of the lens, a somewhat terrified but excited expression on his face.

'Yes. Dad has quit his job,' Holly repeats, patting him on the shoulder.

Scott looks at her. 'Are you going to show the video of me doing it?'

'Yes, Dad. I'm going to cut it into this clip right about now, once we're finished.'

Scott smiles. 'Cool!'

Holly's bedroom disappears, to be suddenly replaced by Charlton Camberwell's office.

Scott stands in front of his boss's desk.

'Shove your job up your arse, you big fat pig!' Scott shouts, causing Charlton to recoil in his chair. Scott then turns towards the camera and looks over it at his daughter. 'Run, Holly! Run away!' he yells, before rushing past, with maniacal glee writ large across his face.

Scott has done quite a lot of running away recently, but this just might be a case where it's very much the right thing to do.

Back in Holly's bedroom, Scott looks quite pleased with himself. 'I thought I handled it very well,' he says, nodding to himself.

Both Holly and Kate tut and roll their eyes in exactly the same manner.

Like mother, like daughter indeed.

'Dad was able to quit the distillery because we've managed to work out how to make money from being on YouTube,' Holly says, by way of explanation.

'Pfft,' Kate interrupts. '*You've* done all the work, sweetheart. We've just gone along with you. You are very much the brains of the operation.'

'That's right, Hols,' Scott agrees. 'It's all thanks to you, really. You're the one that created Dry Hard, you're the one that kept it all going, despite our best efforts, *and* you're the one that's managed to nick most of PinkyPud's audience, now he's been shown up as the twat he most definitely is!'

Which is all very true.

With the demise of Jasper the Grasper's YouTube popularity, thanks to his expletive-filled rant, a distinct gap has opened up in the market. A gap that Holly Temple has jumped into with both feet. *The TempleGurl* is the fastest-growing YouTube channel in the whole country. And every penny made from monetising it is going right into her pocket, now that the manipulative little turd PinkyPud has been left in the dust.

Good old Pinks must be chewing on his own liver, wherever he may have ended up.

And who better to help Holly create her content for her rapidly growing channel than her father? What he lacks in experience, he more than makes up for with the enthusiasm of someone who knows that he never has to do what Charlton Camberwell tells him *ever again*.

'I'm really excited to be making stuff for the YouTube!' Scott says, with barely concealed delight.

Holly laughs. 'Yeah. You sound it!'

'Er . . . I haven't been able to quit *my* job,' Kate says, shaking her head and rolling her eyes again. 'I just thought I'd point that out.'

Her daughter gives her a sympathetic look. 'That's true, Mum . . . but you have got a brand-new client, though, eh? A rising YouTube star, who needs the right PR advice!' There's a deep sense of pride in Holly's voice.

Kate puts an arm around her daughter. 'I have. And I couldn't be happier about it.' The pride in Kate's voice is deeper than the Mariana Trench.

'And that's where we are,' Scott says. 'That's what's been happening over the past few weeks. It's been a rollercoaster, and no mistake.'

'It has. But that's not why we're here today,' Kate adds. 'We're here today to talk about Dry Hard.'

'We are,' Holly agrees. 'Because it's been a whole year since we started this thing.'

Scott looks amazed. 'Can you believe it? A whole *year*?'

'I can,' Kate says, with a wince.

'And despite a few very small setbacks . . .' Scott continues.

'*Very small setbacks??*' Kate says in disbelief, looking over at her husband.

'. . . we've made it to the end of the year,' he says, ignoring her. 'A year in which we have been sober almost the whole time!'

'Despite some very small setbacks,' Holly says with a grin.

Scott pinches his fingers together. 'Very, very small.'

'Which means that Dry Hard is coming to an end,' Kate says, with a slightly melancholic tone to her voice. 'We've done what we set out to do – more or less. We've taken the alcohol out of our lives and done everything we can to live without it.' She holds up her hands. 'I'm not saying everything is wonderful and perfect – there's still some work for us to do, but all things considered, we're doing okay.'

'That's right!' Scott says, with a smile. 'Everything is different now. Everything is *better*.' He looks over at his wife, an almost shy expression on his face. 'And that's just about all you can wish for in this world, isn't it? That things just get *better*. That when you try to make a change, that when you make an *effort* . . . you get some results. Something to show that you've done the right thing.'

'We have done the right thing, sweetheart,' Kate tells him. 'Not drinking for a year has shown us that we can live our lives without it, if we want to.' Her eyes blaze. 'We don't *need* it. It's not important. This has hopefully changed our relationship with booze enough that we can now enjoy a drink, without it taking over our lives again.'

'That's right,' Scott says. 'That's what we're hoping.'

'We really, really are,' Kate says, trying to sound matter of fact – but there's an almost imperceptible wobble there at the back, if you listen hard enough.

'Absolutely,' Scott agrees. 'We have learned our lesson.' The wobble in *his* voice is *easily* perceptible. 'So, to celebrate coming to the end of the year, we're all going out for a nice meal – somewhere that doesn't serve insects or Venezuelan chips. And we're going to have a glass of wine with that meal, to toast our future!'

'Yes!' Kate adds, sounding a little more sure of herself.

Holly leans forward. 'And we wouldn't dream of doing it without you guys coming along . . . one final time.'

'No, we wouldn't!' Scott agrees and smiles at the camera.

A brief silence then descends.

'What do we do now?' Kate asks, from the side of her mouth.

Holly chuckles, wraps her arms around her parents to give them a hug, and then leans forward to turn the camera off.

***

So.

Here it is then.

At long last.

The final Dry Hard video.

The final time the vast, faceless online community will get to watch Kate and Scott Temple's battle with the demon booze.

Except . . . it's not a battle any more.

Lessons have been learned.

Mistakes have been made.

Significant revelations have been had. Mainly wearing adult onesies, admittedly – but *significant* revelations, nonetheless.

A rocky road has been navigated by two people – no, sorry, *three* people – who have come to understand and appreciate each other more, thanks to the various trials and tribulations (most of them self-inflicted, if they're being honest about it) that have beset them along the way.

It's all made for some bloody good entertainment, that's for certain.

So much so that the Temple family find themselves at the start of a bright – and potentially very *lucrative* – future, if they play their cards right. Hundreds of thousands of people have been entertained by their mishaps and shenanigans, and there's gold in them thar online hills – if you're savvy enough to know how to get at it.

Holly Temple certainly is. She learned everything she needed to from PinkyPud, before she kneed him in the balls.

So, there's much to celebrate.

Much to be proud of.

Much to raise a glass to, if you will.

. . . and here are those glasses!

Look at them.

Look at how they gleam in the soft restaurant light.

And here is the waiter with the bottle of fifty quid Bollinger. Look how the champagne bubbles merrily as it pours smoothly into the glass.

Have you ever seen such a clear, crisp and lovely liquid in your life? It's the stuff of dreams.

'Well, go on then, you two,' Holly says encouragingly, from behind her camera. 'Drink up.'

Scott and Kate smile and lean forward to pick up their glasses.

Is there a look of relief on their faces as they do so?

Probably.

It certainly looks like it.

The Temple Twosome stare at each other over their raised glasses, as their daughter records the moment for posterity.

Everything is set.

Everything is right.

This is the moment.

'Here's to the future,' Scott says to his wife.

'Yes. Here's to it,' Kate replies.

Scott smiles. 'Things are looking good, aren't they?'

Kate smiles back. 'They absolutely are.'

'We did it.'

'We did.'

'Together.'

'Together.'

Both of them stare down at their glasses again.

They continue to stare.

The stare goes on for so long that it starts to become ever so slightly uncomfortable.

There are thoughts going through their heads that nobody else can truly understand, no matter how hard they try. Not unless they've been where the Temples are right now.

On the cusp. On the edge. On a fork in the road.

Silently, between them, a decision is made. Not the right decision. Not the wrong decision. Just *a decision*.

Life is full of these, whether we like it or not.

Decisions and choices, each one shaping who we are.

Who we choose to love.

Where we choose to live.

Who we choose to trust.

Where we choose to work.

. . . what we choose to drink.

We are strange, frail creatures, by and large, all of us stumbling through life with no guidebook or roadmap to tell us where to go.

There are many choices out there ahead of us – every single one a crossroads on the path of our lives. Some decisions are taken lightly, some are deeply thought about. But all are *important*, in one way or another. All are *significant*.

Scott swallows hard, looking over at his daughter, and her all-seeing, all-knowing camera lens.

'I don't want this,' he declares, with surprise in his voice.

Kate looks over too. 'Neither do I,' she says, equally amazed.

ACKNOWLEDGMENTS

Writing comedy novels is one of the easiest things in the world to do – while at the same time being incredibly difficult. The fact that I haven't gone entirely insane while doing it is largely down to the following people:

My agent, Jon, and his assistant, Rosa; my editors, Sophie and Victoria; the rest of the team at Amazon Publishing; and everyone else involved in the production and distribution of this novel. Also, my mother, Judy; my sister, Sharon; and all my close friends. A special thanks to my gorgeous, funny and above all patient wife, Gemma.

And, of course, there's you. Yep, you. The one reading this book right now. Without you, there is no Nick Spalding. Please bear this in mind when things go horribly wrong. It'll mostly be your fault.

ABOUT THE AUTHOR

Photo © 2017 Chloe Waters

Nick Spalding is the bestselling author of eleven novels, two novellas and two memoirs. Nick worked in media and marketing for most of his life before turning his energy to his genre-spanning humorous writing. He lives in the south of England with his wife.